The Insistence of Memory

Susan Quilty

The Insistence of Memory
Copyright © 2017 Susan Quilty
All rights reserved.

Cover by Angel Fischer, Halo Designs

This is a work of fiction. Names, characters, places, and events are products of the author's imagination or are used fictitiously.

ISBN: 1976566258
ISBN-13: 978-1976566257

To Brian and Michael,
Never be afraid to tell your own story
and
To Peter,
For listening to mine

CHAPTER ONE

The ceiling is smooth and white above Joanne's head. There is a play of shadows on the wall as light filters in through the partially drawn shades. Joanne doesn't notice the worn paperback that lies open, its pages bent, less than a foot from her head. She doesn't notice the book light that lies forgotten on the floor, still shining faintly in the morning light.

While her eyes skim the surface of the ceiling, her inward gaze focuses on the blue pickup truck from her fragmented dreams. She sees it driving away, in stages, down a long dirt road. She knows that Jeff sits behind the wheel. Every night, driving away.

The images blur as little-girl chatter filters in from the bedroom down the hall. The truck loses shape. The road fades away. Joanne can't make out the words, but she knows the familiar cadence. There's a lilting quality to the conversation, a rise and fall that's almost like a song. As Joanne listens, she wonders if she did that to them. To her daughters. She wonders if their speech patterns have been affected by the years of poems, fables, and nursery book rhymes.

She wonders if she had the right to fill their heads with fairy tales.

When she reaches the kitchen, Joanne's socks—Jeff's socks—pad softly against the yellowing linoleum. The mottled gray and white wool bags and pools around her feet. The sewn red lines lie loosely crooked across her toes, while floppy heels stick out along the backs of her ankles. The heavy socks are too warm for late spring, but she wears them every night. She wears them because they were Jeff's. Keeping him close, even as she dreams of him driving away.

Breakfast is a practiced routine by now. There are no thoughts as Joanne lays out the table: two ceramic bowls, two metal spoons, two glasses of juice, a box of cereal, and the milk. She puts on a pot of strong coffee and fishes a cold bagel out of a paper bag on the counter. She looks at the bagel, sniffs it, feels its cornmeal-dusted texture, and puts it back in the bag uneaten. She stares at the brown paper bag for several long, slow breaths.

The bag sits in a ray of sunlight. Crumpled folds take on greater depth in the slanting light, while Joanne's restless eyes mindlessly follow their maze of soft creases.

She is pouring her second cup of coffee when the girls tumble into the kitchen. They are laughing as they cross the threshold but stop when they catch sight of Joanne. Smiles pass uncertainly between mother and daughters. There was a time, not long ago, when the girls would have ambled over for hugs and kisses. Now they are wary. There is hesitation, just inside the doorway, before they take their usual places at the table.

Joanne watches her daughters with a new detachment.

The same straight hair trails down both of their backs. The same dark eyes assess the world around them. They are identical, in appearance if not in temperament, but they have always been unique in Joanne's eyes. Until lately. Now she has begun to see them as one unit. One responsibility to be fed, and clothed, and tucked into bed.

The girls are somewhat small for their eight years, but they have a way of filling the room, of filling the house, with more than their physical size. Everything about them is larger to Joanne. More significant than Joanne herself has become. It happened gradually, she thinks, or maybe it happened all at once. Maybe it began the day they came home from the hospital, or the moment they took their first breaths, or in the instant when she first felt their fluttery movements inside her body.

"You always get the blue bowl," Sarah grumbles while watching Ruthie pour cereal. True to form, Ruthie quickly offers to switch.

"Not after you've touched it," Sarah scowls, while taking the cereal box from her sister's hands.

Ruthie, more sensitive these past weeks, blinks back tears and quietly waits for Sarah to finish with the milk before filling her own bowl. In another time, Joanne would have stepped in. She would have scolded Sarah and encouraged Ruthie to stand up for herself. She wants to step in now, but the unformed words get lost in her throat. By the time she feels ready to speak, the moment has passed. The girls are eating together and softly giggling over a quiet conversation. The argument short-lived and already forgotten.

Their words are barely audible now and Joanne wonders if their whispers are for her benefit. She turns away to pack their lunches. Breathing to steady herself for the next several minutes of active mothering.

No matter how early the girls get up in the mornings, they are rarely waiting at the curb when the school bus arrives. Today is no exception. Ruthie waits impatiently by the front door, glancing down the street every few seconds, while Sarah ties her shoe with no sense of urgency. Joanne stands quietly beside them, a lunchbox in each hand. She's not prodding them along, the way she once did, but their pace, prodded or not, has not changed.

And then, all at once, the wait is over. Ruthie yanks open the front door, snatches her lunchbox, calls a hasty goodbye, and hurries down the front path. She hits the sidewalk just as the yellow bus pulls to a stop before their house, and she glances back with a look of anxious desperation. Sarah ambles behind, lunchbox swinging at her side. Joanne can't see Sarah's face, but she knows that it is calm, unconcerned about making the bus driver wait. For the second time this morning, she wants to reprimand Sarah, shame her even, but the idea is too big. It takes too much effort.

Both girls are on the bus now and the door cranks shut. A cool breeze blows gently across the front porch as Joanne pulls her flannel bathrobe a little tighter. She could go back inside the house, but she doesn't. She feels compelled to stand on the porch until the bus drives out of sight. It's a tradition that she will not change. One small moment that feels almost the same.

With the morning light reflecting off the dark windows, Joanne cannot see inside the school bus. She has no way of knowing if the girls are looking out at her, or if they are even sitting on this side of the bus. Yet she steps to the edge of the front porch as the bus begins to roll away. She raises her hand in a silent wave, feeling the smile stretch encouragingly across her face. Her eyes go slightly out of focus and her mind, for a moment, mercifully forgets everything else. Joanne waves until the school bus is out of sight, then lowers her hand and wonders what she will do until it returns.

CHAPTER TWO

There is a commotion at the kitchen door. The jangle of keys and the thud of a small, sneakered foot banging against the soft wood. Joanne passes through the dining room just in time to hear a key twist in the lock and then see Eleanor breeze into the house with two-year-old Nolan perched on her hip. Sunlight streams around them making the day seem warmer than it had been just moments before on the shaded front porch.

"Morning, doll," Eleanor calls out a happy greeting while plopping Nolan onto the nearest kitchen chair. "The girls get off to school okay?"

Joanne nods, but Eleanor doesn't see. She's already busy bustling around the kitchen, clearing the table and rinsing the girls' breakfast dishes in the scratched steel sink.

"Is this dirty or clean?" The dishwasher drops open and the dirty dishes are quickly loaded.

Behind Eleanor's back, Nolan slaps his hands on the table in a somewhat rhythmic beat. *Whap! Whap, whap.*

Whap, whap! Whap, whap. The table is solid, indifferent to his banging, though the sudden sounds rattle Joanne, making her draw further back.

The doorway between the kitchen and dining room provides some shelter. It lets Joanne hover outside the activity, observing without participating. Her gaze takes in Eleanor's vivid style. Today it's muted purple jeans with a green shirt layered over a burnt orange tank top. A tangle of her own homemade necklaces string around her neck in coordinating shades. It's eight o'clock in the morning, but Eleanor is in full make-up with glossy lips and lightly shadowed eyes. Her short auburn hair sticks up in carefully styled spikes and waves.

Eleanor's deliberate appearance makes Joanne uncomfortably aware of the tee shirt and flannel pajama bottoms she has on under her dingy bathrobe. It makes her aware of her unbrushed teeth and uncombed hair.

Eleanor shows up this way each day, without invitation or advance notice. Her arrival has become part of their new morning routine. Though Joanne has begun to wonder how long this will last. She has begun to imagine the day when she will once again face the empty house alone.

Today, there is something appealing in the idea.

Eleanor keeps up a steady chatter while scurrying around the kitchen. She talks about her latest jewelry party and how she's building inventory for a craft show at the end of August. It's the kind of event where Joanne would have helped. In the past. They would have left the kids home with their husbands. Or with Eleanor's mother. They'd have unpacked the booth in the early hours, then spent the day smiling with strangers and chatting up customers. They'd have brought sandwiches in their little green cooler and sipped water from plastic sports bottles. They'd have laughed at whatever went wrong. At a wobbling table leg or a sudden burst of rain. Normal problems.

"Speaking of parties," Eleanor's segue pulls Joanne back from the craft fair memories. She watches Eleanor set a bowl of dry cereal in front of Nolan and wonders when they had been speaking about parties.

"Have you thought about Diane's jewelry show? Next Thursday?" Eleanor persists. "It's out in the sticks, but some of the old crew will be there. Bethany, Lynn, maybe Katie."

Joanne pictures Diane's rustic living room, set in a log cabin out in the woods. Two walls made of exposed timber. A stone fireplace with a rough-hewn mantle. She pictures their old high school friends gathered around the coffee table, holding glasses of wine and looking past Eleanor's jewelry to ask their questions about Jeff. Or to carefully *not* ask their questions about Jeff. She pushes the image aside without responding.

In minutes, breakfast is nearly ready. Eleanor has a pot of oatmeal bubbling on the stove, two glasses of juice on the table, and has poured herself a cup of coffee. She fishes a bagel out of the bag on the counter, slices it, and drops two halves into the toaster. A second bagel is plopped onto the table beside Nolan. Uncut. Untoasted.

Joanne's eyes dart from one item to the next. From the stove to the juice to the bagels. The sun streams into the kitchen. Nolan gurgles. A whining ache grows in

Joanne's right temple, while heat rises through her ribcage, bringing a flush to her cheeks. Her lips press together. Eleanor is ladling oatmeal into two bowls when Joanne finally speaks.

"I can do that myself."

The words are gruff, impatient and overeager, but Joanne doesn't back them up. She doesn't reach for the pot or take the bowl from Eleanor's hand. She doesn't move from the doorway at all.

Eleanor looks her way and smiles carefully.

"I know that." She straightens the bowls on the table and returns the empty pot to the stovetop. "Are you ready to eat?"

"No," Joanne tells her. She looks at the steaming servings of oatmeal, at the bright orange juice, and at the napkins folded beside each bowl. It's too neat, too carefully prepared.

"I don't want oatmeal," Joanne continues, getting louder. "I don't want a bagel. And I don't want you making my breakfast, okay?"

"Okay," Eleanor settles into the chair on the far side of the table and begins to stir her own oatmeal. She forces herself not to look at Joanne, turning to ruffle Nolan's hair instead. Her smile is strained, but she lets Nolan push a piece of cereal into her mouth, then laughs, sensing the anger, the tears, building in Joanne.

"Damn it, El," Joanne stamps a foot, her arms now clenched over her chest. "You can't come in here like this, day after day, and just pull me along like… like…"

"Like what?" Eleanor prods, but it isn't enough. Joanne's small flare of anger settles into the resigned calm that keeps Eleanor awake at night. Her eyes close and she breathes to settle her roiling stomach.

"Dammit," Nolan parrots from his place at the table. "Dammit, dammit, dammit."

They both ignore him.

Standing now, crossing the room, Eleanor tugs at Joanne's sleeve, unwinding the protection of her crossed arms, and takes hold of her right hand. Joanne's left hand, with its single diamond and thin gold band, hangs limply by her side. They've stood like this before. In this kitchen. In childhood, in their teen years, and in the early days of motherhood.

"You can't fix this," Joanne speaks plainly. Her voice is flat, but tears have begun to roll slowly down her cheeks. "Jeff is gone. And you can't fix that."

Nolan watches them quizzically while pushing bits of cereal through the hole in his bagel. The near-silence of the kitchen waits around them. The smell of coffee fills the air.

"I know," Eleanor's eyes begin to swim, reaching back through the years of their friendship. "But, Jo, you're not going through this alone. I won't let you."

Joanne nods and the tears come faster. The kitchen sways slightly, fading away, as she focuses in on Eleanor's damp eyes.

"El, Jeff is-- Jeff isn't coming back."

Her teeth begin to chatter as she leans into the doorframe. Eleanor stands beside her, nodding helplessly, twining their fingers together.

"No," she agrees softly, "he isn't."

Eleanor kisses the back of Joanne's hand, feeling her fingers go slack. Joanne's lungs feel too big for her chest, yet they struggle to take in air. A voice inside tells her that she has to say it. That she has to hear it out loud. Again. That she has to make herself wake up.

"Jeff is dead."

The words are clipped. Loud in the quiet kitchen.

"Yes," Eleanor agrees, speaking firmly. "Jeff is dead."

CHAPTER THREE

From his place at the kitchen window, Andy watches Joanne leave her house and walk slowly toward her car. The keys are in her hand, but she pauses by the driver side door to check the writing on a manila envelope that sticks partially out of her bag. She begins to reach for the door handle, stops, and looks up sharply.

Andy doesn't move, doesn't step back from the glass. He watches her hair blow in the wind as she scans the area. A cloud passes over the sun. After a moment, Joanne shrugs, visibly shaking away her apprehension, then gets into her car and backs slowly out of the gravel driveway.

Andy is still standing by the window, still staring at the wide, empty driveway between their houses, when the sound of shoes clatters on the stairs. The muscles at the back of his neck tighten.

"Mission accomplished," Eleanor sighs as she plunks the baby monitor on the countertop and rolls her shoulders up and back to stretch out the kinks.

"He's finally asleep, but probably not for long." She shakes her head, frowns. "I will not survive when he stops napping altogether."

"Mm hmm," Andy isn't listening. His hands clench by his sides as he looks down at his work boots. The stained brown leather matches some of the darker flecks in the worn linoleum floor.

Eleanor reaches a can of lemonade drink mix out of a cabinet and starts measuring scoops of sugary powder into a plastic pitcher, continuing her thought.

"A kid at the library stopped napping, and now he's terrorizing everyone at Story Time. Last week, he kept crying for a clown story. Yeah, clowns. And when Gina finally pulled out a book about the circus, he had a total meltdown. He kept screaming, 'Not those clowns! The clowns with wings!' Can you believe that?" She grimaces. "What the hell are clowns with wings?"

Andy doesn't reply. His focus is back outside the window where their shared driveway shows thinning strips of worn gravel. Inside, Eleanor's laughter fades. The kitchen grows quiet except for the gritty scrapes and rhythmic swish of the lemonade being stirred.

"Jo just left to go somewhere," Andy offers at last.

"Yeah, she has an appointment with her lawyer today."

"Something about the settlement?" Andy's hands dig deep in his pockets.

"I guess," Eleanor shrugs off the question, sets the pitcher aside and rummages through the refrigerator. "When are you going in today?"

"Not until two."

Andy is distracted, but Eleanor is, too. She's perplexed

by the winged clowns and bothered by the memory of the poor mother who had to carry her wailing child out of the library. That could be Nolan, it *has been* Nolan, and the thought makes her second-guess the appeal of motherhood. The doubt stays with her as she lays out what she needs to make sandwiches, slips a green apron over her white shirt, and begins slicing a tomato.

Finally turning away from the window, Andy notices the wrapped lunch meat sitting on the counter and tells Eleanor that he would rather have a BLT. She finishes slicing the tomato without comment, but eyes the turkey and ham that he had asked her to buy yesterday with a frown. A soft snuffling passes through the baby monitor.

"How's she doing?"

Eleanor stands in front of the open refrigerator, swapping the lunch meat for a package of bacon. She glances over her shoulder quizzically.

"Jo," Andy clarifies. "How was she today?"

"Oh," Eleanor shuts the refrigerator and sees the collage of pictures covering the door. She and Jo. Nolan. The girls. A plastic framed wedding photo that shows a leaner, younger version of Andy. One whose face and belly haven't softened with beer and age. One whose eyes aren't hardened by disappointments.

Chasing away the thought, Eleanor opens the package, drops a few slices of bacon into a heavy cast iron skillet, and considers his question. She doesn't want to tell Andy that she didn't go over there this morning. That she watched the girls get on the bus, then took Nolan out for a walk alone. She doesn't want to admit that Joanne had asked for some space.

"She's getting better," Eleanor says instead. "Slowly. It's going to take time."

"Right, yeah, of course." Andy stands, paces the room, and stops to peer into the skillet. "But she's stronger now?"

Eleanor narrows her eyes and gives Andy her full attention. He's only 27, but his hair has begun to thin and there are hints of gray in the scruff on his chin. The bacon sizzles between them as Andy begins unconsciously curling and flexing his fingers.

"And you're asking because...?"

"Well, I--" Andy stops. He looks over her head, back toward the window and the house beyond.

"Andy?" Eleanor scrutinizes his face, searching for truth, until Andy blurts out the first words that come to mind.

"Okay. So, Jeff was a genius." Eleanor frowns and flips the bacon.

"Yes. We all know how smart Jeff--"

"No. Not smart," Andy's eyes gleam. The secret builds in his chest, expanding his ribs. It's all right there, ready to come tumbling out. "El, he was a fucking *genius*. Smarter than any scientist at that fucking lab."

"Andy," Eleanor prods the bacon with a fork. "Jeff really appreciated you getting him that job. He didn't care that it was on the maintenance crew. Someday he would have finished night school, and--"

"El, please!" Andy slaps his palm on the counter for silence. "I need to tell you something important. About Jeff. And me." Eleanor clamps her lips together, eyes trained on the pan. "Okay, the thing is we built something. Me and Jeff. See, we, uh, built something in his basement."

"In his...?" Eleanor lays the cooked bacon out on a stack of paper towels as Andy's words come together. She hesitates, her hands hanging in mid-air, and a cold, prickling sensation breaks out across her collarbones. "You and Jeff built something?"

"Yes, babe, please, just let me explain." Andy cracks his knuckles, pacing. "We built this computer thing. Okay, I mean Jeff built this computer thing, but I helped."

"How would you--"

"I got the parts and stuff," Andy cuts her off, but his answer only makes Eleanor's eyes widen in fear.

"Andy. What did you do? Where did you--?" Her voice drops to a shocked whisper. "Did you take equipment? From the lab?"

Andy runs his hands over his face and looks toward the ceiling. A long, thin crack crosses overhead, nearly meeting the glass covered ceiling light at the center of the room.

"That's not the point," he tells her. Eleanor tries to argue with him, but Andy grabs her by the upper arms. "Listen, El, it's what we made that's important. It's what Jeff discovered.

"Babe, this will change the world."

The look in Andy's eyes makes Eleanor forget the stolen equipment. She forgets the fear that Andy will end up in prison, that she and Jo could be accessories after the crime. The wild look in his eyes raises her curiosity above all the rest. She feels his fingers digging into her arms, leans closer and has to know.

"What did you do?"

CHAPTER FOUR

Joanne's lawyer has a small office on the west side of town. It's in the same complex as her dentist and insurance agent, but on the far side of the tan brick building, where a winding stone path separates its entrance from the other business fronts. Flowers in stone urns flank either side of the painted black door and a thick coir doormat centers between. The mat has a bold black outline and an elegant *M* at its center. Joanne lingers in front of the door, reading its small brass plaque: *Doug Mitchell, Attorney at Law*. She remembers how the plaque had impressed her when she was thirteen.

Inside, the furniture is the same as it had been on her very first visit: leather couches in the waiting room, a simple wood desk for Doug's paralegal, and metal file cabinets on the far wall. A large abstract oil painting hangs over the couch and porcelain figurines stand in a corner curio cabinet. By now, Joanne knows the history of that collection. She knows that Doug and his wife, Evelyn, had purchased the first figurine on their honeymoon and the others each year after until the year their daughter was born. Joanne doesn't like the statues any more now than she did as a teenager.

Although the décor is the same, the paralegal has changed. Several times. This one, Kara, is perhaps a year or two younger than Joanne, though Joanne feels much older when attempting to return her eager smile. After leading her into Doug's office, Kara rattles off a long line of drinks, counting them on her fingers, until Joanne interrupts to say that water would be fine.

Doug winks at their exchange, then greets Joanne gently, kindly, as she takes her seat on the opposite side of his desk. Joanne is now twice as old as she was when they first met, but she hasn't aged in Doug's mind. From Joanne's perspective, Doug hasn't changed much either. Same gray hair, same blue eyes. Instead of looking at him, she lets her gaze rove over his bookshelves, sharply aware of the empty chair beside her. It feels strange to be here alone.

"Joanne," Doug says her name heavily, with a compassionate look that makes her want to apologize. "How are you holding up?"

She pauses at the question, lightly lifting her shoulders, and it's a relief when Kara's return saves her from actually answering.

The glass of water is cold in Joanne's hands. Tiny droplets of condensation slowly wet the small napkin she holds under its base. For a moment, Joanne lets her eyes stray toward the empty chair, her grandmother's chair, and that's all it takes to become a teenager again. Wisps of memory wash through her mind. Cheap beer and parties by the lake, musky cologne, and an overwhelming sense of fear.

"Joanne?"

She blinks to clear the past and sees that Kara has left the room. They are alone.

"I've talked to the lab and the proposal looks good," Doug begins directly. "They are eager for you to settle."

"Okay," Joanne is only half-listening. "Do I have to sign something?"

"Well, there are a few things I have to check over first," Doug pauses to consider Joanne's roving eyes, her lack of interest. "It's a good offer, but they could do better."

Joanne doesn't acknowledge that she has heard him. Her eyes are back on the adjacent chair.

"I've talked to their lawyers about your situation, about your past--"

This gets Joanne's attention, but Doug raises a hand, holding off any response.

"It's public record. They were bound to look into you on their own, and your story can only help us." He leans forward. "Joanne, you have, what I'd call, a very sympathetic case. If this goes to court, any judge would be likely to hand you a fat settlement. The lab knows that."

Joanne shakes her head the whole time Doug is speaking, but the gesture is small, impatient.

"This isn't about me. It's about Jeff and the--" she can't bring herself to continue the sentence. "I don't care what they want to give me. None of it matters when--"

Joanne's words choke to a halt again. Her eyes close

for a moment and when they open, Doug sees a familiar anger smoldering under their watery surface. A lake of pain. He presses his lips in a tight line, tells himself she is a client and this is her choice, but it doesn't work. Sitting there, with her straight spine and glittering eyes, Joanne might as well be his own child.

"You have other things to worry about," he tells her. "Let me handle this one."

"I don't need more money." Joanne sets her glass carefully on the edge of his desk. She folds her hands in her lap. "I just need this to be over."

"No." Doug waits until she meets his eyes. "What you really need is time. You need time to heal and to help your girls heal. But that takes money.

"Without this money, you'll have to get a job before long. Any job you can get. You'll have to put your girls in an after-school childcare program, in full-time childcare in the summer. You'll struggle to pay the bills while juggling all the responsibilities of single parenthood."

Joanne swallows hard, thinking that maybe it's time for her to do exactly that, but Doug is already ahead of her.

"You could do it," he continues. "I've seen you survive worse. But you don't have to. Once this settlement is worked out, it will let you stay home with the girls for several more years, maybe go back to school yourself. It will let you get back on your feet and start over on your own terms, when you're ready. All you have to do is let me handle this on your behalf."

Joanne is quiet after Doug finishes his speech. She hasn't gotten past what he said earlier. About her story.

"Doug, I--" Joanne pauses, weighing the words that

need to be said against the information that they've agreed to never discuss. "If they're looking into my past--"

Realization comes over Doug's face.

"They won't ask about that."

"You don't know that."

Doug taps his pen against the legal pad in front of him. The lab's lawyers could try to cast a shadow over the young, orphaned, widowed mother, but he doubts they would. Still, his mind turns over the possibilities.

"I didn't get to see Jeff," Joanne's voice is hollow now, her gaze back on the bookshelves. "After. They said he was too--"

"Joanne," Doug cuts her off with a promise that he hopes he can keep. "I'm going to get you a better deal, but this will be settled out of court. Quickly and quietly. Just give me some time and let me take care of it."

Joanne nods and relaxes her fingers, noticing the half-crescent grooves that her nails had dug into her palms. There's a small window in Doug's office, partially blocked by the branches of a fruit tree that are heavy with white blossoms. Joanne looks at the flowers and sighs.

"Thank you," she tells Doug, while still looking out the window, her mind on other things.

CHAPTER FIVE

Soft mumblings carry over the white noise of the baby monitor, announcing that Nolan is nearly awake. Eleanor pictures him stretched out in his small bed, his fringe of hair plastered to his warm temples and his cheeks flushed from nestling under his blankets. She can't imagine how she will pick him up, breathe in the sweet warmth of his toddler skin, and go about their day as if the world were the same place it had been less than an hour earlier. It's different now and she feels exposed. Vulnerable.

Eleanor turns her attention to Andy, sitting across the table from her. He chews his cold BLT quietly as she tries to understand how he can manage to eat and breathe and act like everything is normal. But then, this is normal for him, she remembers. The world has only changed for her. He has been hiding this secret. He has known.

What else does he know?

The question keeps repeating, now that Eleanor knows this much. Now that Andy has taken her to Joanne's house, baby monitor in hand, lunches left on the table, to show her Jeff's discovery. She doesn't want to believe it's real, but she has no choice.

"How--?" Eleanor starts to ask another question, but the words fade away.

Andy sighs and shakes his head at her. He had sat her down at the table, as soon as they returned, made up their plates and poured them each a glass of lemonade. She knows that he's trying. He's doing his best to make this easier on her. In his own way.

"I already told you," he replies. "I don't know how any of it works. Any of the science stuff. That was all Jeff." Sandwich finished, he moves on to his pile of barbecue chips.

"But I--" Again, Eleanor's words fail to form a full sentence. Her thoughts jump madly from one question to the next.

Their kitchen is sunny and bright. The deep blue cabinets, painted by Eleanor and Joanne just last year, stand out against the soft green walls and it feels like the wrong setting for this conversation. Eleanor's eyes linger over a large, framed picture of a single white daisy, a gift from Joanne, and, for the first time, she sees sadness in it.

"It's something about making a map," Andy talks into the uncomfortable silence, making an effort. He tries to remember the way Jeff used to explain it to him, but it had never made much sense and he'd never really cared how the thing worked.

"But it's like a thinking map," he continues. "And everyone has one that's not exactly the same and, the map thing, it's real complicated. But then Jeff found some easier way. He said the science guys were all making it too complicated. With what they were looking for, and how, and all. But they missed something because, uh, because Jeff found an easier way."

Eleanor can only stare, her mouth slack and brows lowered, but Andy doesn't notice her reaction. He's talking with his head down now, pushing broken chips around his plate.

"For a long time, it only worked for Jeff. The playback part, I mean. But then he figured out some stuff. Translating, transcoding stuff, or something. And then it worked for me, too, even though my thinking map thing is different. Or-- Fuck, I don't know. The science shit was Jeff's thing."

He drops the chip he was holding, frustrated, and reaches for half of Eleanor's sandwich, feeling the cold toast rough like sandpaper under his fingers. She hasn't taken a single bite and he's starting to get angry. He knew she'd have questions, knew she'd be shocked, but he hadn't expected this blank stare of a non-reaction.

He had thought she would at least be excited.

Eleanor's eyes drift across the table, taking in the placemats, the wooden napkin holder, and the set of glass salt and pepper shakers. The salt is nearly empty and she makes a mental note to refill it before dinner. Dinner. The idea of meatloaf and potatoes, green beans, and lemon pudding works its way into her mind. Whatever else happens, they will still need to eat.

With a few rapid blinks and a deep sigh, Eleanor can feel herself coming to terms with the situation. This is real, she tells herself. This is their new reality. Soon, her son will wake from his nap. Her husband will leave for work, at the place where he could probably be arrested for grand larceny, and her best friend will come home to a bigger shock than the life-altering crisis she is already facing. And Eleanor will make meatloaf.

A breeze flutters the white curtains on either side of the open window and they hear a dog barking in the distance. Andy chews through the sandwich. The yellow ceramic of Eleanor's plate reflects a half-moon of light around the wilting lettuce of the half-sandwich he left behind.

"But what you showed me," Eleanor clears her throat. "Those are the only memories? That Jeff… left?"

"Yeah, it's not that easy," Andy sets down the sandwich, frowns. "To record them and all."

He keeps talking, stumbling through an explanation, but Eleanor's mind travels on without him. Could they just get rid of the equipment? Could Andy sneak it back into the lab or just throw it away? Bury it somewhere or toss it in a lake? But then Joanne would never know. Never experience what Jeff had left for her or know what he had accomplished. Caught in those thoughts, Eleanor misses most of Andy's response.

"--and I think he's the right guy. The only guy really."

"The guy?"

"The scientist. The brain guy? David Tyler? Fuck, El, are you even listening to me?"

Eleanor stands up to bring their plates over to the sink. She doesn't want to hear more, but asks him to tell her again.

"Look, it's simple." Andy is on his feet now, crossing

the room to face her. "We need to get a scientist on board. Someone who can figure this shit out and finish what Jeff started."

"Finish what--" Eleanor's already churning stomach drops with a sickening thud. "You mean? What are you talking about?"

"Babe, come on! This is a huge fucking discovery!" Andy is pacing now, barely containing himself. He wants to shake Eleanor, to make her see the possibilities.

"Babe, Jeff figured out how to record his memories and then play them back. In. Someone. Else's. Head. How are you not fucking blown away by that?"

"I--" Eleanor can still feel where the electrodes were stuck to her temples, still see the images playing out behind her eyes. Jeff's memories mingling with her own. She *is* impressed. She *is* blown away. But any glimmer of excitement has been swallowed up by an unrelenting parade of disjointed thoughts. She can't stop thinking about Marie Curie being radiated by her own discovery, about tabloid newspaper headlines, sleazy reporters, angry men in white coats who own the lab, and another fear too dark to acknowledge.

"Think about what this could mean for the world!" Andy does not see the danger of their situation. He paces and gestures, his voice getting louder. "Think about what this thing lets us do. Actually *seeing* other people's thoughts? It's better than TV or movies or... Fuck, I don't know, it could even help people with old-timer's disease or be used in court cases... Can you even imagine what people would pay for this?"

"Pay?"

The room feels too big, too far away, as Eleanor tries to process this development. Andy is moving too fast and all she can think about now is smashing the equipment with a baseball bat. Utterly destroying it before Joanne gets home. But it's too late.

Stepping over to the window, Eleanor sees Joanne's blue car parked in the driveway. The wind chimes near the kitchen door are swaying slightly, as if she's just walked past. She's in the house now. In the house with Jeff's memories under her feet. Eleanor closes her eyes, reliving the sensation of being inside Jeff's memory. Of feeling the way he felt when looking at Joanne.

"All right," Eleanor speaks slowly, forming a plan of her own. "But first we tell Jo. *I* tell Jo. Alone. Tomorrow, after the girls leave for school."

Andy is nodding from the center of the room. A cough through the baby monitor warns them that Nolan is waking up and they don't have much time.

"But, we tell Jo first and go from there." Eleanor turns from the window to meet Andy's eyes. "No bringing in anyone else until we all agree that it's the right thing to do. Understood?"

"Yeah, of course, sure." Andy crosses the room to wrap his arms around Eleanor. "We do this when Jo's ready. We do it together. But, babe," his face breaks into a smile and he lifts her off the ground, nearly shouting, "We're going to get so fucking rich from this!"

CHAPTER SIX

In the cool of the basement, Joanne feels Eleanor apply the electrodes to her temples. Her gaze darts around the unfinished room. Jeff's room. She hasn't been back here in ages and it feels odd to realize that there is a room in her own home which has become completely unfamiliar. There are open rafters over their heads and rough wooden shelves along one wall. Everything in the room is practical and orderly. Neat stacks of notepads, even rows of secondhand books. A small, framed photo of Joanne and the girls sits beside the clunky beige machines.

In the center of the room, Joanne lies in a reclined chair that has a black leather seat attached to a metal frame. There is a rip along the back cushion that Jeff has covered with a strip of black duct tape. The matching ottoman has a small, unpatched tear along one of its seams. As Joanne lightly clutches the padded armrests, she tries not to remember Jeff bringing the worn chair set home soon after they were married. She knows they had a fight about it, but now she can't imagine why she had cared so much about a stupid chair. She doesn't want to remember the things she may have said.

Focusing on the feel of the chair helps Joanne forget the wires running from her temples and the rack of unfamiliar machinery by her side. Eleanor had said that Andy helped Jeff get the equipment in here and Joanne knows there is only one place where they could have gotten it. But that's something to deal with later, after she confirms the fantastic story Eleanor has just told her.

Beside her, Eleanor flips a central switch that brings the equipment to life with a whir and a hum. Nolan is resting upstairs, curled under a thin blanket in front of a DVD. His cough had gotten worse in the night and now, focused on what will happen in the next few minutes, Eleanor silently hopes that the medicine she gave him this morning has already put him to sleep.

She watches the screen as it glows blue, then flashes to black with quickly scrolling white text. Joanne watches, too, craning her neck to see around Eleanor's body. An instant later the monitor displays a gray-and-black checkerboard background. A single black window opens in the center of the virtual desktop and a cursor blinks slowly, waiting for direction.

Eleanor hesitates over the keyboard, still feeling the overwhelming sensations from when she was the one in the chair. Still worried about how Joanne will react. With a deep breath, she types "go" and presses enter. The tiny white arrow becomes an hourglass that rotates in jerky, 90-degree turns. Joanne begins to tremble. A second window appears with rows of reassuringly labeled icons.

Eleanor exhales slowly.

"Okay," she turns to face Joanne. "This is it. Are you ready?"

Joanne nods tightly and Eleanor positions the cursor over one of the icons. She pauses before clicking the mouse.

"Close your eyes."

In the darkness behind her eyelids, Joanne sees fading, shimmering oblongs of bluish-yellow light. The decaying reflection of the basement's bare lightbulb. Her head rests against the padded support as she waits, feeling nothing.

"*Joanne...*" Jeff's voice echoes faintly, and Joanne's eyes pop open.

Eleanor clutches her hand, squeezes reassuringly.

"Close your eyes," she repeats in a hoarse whisper, but Joanne's eyes stay slightly cracked, her mind struggling to stay in the basement with Eleanor.

Phantom sounds ring in Joanne's ears, soft at first but growing louder. There are birds chirping, and a... a waterfall? A river? A feeling surges upward, through and above her, overwhelming her panic with a calm sense of wonder. As the feeling infuses her body, her gaze loses focus and Eleanor blurs into the background. *Happy.* It's a feeling of happiness. Disoriented, Joanne sinks back into the emotion and closes her eyes completely.

It's a sunny day. Warm. There is fresh-cut grass and a worn pink blanket covered in fine, web-like patches of balled up lint from multiple washings. Joanne knows that blanket. There are paper plates and napkins, plastic containers, and an open bag of potato chips. There is laughter and there is a girl sitting on the other side of the blanket. The stream flows behind her, sunlight glinting off ripples as the water trickles down graduated lines of flat, wet rock.

"*I love it here.*" Jeff's voice again, soft and faint.

The laughter is distant. More of a sensation than an actual sound. Joanne knows that it is close. She can almost feel it bubbling up in her own chest. It's the sensation of watching someone else having a good time and feeling drawn in. It's catching sight of cute kids playing in a park, their parents laughing from a nearby bench, and forgetting yourself long enough to join in, smiling and laughing for just a moment—that brief moment—before remembering that you aren't with the people you are watching. That you are intruding.

She can feel the smile on her face, but there is something… *different*… in the smile. Something *different* in the feel of her own facial muscles. Something not quite… Looking at the girl brings a warmth through Joanne. A desire which may not be her own. The girl across from her is-- The girl is familiar and unfamiliar at the same time. The sensation is like seeing someone across the room at a party, someone you had known, known well, but can't place. It's the knowing that you *should* know that person, knowing that you did or do, but didn't and don't, all at the same time.

The girl across from Joanne *is* Joanne.

Her eyes fly open again, but Eleanor has been standing watch, as if waiting for this reaction. She covers Joanne's eyes with her cool hand, gently urging her to keep them closed.

"Shhh…" she murmurs through her own fear. "Relax… It's all right…"

The vision, the sounds, pull Joanne back. No. It's the sensations, the feelings that pull her in. It's like waking from a particularly strong dream and feeling caught in its grasp. Her mind is at odds, feeling both the reality of the basement and the pull of the dreamworld. She is aware of the feel of Eleanor's soft hand. She is aware of the cold, faintly acrid smells of the cement floor and the metal equipment rack. But there is also something beneath Joanne's hands. Not beneath the hands that rest on the leather chair, but under the strong hands that she suddenly feels as her own.

The hands are moving. Her right fingers are swiping, up and down, grasping something lightly. Her left fingertips press against an uneven surface that causes a strangely vague sensation. Guitar music. There is guitar music, coming from her own hands, as if her hands had always held this power.

Jeff's voice sings lightly, "Joanne... Jo-oh-anne... How I love, to be your man..."

On the blanket, the other Joanne laughs, rolls her eyes, reaches for a handful of chips, makes a playful face and looks away--

"Stop!"

Joanne sits upright, slapping away Eleanor's hands and clawing at the electrodes. "Stop it! Just-- just stop it!" Her breath is shallow and the room is hazy. A ghostly image superimposes itself over the bleak surroundings of the basement room: the sounds—*that voice*—mixing and merging with the hum of the equipment by her side.

She can't get away. She can't breathe.

Eleanor springs into motion, scrolling the mouse

frantically across the screen to click on the digital controls. By the time she turns back, Joanne has peeled off the electrodes. She stares at the plastic squares, lying limp in her shaking hands. Her entire body trembles as her head shakes slowly from side to side.

"What was that?" She asks at last, her voice strained. Shaky and shrill. Eleanor sits down in the desk chair, wheeling it closer and cautiously placing her hands over Joanne's. The thin wires from the electrodes tangle between them.

"What was that?" Joanne repeats, softer now, hoarse and desperate.

"That was Jeff's memory."

Joanne continues to shake her head, though she appears to be unaware of the motion.

"That's impossible."

Eleanor's eyes are steady, relying on her gaze to transfer the truth.

"But you remember that day?" She doesn't have to ask. The answer is painted across Joanne's face. She was there, in her own memory, and in Jeff's. Eleanor suddenly wonders if there's something dangerous about seeing your own memory through another person's eyes.

"You've watched it?" Joanne's eyes cling, looking for a moment's hesitation, any flicker to betray her words. Eleanor's stare softens with compassion.

"Once." She's already answered this question. But that was before.

Joanne has no choice but to believe her. Now. She sits for a moment, digesting the information, feeling it tumble through her brain, disrupting previously formed beliefs and raising half-formed questions.

"How many are there?"

"Three," Eleanor tells her promptly, gauging Joanne's reaction. Something has shifted. She senses that Joanne is okay, or will be okay, but sees that her heart is still pounding. Her eyes are still wide and wild.

"You've watched them all?"

"They're very short," Eleanor nods.

"And there isn't--?"

"No," Eleanor reassures. "There isn't." She tries to gauge Joanne's shock and decide how to help. "Do you want to try again? To see the rest of this one?"

"No," Joanne answers quickly, before considering the question. "Maybe," she adds. "But not yet. Not now."

Eleanor nods. There is a thump through the floorboards above. Nolan calls out for Eleanor.

"Damn, I thought he would sleep." She starts to rise, but Joanne grasps her wrist.

"How did he do it?" She needs answers that Eleanor doesn't have.

"I don't know. Andy is the only person he told, and well… You know Andy. He couldn't begin to understand something like this."

They sit together while Joanne thinks about Jeff's dreams, his fantastic ideas. She thinks about all the hours she thought he had only been studying in here. There are textbooks still stacked on the shelves and piled on the table. More textbooks than he would ever need for his night school classes. But he had said the classes weren't moving fast enough. That he needed these secondhand books. That he had his own theories.

When Nolan calls for her again, Eleanor pats Joanne's hand reassuringly and says she'll be right back.

"Why?" Joanne speaks into the silence, stopping Eleanor at the door. "Why did he tell Andy?" *And not me*, she doesn't say aloud.

"I don't know. He needed help getting the equipment."

It isn't much of an answer, but Joanne nods anyway.

"I guess they had big plans for it," Eleanor adds in an attempt to explain. But an unrelated image has appeared in Joanne's mind: Jeff's clothes hanging neatly in their closet, just beyond his empty side of the bed.

"And then Jeff died," she says flatly. For the first time, she feels nothing when the words pass through her lips.

"Yes," Eleanor agrees. "Then Jeff died."

CHAPTER SEVEN

Nolan is asleep in his small bed, nestled under a blue blanket with swirling airplane designs. The nightlight glow highlights his rounded cheeks and fringe of dark lashes. The airplane blanket is one of the few gifts from Andy's mother that Eleanor hasn't quietly exchanged for store credit. She tries to forget where it came from as she lingers in the upstairs hallway, watching her son sleep. She doesn't want to go downstairs, back to the adult world, but she forces herself to move, making a detour through the kitchen to pour a glass of red wine.

In the living room, Andy sits on the couch, listening to Eleanor move through the kitchen as he lights up a joint. He waits, patiently, as she rattles glassware in the next room, straightening up something in the already clean kitchen. He watches, when she finally appears, as she turns the radio on softly and sets the baby monitor on the coffee table. Music mixes with the gentle static, periodically disrupted by the familiar sounds of Nolan's snuffling sleep.

Eleanor sets her glass of wine next to Andy's shoebox stash, pretending not to see it. She thinks people who have become parents are too old to be smoking pot. He thinks there are too many empty wine bottles going out with their trash. But they've stopped arguing about both ideas. Mostly.

Silence stretches between them as Andy slouches back to get a better read on Eleanor's posture. Her back is straight, shoulders down and chin jutting slightly forward. She's perched on the edge of the couch, ready to move.

"Well?" Andy knows that Eleanor won't tell him on her own.

"Well what?"

Andy lifts the joint and inhales slowly, willing himself to be patient. Eleanor knows what he is asking. He lowers his hand to the ceramic bowl that sits on a cushion between them and Eleanor reaches forward for her glass of wine.

"Okay," she says after a quick swallow. "I told her."

"Good," Andy nods. "Good. How'd she take it?"

"How do you think?" The words come out harsher than Eleanor intends. She drinks the rest of her wine and realizes that the empty glass is shaking in her hand. She wants to pour a second glass, but doesn't want to see the judgment in Andy's eyes.

He holds the smoke out to her and she slaps it away.

"Oh, come on, babe," Andy takes another long inhale. "You know we had to tell her."

"Don't say it like that."

"Like what?"

"Like," Eleanor clutches her fingers around the base

of the glass, searching for something to say. "Like it's some normal thing. Like it's not completely insane to have to tell my best friend that there's a computer in her basement that holds her dead husband's memories. And, oh yeah, by the way, my husband wants to use those memories to make lots and lots of money."

When she finishes speaking, Eleanor springs off the couch and heads back into the kitchen.

"Damn it, El," Andy's voice is low and hollow, more musing than upset.

"Why do you do that?" He asks the empty room, then clarifies when Eleanor returns with a full glass and the open bottle. "Why do you always make me the fucking bad guy?"

"I don't *always* do anything." She stands across the room from him, in the doorway, drinking her wine and glaring toward the front door. "But maybe, in this case, you kind of are the bad guy."

Instead of taking offense, Andy settles back into the couch and quietly presses out the joint, leaving it in the ceramic bowl. He considers what she said, looking up at the ceiling. A feeling of distant calm washes over him.

"Well, fuck. Maybe I am the bad guy. This time." He says it in a mellow tone which only infuriates Eleanor more. "Doesn't change anything though."

Eleanor ignores him to focus on the slight spinning that has started in her head. She's tempted to pour another glass of wine, but she can't now that he's stopped smoking. Her eyes drop to the green shag carpet and the question echoes in her head, wanting to come out.

"Come on, babe," Andy gets up slowly and moves

across the room to take the empty glass and half-full bottle from Eleanor's hands. "Let's not fight."

"It was just--" Eleanor remembers Joanne's face, tear-stained and helpless. "You weren't there. You didn't have to see her pain."

"I know, I know," Andy consoles as he leads Eleanor back to the couch. "But it's done, and once she gets used to the idea, it will be good. We had to tell her."

Eleanor nods, but her thoughts are fuzzy now. The room is dimly lit, the radio is playing slow jazz. Eleanor's mind is softening around the question. She relaxes into the couch and narrows in on Andy's eyes, seeking out the golden flecks within the hazel, feeling an echo of the first time she noticed those flecks, back when they were kids on a school picnic, shy and nervous to be alone together. The memory weakens her defense and the question escapes.

"Those are the only memories?"

Andy's brows come together questioningly.

"The three you showed me?" Eleanor clarifies, but there's an edginess creeping into her voice. A jittery sensation climbs up her ribs and sharpens the angles of her mind, now that the question has been asked.

"Yeah, it's just them." Andy tenses, without moving from his comfortable slouch. "Why would that matter?"

"It's just--" Eleanor's cheeks flush. She casts around for steady footing. "I don't know. It's like reading someone's diary, but worse. You expect thoughts to be private... Protected."

"Oh," Andy shakes the idea away. "Babe, Jeff chose to share these thoughts. They weren't private anymore."

"Yeah, but," Eleanor looks down at their hands, side

by side on the couch. A voice tells her to let it go, but the question slips out again. "But those are the only memories? Those three?"

Andy turns her face to look up at him. His body stays settled, but his jaw is clenched and his eyes are probing. For a moment, dread slices through Eleanor's chest. And then Andy smiles. He slides his hand down her neck and squeezes her shoulder gently.

"Just those three. That's all."

Eleanor smiles back, weakly, before her eyes drop and she settles into the couch. They sit that way for a few minutes. The soft music and haze of wine lulls Eleanor into her day's first calm moments. Andy feels her relaxing beside him and shifts closer.

"Remember the guy I told you about?" Andy is leaning toward her. His right hand is on her thigh now, while his left is gently holding her hand. The cushions are soft behind her back. Relief is spreading throughout her body.

Eleanor nods vaguely, though she doesn't remember at all.

"I talked to him at work this morning. I told him Jeff left a bunch of research stuff that might mean something to him." Andy nuzzles her neck, bringing his hand higher on her thigh.

"Mmmm," her shoulders are melting beneath his warm breath, while his words seem to drift in from a great distance.

"I think he's taking the bait." Andy's lips move down her collarbone. His hand reaches its destination. "Just need to reel him in."

"Mmm hmmm," Eleanor sinks deeper into the

cushions. Her hand reaches for Andy's waist and his words begin to take shape.

"Wait, what?" Eleanor opens her eyes, sitting up and pushing him away. "Who are you--? Who did you talk to?"

Andy sighs, attempting to press her back into place. His voice and eyes are deliberately soft.

"The guy. Tyler," he runs his hand back up her thigh, but Eleanor hardly notices.

"Tyler?"

Andy makes a soft, shushing sound as his hand lifts to cup her breast.

"Relax. It's nothing. We can talk about it later."

"No," Eleanor brushes his hand away. "Let's talk about it now."

"Tyler," Andy sighs. "The brain guy. I told you about him."

"Wait," Eleanor sits up, shifting her body out of reach. "Are you saying that you talked to a scientist? At the lab? You said you weren't going to do that yet."

"Babe. El," Andy tries to recapture her hands, but Eleanor rushes to her feet, bumping the coffee table and knocking over the open bottle. Wine pools across the wood veneer and drips slowly to the carpet below. Eleanor doesn't notice and Andy doesn't care.

"El, come on," Andy sinks back into the couch with a groan.

"Andy," Eleanor speaks slowly, making each word count. "You promised me."

"Yeah, okay, maybe," Andy shakes his head, not understanding her anger. "But I didn't tell him about the fucking memory machine. I just laid some groundwork.

Said there were some notes and shit."

Eleanor runs her hands over her face, letting her fingertips comb through her spiky hair and massage into her scalp.

"El, look," Andy begins crossing toward her slowly, hands raised. "Tyler liked Jeff, okay? They were like work friends and shit. Go to lunch and whatever, so the doc knows how smart he was. Even used some of Jeff's ideas in a research thing, or something. So, it's not a big thing for me to ask if he wants any notes Jeff left behind, you know? And if I can just get him over here…"

"Then what?" Her voice snaps. "What is this master plan? Going to pin him down and slap the electrodes on him?"

"Fuck, El, of course not."

Andy sighs. Eleanor waits.

"Alright, fine. You know he was at Jeff's funeral, right?" His tone shifts as excitement creeps in. "And I saw him looking all sad-eyed at Jo. So, I figure, he comes over, and she tells him the rest. More chance he'll listen. And it's not like he's going to turn in the pretty, little widow for grand fucking larceny, right?"

Eleanor drops her hands to her side and stares, lips pursed and head cocked to one side. The room rocks lightly.

"So, let me get this straight. In your brilliant plan, Joanne—my best friend—is the *bait*?" She spits the last word at him in disgust, but Andy shakes his head, then wobbles a bit on his feet.

"No. The *notes* are the bait," he corrects. "Jo is just… Okay, wait, so the doc is a cat. And I'm a dog. He's not going to trust me because I'm a dog. But Jo is a mouse, so she's not a threat to a cat, and it's like she's... uh..."

Eleanor raises an eyebrow.

"Bait?"

"No, not bait. She's like..." Andy meets Eleanor's eyes. "Okay, look, we need this guy's help and I'm just saying it's a lot harder to turn down the widow who's all vulnerable and shit. And, yeah, it doesn't hurt that she's pretty and sad and shit."

"You're an ass."

"I'm an ass?" Andy sneers, shaking his head. "Maybe I'm doing Jo a favor. We know she likes smart guys. And it's not like it takes her long to move on."

The shove comes so fast that Andy stumbles backward, nearly falling to the floor before catching his balance. Eleanor's hands are clutched in fists and her breath is short and fast. She's shaking with the effort to hold herself back. Andy's mocking laugh has stopped. His eyes are cold and hard.

"Right. I'm not supposed to care, when it's *my* best friend who's dead."

Eleanor freezes. She drops her fists and they stare at each other across too many years of memories. Gradually, her spine straightens and her chin lifts.

"You're high," she tells Andy simply. "You're impossible. This is pointless to get into. Again. And I'm going to bed."

As she turns to leave, Andy reaches for her arm. She tenses but his touch is tender. He pulls her close and whispers an apology. He kisses the side of her face, her neck, her jaw. His body is fluid, his eyes damp. She wants to resist, but his words still repeat in her head. She knows that he's vulnerable, underneath it all. And she knows why.

His lips move across her cold skin. His hands roam over her body, pulling at her clothes, lifting up, sliding in. And Eleanor lets him, thinking that she owes him that much, at least.

CHAPTER EIGHT

Joanne's feet pound the treadmill while the driving bass echoes through her headphones. For weeks, she has felt left behind, frozen in place while the rest of the world has kept moving forward around her. Rushing past her with the momentum of those who have places to be and people to see. It feels personal. It feels like time has refused to stop and wait for her to get her bearings. Like time has been mocking her for being out of step. But here, in this moment, the music spurs her to catch up. To overtake time itself.

As Joanne runs, the violent, throbbing rhythms of the music shut out all other thoughts, all memories of the day. The music lifts her up. It fills her. It moves her as if the rhythm itself is speaking to her muscles, bypassing her tired brain. For a moment, it feels as if she's stolen time from a past when she was alive. When Jeff was alive. She can almost believe that it's true. That he's here. That she has turned back time.

Until she looks across the room.

The door to the back room is on the left side of the basement, in sight of the treadmill. Joanne wonders how many nights she had been down here, running, while Jeff was shut away behind that door. She wonders if she had been right here when he captured his first memory. Had he wanted to celebrate? Had he even wanted to tell her? Why had it been a secret? From her. What else hadn't he told her?

Closing her eyes, Joanne wills her mind to stop thinking, and grips the padded sidebars to fight the dizziness of running blind. Her fingers curl around the bars as they had curled around the padded armrests of the leather chair earlier today. Flashes enter her mind, despite the blaring volume of her running music. That picnic. That summer. The summer before Jeff left for college and before Winter Break. Before she had gotten pregnant and before they were married. Before he quit school to take a job at the lab. Before the pain of watching his hope erode as the bills came in, as the sonogram showed *two* little growing blobs, *two* heartbeats. Two little people dependent on them both.

The music swells as Joanne stumbles blindly forward. The driving beat yields to a woman's voice, rising and falling in wordless surrender. Only the barest rhythm keeps time below her primal song. It's music without time, sensations without meaning. Through the hazy view of her music and motion-induced trance, Joanne opens her eyes and again sees the door. Jeff's door.

A quick pull on the safety cord causes Joanne's sliding world to jerk to an abrupt halt. Her body pulses with the

The Insistence of Memory

abandoned movement, with the driving force of the persistent bass line. When she pulls off the headphones the silence is overpowering.

Her feet echo on the cement floor.

The back room's secret equipment turns on easily with the flick of one switch on a central power strip. In minutes, Joanne has the electrodes attached to her temples. She types "go" at the prompt, just as Eleanor had done nearly twelve hours earlier. From there, a pair of clearly labeled icons appear. The icons Jeff had labeled. One is marked "program_start_click_first," another "list_of_memories." After clicking the *program_start* icon, three more files appear: *memory_1, memory_2, memory_3*.

Joanne's hand hesitates over the mouse. Three memories. Just three.

She watches the cursor hover near the icons, waiting for something to happen on its own. Waiting for something to take the choice away. But nothing happens.

She doesn't know how much time has passed. She doesn't know how long she has stared at the dark screen before finally choosing memory_1 and settling back into the chair.

The picture is clearer this time. Once her eyes adjust enough to make out the image, Joanne finds that she can shift her vision around, bringing out the details. There is a bridge not far from their picnic, and kids are dropping rocks into the stream beneath it. She can't exactly see them, as the vision within the memory is looking forward at the girl on the blanket, at her own young self, but Joanne senses they are there. Maybe Jeff saw them earlier or maybe they wandered in from her own memory. With that thought, she stops examining the background, wanting to see Jeff's memory alone.

Looking at herself from the outside is less startling this time around. It isn't like looking at herself in a mirror, where the part of her hair and the slant of her nose are backward, and it's not quite the same as seeing a picture or a video of herself either. Everything about her seems softer, prettier. She fights the urge to pick out the flaws and bring in the details of the flyaway hairs, the acne, and her crooked front tooth. She wants to surrender to the experience of being Jeff. Of seeing herself the way did. In that moment.

"Joanne... Jo-oh-anne..." Jeff's teenage singing voice is exactly the way she remembers it, reedy and thin, though he drops it as much as he can, striving for a full, deep bass. *"How I love, to be your man..."*

The Joanne in the memory puts down her chips, stops laughing and leans forward, past her crossed legs. She puts her hand over Jeff's to stop his strumming, while real-life Joanne wants to cut her off.

Don't say it, she wants to yell, just listen to him sing. Just be young and happy and don't make him feel bad about chasing his dreams. But the memory has already happened and she is powerless to change it now.

"Do you have to go?" Young Joanne asks with large, pleading brown eyes. There is a physical catch, a twinge in Joanne's-- in *Jeff's* chest. "Can't you stay with me? Wait and go to college with me next year."

Jeff's voice laughs, gentle and soothing, but Joanne now feels the pain behind his smiling face. Happiness and regret, excitement and sadness all mixing together under the warm sunlight. His hands reach out to pull Joanne close and the smell of her hair, like strawberries and vanilla, fills the air.

Joanne remembers that shampoo and wonders when she stopped using it. Why she stopped using it.

"Aw, Jo, it's only a year. I'll visit at Christmas and Easter... It will go by so fast, I swear."

They nestle together, Joanne's face buried in Jeff's chest, his guitar now forgotten on the blanket. Across the water, an old couple walk, hand in hand. The Joanne cuddled against Jeff's chest can't see them, but flesh-and-blood Joanne, now looking through Jeff's eyes, sees their contented smiles, their comfortable gait. She hears Jeff's internal thought as he watches them pass. *That will be us someday.* Joanne feels her own soft hair snagging under her *(his)* callused fingertips. As the trees rustle gently overhead, Joanne feels the warmth swell Jeff's chest as he inhales her sweet, teenage scent. The simple beauty of the moment takes her breath away, even before she hears Jeff's last recorded thought:

This is the girl I'm going to marry.

CHAPTER NINE

The next morning, Eleanor approaches Joanne's side door cautiously. Nolan is perched on her hip, she has her keys poised to unlock the door, but her stomach is clenched against the fear of facing Joanne.

Focused on what she will say, how she will act, Eleanor startles when Ruthie jerks the door open. The small face stares up with pale worry and a quick glance around the kitchen sends Eleanor's heart into her throat. Cereal flakes and splashes of milk spill across the table. A drawer is half open, revealing the tray of silverware inside. There is no coffee brewing on the counter. Joanne is nowhere in sight. Sarah pouts in front of her soggy bowl of cereal, while Ruthie stands her ground, trembling by the back door.

"Where's your mommy?" Eleanor struggles for a bright tone as she carefully deposits Nolan in an empty chair. She tells herself that everything is fine. That Joanne is back in bed with the covers pulled over her head. That this is just a setback.

The girls shrug. Ruthie's eyes are wide with terror and Sarah's pout turns to an outright scowl. Eleanor frowns.

"You haven't seen her?"

"No," Tears spill onto Ruthie's cheeks as she shakes her head. "She's not in her room or anything. She's gone."

"She's dead, like Daddy," Sarah adds in a matter-of-fact tone that sends chills through the room.

"She's not dead!" Eleanor rushes to wrap her arms around Ruthie, who has begun sobbing, and fixes Sarah with a scolding look. Sarah's arms are crossed in front of her small body and her face is screwed up in a tight frown, but her eyes begin to show a glimmer of hope. If Aunt El is cross with her and showing it, she decides, then she must think her mother is still alive. People are nicer when parents are dead.

"Really?" Sarah narrows her eyes to better catch a lie, but Aunt El has always been hard to read.

"I'm sure she's fine," Eleanor insists, despite the images whirling through her mind.

Sarah and Eleanor lock eyes, while Ruthie continues to whimper. After a moment, Sarah nods, satisfied, and turns back to her bowl. Nolan picks dry cereal off the table, half-crawling to reach the pieces farthest away, and shoves them into his small mouth. A moment later, a horn blares from the front of the house causing Ruthie to jump out of Eleanor's embrace.

"Oh no! The bus!" Her eyes slide around the kitchen, frantic. "We don't have lunches!"

"It's all right," Eleanor assures her, while Sarah simply sinks deeper into her chair. "Don't worry about the bus. I'll pack your lunches and drive you to school today.

"Now, did you check the basement?"

Ruthie shakes her head, reminding, "We're not allowed down there."

"We yelled down," Sarah adds in a sarcastic grumble, implying that *she* wanted to do more.

"Okay, well, you two keep an eye on Nolan for a minute and I'll go check it out. Your mom's probably just... lost track of time... doing the laundry."

"Maybe she's running?" Ruthie asks, wiping her eyes. Her small brow screws into a thoughtful frown. "Though she doesn't at breakfast. Not when there's school."

Eleanor squeezes Ruthie's hand reassuringly and looks between the two girls, but she doesn't know what else to say.

Downstairs, the empty treadmill sits directly across from the bottom of the stairs. Eleanor doesn't see the abandoned mp3 player or the safety cord strewn on the floor. She scarcely notices that the lights are on. All she sees, as she rounds the corner, is the door to the back room standing wide open. She pauses then, bracing herself.

In Jeff's room, Joanne sprawls in the leather recliner, electrodes pasted to her temples. Her hair has escaped its ponytail to tumble around her shoulders, her arms are crossed loosely over her middle, and one leg is bent at an odd angle. All of the equipment is on and Joanne is fast asleep.

As Eleanor looks down at her, she steels herself against rising feelings. Her mind holds too many other images of Joanne sleeping. Memories of waking up together in this very house, in the room now shared by Ruthie and Sarah. Joanne's old room. Memories of

Joanne's grandmother making them pancakes and eggs on Saturday mornings. Waffles and bacon on Sundays.

In those days, Eleanor had felt more welcome in this house than in her own. She'd lie awake at night wishing that Joanne's grandmother could take her in, too, but she would have never said it out loud. She didn't have to.

"Joanne," Eleanor shakes her shoulder, harder than she should. "Joanne, wake up."

After shifting awkwardly in the firm chair, Joanne's eyes part just a crack. She lifts an arm and it catches in the wires running from the electrodes. Her mouth is dry and she presses her lips together, squinting in the light. Eleanor carefully removes the electrodes from her temples, wrapping the wires into hasty bundles.

"Wh-what happened?" Joanne is groggy, disoriented.

"You fell asleep." Eleanor pulls the desk chair over to sit at Joanne's side. "It's morning."

Joanne's head swivels to take in her surroundings. The concrete walls, the whirring computers. Realization clouds her face. "The girls?"

"They're upstairs. Okay, but worried when they couldn't find you."

"What time is it?" Joanne wipes the crust from the corners of her mouth and blinks her eyes. Sleep still clings to her and it draws Eleanor in, soothing her earlier panic and taking her back to the time when it was just the two of them facing the world together.

There is a clock on the wall. Joanne bolts upright when she sees the time.

"Oh, the girls! The bus!"

"It's okay," With a restraining hand on Joanne's arm,

Eleanor repeats the reassurances she had given upstairs. "I'll get them to school."

Joanne settles back, nodding, still caught in the memories she had experienced the night before. The sound of Jeff's voice haunts her mind. The feel of his body, warm and taut with restrained energy, still tingles under her own skin. She isn't ready to remember the years in between or the pain of the past few weeks. She sits with her eyes half-closed, letting the sensations flow through her.

There's something that Eleanor wants to say, but she bites it back.

"We'll go up now," she says instead. "We need to let the girls know that you're okay."

As they move toward the stairs, Eleanor keeps her hand on Joanne's arm, guiding her, even as Joanne pauses to stretch muscles that are stiff from her night in the rigid chair.

"I'll take the girls to school," Eleanor repeats softly, then adds, "You had me worried, too."

"I'm sorry," Joanne's words are a reflex and she fleetingly wonders what she really means. There are too many things to be sorry for.

As if reading her mind, Eleanor stops in the doorway, holding Joanne back. She knows the girls are waiting anxiously, but she can't wait any longer herself. If she doesn't say it now, it may be too late.

"Jo," she hesitates, channeling all of her conviction into one steady look. "We have to destroy it."

"What?" Joanne stares back, searching for understanding.

"We have to dismantle it. Get rid of it. The whole thing, before this goes any further."

In the weak morning light, Joanne can see Eleanor's fear. She tries to feel it for herself, tries to be pragmatic and protect Eleanor the way Eleanor has always protected her, but Jeff's memories are too fresh. Joanne shakes her head, holding Eleanor's gaze. She won't let these memories go. They're too precious.

"El, they're just a few memories. Who does it hurt to keep them?"

"Jo," Eleanor grips Joanne's hand. "Andy wants to bring in a scientist from the lab. Someone who can make sense of all this. And... And turn it into something more."

"Someone from the lab?" Joanne recoils at the thought of a stranger watching Jeff's memories. "Who?"

"I don't know. A neuroscientist, I guess. Tyler something or something Tyler?"

"David Tyler?"

"I think so. Why? Do you know him?"

"Jeff did," Joanne remembers him from the funeral. Tall, thin, and soft-spoken. Curly brown hair and wire-rimmed glasses. Maybe five to ten years older than Jeff, but different than the other men from the lab who had come to pay their respects. Quieter. And he stayed the longest, sitting alone in the back row of seats as everyone else filed out.

"He listened to Jeff," she tells Eleanor now. "He encouraged him and listened, and Jeff looked up to him."

"Well, that--" The expression on Joanne's face worries Eleanor. "That doesn't matter now. Jo, we don't really know this guy. We can't trust him with this. What if he turns Andy in? What if it affects your settlement with the lab?

"We just can't let this go further," she insists. "We have to get rid of it all. Soon. Today, even."

Joanne shakes her head more firmly and, for the first time since Jeff's death, Eleanor sees real strength behind her eyes. Her heart sinks at the sight, not wanting to be the one to take that courage away.

"El, how can I do that? Give this up? You can't give me back a piece of Jeff and then expect me to just throw it away. You can't ask me to do that.

"Besides, Jeff trusted David--" Eleanor doesn't let her go on, putting as much gravity as she can muster in her next words.

"No, Jo, he didn't. If he had, he would have told him about all of this himself."

They stand in the doorway together, silently weighing the situation. Silently weighing each other's will.

"Aunt El?" A thin young voice calls down, breaking the tense moment. "Mommy?"

"It's okay, Ruthie," Joanne calls back. Her voice is bright, cheery, and Eleanor knows that Joanne is going to win this fight.

When they reach the kitchen, both girls run into Joanne's arms, knocking her to the floor as they fold together in a tearful embrace. They haven't clung to Joanne like this in weeks. Not since before the funeral. They haven't cried this freely or shown such pure relief.

"It's okay," Joanne repeats over and over. "Mommy is fine. Everything is going to be just fine."

Closing the basement door, Eleanor watches them, vowing to make those promises come true. Even if Joanne can't.

CHAPTER TEN

The morning air is crisp and cool when David climbs out of his dark green hatchback. It feels more like fall than spring, but he knows it will be warm by noon and wishes that he could have taken the day off. These longings to be out of the office have gotten stronger and they bother David. He remembers better days. Days when he was eager to be at work and proud of being on Keller's team. He perches his metal travel mug on the roof of the car, reaching into the backseat for his laptop case, and doesn't see Andy's long strides closing in across the blacktop.

"Hey, doc!"

The twisted strap of David's laptop case digs into his shoulder as he turns toward the voice.

"Ah. Morning, Andy."

David gestures toward the lab and starts walking, letting Andy fall in step beside him. The watery morning light glints off the security fence and casts a platinum haze over the building ahead. Normally David enjoys the walk in from the parking lot. He likes the imposing look of the stark brick building with its angular lines and darkly tinted windows. He likes having these few minutes of quiet to look at the building and remember why he wanted to work here.

"So, you remember that stuff I told you about?" Andy begins. "Jeff's notes and stuff?"

"Oh, uh, yes, of course," David takes a sip of his coffee to hide his ambivalence. "Did you bring them in?"

"Well, no." Andy stops walking. He lets his gaze drift toward the south end of the complex where the construction work on the farthest building has come into view. David pauses to see what has caught Andy's attention, then swallows a lump in this throat. The reconstruction is the last physical reminder of the explosion that killed Jeff and left two scientists badly burned.

"They're making good progress."

Andy's words hang between them.

David shifts his weight and hitches the laptop strap more firmly onto his shoulder. Metallic clangs drift across the empty expanse. They are the only ones in the parking lot, other than the guard in his gate booth.

"It's a damn thing," Andy continues. "You know he left twins behind? Eight years old. Every time I see those girls I think how they probably won't even remember Jeff. Not really, you know? And another accident? It's gotta be extra hard on Joanne. Considering."

David doesn't respond. Andy glances his way, as if just remembering who he's talking to, and shakes his head.

"I guess you wouldn't know about that, though. About her past?"

David remains silent, but Andy continues to stare until David eventually meets his eye. There's a vague curiosity in David's look, which Andy takes as encouragement to go on.

"Joanne's parents died in a car accident when she was a kid. Both of them."

"That's--" David clears his throat. "That's terrible."

"Yeah, she's had it pretty rough. And then there was--" Andy trails off.

"Was?" David prompts, just as Andy expected he would, but his question is more polite than genuinely interested and the detached tone throws Andy off pace. It brings a surge of anger that he forces himself to swallow back.

"Well, then there was... well," Andy tamps down his feelings and gestures vaguely toward the construction, "there was this."

David takes another sip of coffee and fidgets with his laptop strap again. He wonders how to extricate himself from the conversation without offending Andy.

"Look, I--"

"Right," Andy rushes to cut him off and they start walking again. "You need to get to work. And you don't need to be bothered with stuff that's not your problem."

"Well, it's not that--" Though it is exactly that.

"No, doc, don't worry about it." Andy waves off David's words, working to regain his upper hand. "You've got important stuff to do and, well, I-- Look, I just want you to know that it meant a lot, okay? You were real good to Jeff and he needed that. Not a lot of people understood him. You know? Hell, I didn't have a fucking clue about what he was saying half the time. But you did and that was good for him. To have someone to talk to, you know?"

David frowns, uncomfortable with the praise.

They are almost at the gate and David pauses to fish his badge out of the front pocket of his laptop case. Andy's badge is already clipped to his shirtfront.

"He had a lot of good ideas," David manages, though it feels inadequate.

"You think? Really?" Andy asks, as if genuinely surprised.

"Absolutely," David straightens up and levels Andy with a look meant to convey his sincerity. "Jeff's insightful ideas have helped me create computational models that could someday lead to significant advancements in cognitive neuroscience."

"Huh," Andy squints and cocks his head to one side, giving David a look that instantly sends him back to a high school hallway where the jocks were happy to copy his homework, but never really wanted him around. And then Andy laughs, shaking his head. "Way over my head, doc. But it sounds good when you say it."

David fumbles awkwardly with his badge, glancing down at his own credentials before slipping the lanyard around his neck.

"You, uh, said something about Jeff's notes?"

"Oh, right," Andy responds as if he'd forgotten about them. "I wanted to talk to you about that."

They both hold up their badges and pass through the gate, but then slow to a stop on the other side, as if knowing the conversation will come to an end the moment they enter the building.

"The thing is…" Andy hesitates, making a show of

being uncomfortable. "Well, I thought maybe you could come by Jeff's house—I mean, Joanne's house—look through this stuff yourself. You know, see if there's anything useful?"

"Oh, I, uh... I thought you would just bring them here."

"Yeah, I would, but, see, there's a lot of stuff and, well, I don't know how Jo feels about me just taking it all away." A look of concern crosses David's face and Andy quickly adds, "I mean, she wants you to have his notes and stuff, but maybe it would be easier if you came out to get it yourself. You know, maybe tell her his effort was worth something? While you're there?"

"Well..." David realizes this is about more than accepting some notebooks and instinctively begins searching for a way out.

"It's not a big deal," Andy backs off, holding up both hands. "It's a drive, and you don't even know her... I just thought it might make her feel a little... but, fuck. Man, it's okay. Don't even worry about it."

"Well, hold on," David remembers watching Joanne and her daughters from his place at the back of the funeral. He remembers his lunches with Jeff and his thoughts of mentoring him, his vague promises of bringing Jeff in as an intern someday.

Was it really so much to ask that he come by to say a few kind words to Jeff's widow? He had meant to say as much at the funeral. He had prepared an entire speech about how extraordinary Jeff had been and how much potential he had had. But the moment he saw Joanne, and those little girls, he had realized how hollow his words would be. What good was potential when Jeff no longer had a chance to use it? Would it matter that David had appreciated her husband when he was now lost to them forever? And who was he to tell a grieving woman anything about her own husband? In the end, he'd sat at the back of the room, mulling it over, until nearly everyone else had left, then muttered some trite words of sympathy and made a quick exit.

He isn't eager to face Joanne again.

"David!"

Fletcher is almost beside them before either David or Andy see him coming. They both turn, instinctively tensing as Fletcher readjusts his badge and stalks their way. He doesn't say hello, or acknowledge Andy's presence, before narrowing in on David.

"Keller called me this morning. Have you finished parsing the fMRI data from last week?"

"Yeah, actually, I did," David shakes off his thoughts about Jeff and Joanne. "I was going over it last night and I think I found something--"

"If you finished," Fletcher interrupts, "why isn't it updated in the central system?"

"Well, I wanted to run an idea past Keller first, because I think I may have found something that might change the model we use to reconstruct the visualizations."

David glances instinctively toward Andy, almost as if looking for an ally, but Andy's eyes are cast down, staring at the blacktop between his feet. Following David's darting gaze, Fletcher shifts his eyes between Andy and David.

"Oh, I'm sorry," his tone carries more sarcasm than apology. "Was I interrupting something?"

"No, man," Andy answers first, lifting his hands and backing away. "I was just leaving."

He's halfway to the front door before Andy hears David calling out to him. When he turns, he sees David trotting to catch up, Fletcher frowning in the distance. David hesitates just a moment before nodding and saying that he'll be in touch about coming to get Jeff's things.

CHAPTER ELEVEN

Eleanor grips the steering wheel as she squints into the overlapping pools of light created by her car's headlights. Trees rise up on either side of the narrow road. Their rough bark and reaching branches are bleached white by the artificial light, while the sky above fades into cloudy blackness.

She doesn't like being out here, in the rural mix of woods and farmlands that fills an expansive perimeter just outside of town. It's unsettling in the daylight, but much worse after dark. Her mind finds it far too easy to imagine deer and bears and long-dead ghosts hiding behind every shadow.

In another mile, the skeletal trees give way to a wide stretch of flat, empty earth, marked with a cluster of oddly sized buildings. Eleanor pulls up to the intersection and gazes toward the empty passenger seat. Joanne would be sitting there, she thinks, if Jeff's accident hadn't happened. She would be scanning through the static in search of a clear radio station. She would be laughing about a ridiculous comment someone had made and telling Eleanor how well the jewelry party had gone. But she's not here. Eleanor is alone in the car. Alone at the crossroads, with no one else in sight.

The longer she sits at the stop sign, her foot firmly pressed on the brake, the more Eleanor begins to realize that the lonely landscape may be the perfect match for her mood tonight. It's the first moment she's truly been alone and idle, with time to process the strange turns of the last few days. It's a chance to gather her thoughts and start making plans. Yet the surroundings also make it hard to hold onto the present, let alone consider the future.

As Eleanor peers into the darkness outside of the car, she struggles to get her bearings. An old clapboard home sits on the corner to her right. It's been converted into a small store and its covered porch boasts an array of signs that Eleanor can't read in the dark. A dim floodlight illuminates a changeable letter board by the road ahead. Its block letters spell out: *Beer wine + DVDs rentals*. The letters are mostly black, though the *B* in beer, the *e* in wine, and the *e* in rentals are red. She's passed this store before. She may have even stopped in once, in another lifetime.

They'd had a different friend who lived out here, back then. She and Joanne. Melanie something. They'd come out here for Melanie's birthday sleepover, just weeks after Joanne's parents had died.

Melanie had been new to their school that year and all the girls in class were invited to her birthday party. Eleanor and Joanne had come along, desperate for a distraction. They'd roamed the woods and run wild, awed to realize how quickly their small town dissolved into this relatively untamed world. They'd walked to this very store, or one remarkably like it, to buy candy and bags of chips. They'd pretended that Joanne could still be happy, like the other girls.

Sitting at the stop sign now, beside the dark store, Eleanor has to make a decision. Turning to the left will take her out to the freeway, bypassing the woods completely. Going straight will lead her to Ridge Road, where she can follow the county line in its winding path back to town. Either route would take her home, but Eleanor's eyes look past the store and toward the road that branches off to the right, deeper into the township. She knows that road will take her on a meandering path, through patches of forest, and out to the bridge at Landon's Hollow. It's a path she hasn't followed in several years, a path tinged with shame and regret, but oddly alluring.

Eleanor's hands hesitate on the wheel, beginning to turn it one way and then the next. The engine idles until she finally lets the memory of her first trip to Landon's Hollow pull her hands to the right, driving into the deeper woods. The winding road brings nostalgia for their high school exploits. The same nervous excitement. The same sense of welcoming fear.

They were supposed to be at a school dance that night—the first night she and Joanne had visited Landon's Hollow. Eleanor, Joanne, Andy, and Mark. They were supposed to be dancing to songs spun by a DJ and feeling grown up because they were wearing fancy clothes in a crepe paper decorated gym. Instead, they had piled into

Mark's car and headed toward a place with more adventure and fewer chaperones.

It was darker that night, in Eleanor's memory. It was moonless and cold with the threat of early snow, making it the perfect time to visit a haunted bridge. They'd passed a bottle for courage—blueberry schnapps because Mark said it was the only booze he could nick without his mother noticing—and they swapped ghost stories that they'd heard from older kids. They'd been a foursome for a while by then, but Mark was the first to reach 16. The first of them to get his license and have a car to drive. Eleanor and Joanne, still freshmen, were impressed by his freedom. They were impressed by his recent drinking and his growing reputation, and also by the sense of danger that had begun to swirl around him.

As Eleanor drives, her tires crunch on the pitted road, sending gravel to skitter in the wheel wells and clatter back onto the ground below. For a few minutes, nothing looks familiar and she thinks she may have made a wrong turn. But then, around the next bend, a rough clearing opens up at the edge of the road. A dirt-packed semi-circle widens unevenly just before the tall framework of an old metal truss bridge. Landon's Hollow. If it was a Friday night, she might have found teenagers out here, drinking in terrified groups or parked in overheated cars, but it's a Thursday and the clearing is empty. Deserted.

Eleanor guides her car gently off the road, letting the engine idle as she stares at the metal bridge. Its pale green frame glows eerily in the glare of her headlights, rough and weathered by neglect.

That first night, the night of the dance, she and Joanne

had sat together in the backseat. They'd shrieked in terror when Andy and Mark decided to leave the car so they could run across the bridge, daring the ghosts to do their worst. They'd huddled alone, whispering over what might happen when the boys came back and quaking with anticipation.

It hurts to look back.

An owl hoots in the distance and Eleanor cautiously lowers her window. The hollow sounds the same as she remembers. There are crickets and frogs, along with the whip-poor-wills that whistle and call at night. The birdsong sounds eerie to Eleanor, just as it did all those years ago. Eerie and incessant, high up in the rustling leaves. As she listens, Eleanor's eyes are drawn to a section of bridge over the middle of the river. The space is obscured by shadows, but she can see it clearly in her mind's eye.

She remembers the winter day when she sat on the edge of that bridge, in exactly that spot, with Joanne pressed against her side. Andy had hovered behind them, while Jeff sat a bit further apart, still hanging back in the shadow of Mark's memory.

That day had been exactly one week after Eleanor's 17th birthday, and she remembers it every year. Even now, Eleanor can feel the cold dampness of the bridge seeping through the plastic tarp that they had pulled off the back of Andy's truck. She can see the metal slick with ice and dangerous in a way they had only recently realized. Everything had been still that day. No birds, no frogs, no passing cars. Silence in the dead of winter. As they sat, Andy had handed out bottles of beer and no one cared if they got caught. They were bold back then, reckless in their teenage rebellion.

Sitting beside the bridge now, alone, Eleanor remembers the feeling of being stretched out on the leather chair in Joanne's basement. She remembers the feel of electrodes on her temples and the sensation of moving within Jeff's memory. She thinks about the memories he chose to record and the memories that he could have recorded. Then she shudders and makes her way home.

CHAPTER TWELVE

There's a wicker wreath hanging on the front door. It's decorated with a faded ribbon and a wooden plaque that has "Jeff and Joanne" painted in pink across a large red heart. Two smaller hearts dangle from the first, bearing the names Ruthie and Sarah. The wood is chipped and worn. David studies the wreath instead of pressing the doorbell, stalling for time. He turns to take in the small porch with its white railing and gently swaying swing. A jump rope is tangled in the far corner and a doll arm is sticking up from the dirt in an otherwise empty flower pot.

David reaches for the doorbell just as the door opens on a pale woman with long, dark hair and sad eyes. Inside, he hears a little girl laughing loudly and is jarred by the unexpected sound.

"Dr. Tyler?" Joanne is wearing a tee shirt, jeans, and thick wool socks. David is in jeans as well, but with a collared shirt because he was worried that anything too casual might be inappropriate. He had almost worn a suit.

The Insistence of Memory

"David, please," he offers a weak smile, wondering if he should shake her hand or if he should have brought her something. A bottle of wine? Flowers? Some small toy for the girls? He sticks his empty hands in his pockets and tries to smile more genuinely when she invites him to call her Joanne.

The house is clean but scattered with evidence of a young family. A play table takes up space in the living room, alongside a cubby filled with bins of small toys. Drawings are taped to the panes of glass on the open doors that lead into the dining room, while framed photos in all sizes and colors cover the walls and tabletops. David stands in the entryway, eyes the pile of shoes by the door, and bends to untie his laces.

"You don't have to," Joanne tells him quickly, but then hesitates in a way that makes him realize she is being polite.

"I don't mind."

He tugs off his shoes, listening to the high-pitched murmurs coming from the kitchen. Ruthie speaks so softly that he can't make out her words, but he hears Sarah laugh again, followed by the deeper sound of Eleanor telling the girls to run get their shoes. And then they are there. Jeff's girls stand in front of David with narrowed eyes and small arms folded over their identical little bodies.

"Who are you?" Sarah's blunt question makes Ruthie nudge her before loudly whispering, "He's daddy's friend from work, remember?"

David is flustered for a moment, wondering if she remembers him from the funeral, before realizing that Joanne must have explained that he was coming by.

"Girls, this is Dr. Tyler." Joanne points to each girl, saying their names before prompting them to say hello. He returns their greeting and tries to mentally note any difference that might make it easier to tell them apart. He decides that Ruthie looks more nervous, afraid of him, while Sarah's expression is downright hostile. He is still struggling for something else to say when David sees Eleanor walk out of the kitchen with Nolan perched firmly on her hip. The introductions continue and Joanne notices that David is anxious, beneath his careful manners.

"So, you and Andy live next door? Have you all known each other long?"

"Practically our whole lives," Eleanor answers flatly, and David wonders if he said something that offended her. He looks at Nolan, who shyly buries his face into Eleanor's neck, rubbing his runny nose against her collarbone. The girls slip their shoes on and eye David skeptically until Joanne begins to shoo them toward the kitchen door.

"Okay, time to go with Aunt El. I'll come get you for lunch in a little while."

"I want lunch at Aunt El's. She's making us pizza!"

"If that's all right?" Eleanor looks from David to Joanne warily. "I wasn't sure how long you would be." Joanne agrees and smiles tightly, watching as Eleanor leads the girls through the kitchen and out the back door. David watches Joanne's smile fade at the sound of the back door closing and questions whether coming over was such a good idea. He's about to offer to simply take the notebooks and go, when Joanne exhales a deep breath and invites him into the living room.

They sit on opposite sides of the room. David perches

in the middle of the couch and Joanne alights on a deep blue recliner. They both sit fully upright, backs straight and nowhere near the plush cushions. Lit only by sunlight, the room dims as a cloud passes overhead. Silence settles like a weight around them. It's the kind of quiet that thickens the air and saps all thought from David's mind. Joanne looks down at her fingers, clasped on her knees, while David studies the way her hair falls around the sides of her face, noting how most of it stays moored behind her gently slumped shoulders. Her eyes lift and David forces himself not to look away.

"Jeff's told me a lot about you," she begins. "He said you're working on a way to keep Alzheimer's patients from losing their memories?"

"Oh, well," David shakes his head and holds up both hands, fending off the praise but happy to have something to say. "Not exactly. I mean, I hope that would be a direction this research could take, but we're nowhere near that stage yet."

"But your research is about preserving memories?"

"In a way."

Joanne narrows her eyes, but her tone is genuine when she says, "I'd like to hear about it."

"Well," David smiles softly, relaxing into the topic. "Let's see. Uh, basically, we work from maps of the brain, which show how certain areas respond to particular visual and auditory stimuli, and then create models which let us decode brain activity to see what a person has been visualizing. For example, if we, um, record brain activity while someone is looking at a photograph or watching a short movie, we can, well, essentially play back whatever they saw on our computers.

"Of course, the picture we get doesn't have much detail, or any really, but we can see the general shapes and colors. Down the road, some day, this same technology may help us decode more complex visualizations, like memories or even dreams. At least, in theory."

"So, you read people's minds?" Joanne nods as she asks, looking for confirmation.

"Ye-es," David draws the word out, hesitating to oversimplify their work. "In a sense."

A car outside revs its engine, bass booming as it passes by. A second car follows a moment later, same thumping bass line and squealing tires. Teens putting on a show. It startles David, but Joanne ignores them, intent on the conversation.

"And for Alzheimer's patients?"

David shifts in his seat, weighing his response. The conversation has begun to vaguely feel like a job interview and David wonders if he is being put through some kind of test before Joanne will trust him with whatever is in Jeff's notebooks.

"Well," he falters over the proper wording, "that's more of a theoretical idea at this point. It's not something we're actually working on yet."

"Yes, but your theory is...?" Joanne leans toward David with her elbows on her knees and her hands clasped beneath her chin. He pauses again, wondering what she expects from his answer.

"I, uh, guess it's not even really a theory as much as a dream at this point, but I'd like to think that someday we could use this technology to let Alzheimer's patients record their memories before losing them." Joanne nods again.

"And then, they'd be able to play the memories back in their minds, with the help of a machine?"

"Well, that's--" David stops himself from discouraging her, knowing that it's difficult for lay people to understand the complexity of the mind and memories. Also knowing that that was exactly what Jeff had suggested. He doesn't want to tell her that they are years from that possibility, decades even. Especially if she thinks Jeff's notes on the idea will lead to some kind of scientific breakthrough.

"If there *was* a machine that could record memories and play them back in someone else's mind," Joanne picks her words carefully. "What would you do with it?"

The room is still around them, silent except for the quiet ticking of a nearby clock. Joanne's eyes are bright and her hair is cascading over her shoulders now, giving her a wild, somewhat mad look. Her intensity worries David, yet he remembers a similar look coming over Jeff's face whenever this subject came up. He decides to treat the conversation like a philosophical discussion without worrying about Joanne's expectations.

"If that were possible," he puts a heavy emphasis on the word *if.* "I would like to think that it could help Alzheimer's patients and others at risk for losing their memories. Although, I think you meant to say that you would be able to play the memories back in their own minds. Right?"

Joanne levels him a strange look before leaning back in the chair and reaching both hands up to smooth her hair into a loose ponytail. Without an elastic band, her hair falls freely down her back the moment she removes her hands, but it lies more neatly now. Only a few shorter wisps slip forward to frame her face. David watches, finding himself strangely mesmerized by the shifting character of her waving hair.

"Can I offer you a drink?" Joanne smiles weakly. "Water? Lemonade? Juice?"

They move into the kitchen where Joanne pours two glasses of water. The door to the basement is in the kitchen and Joanne gestures toward it when telling David that there's a room down there where Jeff used to work. She tells David, while they sip their water, standing across opposite sides of the table, that Jeff had been secretive about his work. She tells him that she only found out about it last week and that it is still something of a shock.

As she talks, David begins to picture a room filled with box after box of notebooks. Perhaps papers pinned to the walls showing inexplicable drawings and figures, maybe even linked with the lines of string that movie set designers use to show the work of geniuses. Or of madmen.

He swallows hard, trying to prepare himself, sensing that there is more to this story than Joanne, or Andy, has let on. Yet nothing David imagines can prepare him for what he will experience when Joanne finally builds up enough courage to lead him downstairs. Nothing will prepare him for the experience of viewing Jeff's memories for himself.

CHAPTER THIRTEEN

David sits at the scratched and scarred kitchen table, poring over an open notebook, while Joanne fills a kettle for tea. They haven't said much since coming up from the basement, and Joanne knows that David will need time to let it all sink in.

When she turns from the stove, she catches sight of Andy through the window. He paces between their houses, chain smoking cigarettes. Joanne watches him drop the spent butt into a stone urn where Eleanor used to plant flowers. She knows that Andy can't see her from where he is standing, not with the sun glinting off the windows, but she shrinks back anyway, pressing herself into the corner of the cabinets where she can turn her attention to David.

"It's a lot to take in," she says softly.

David shakes his head. His fingers ruffle the notebook's pages before he shuts the cover and sets it on top of the stack of identical notebooks on his right. There's a vein in his neck that strains against the clenching of his jaw. As Joanne watches, she sees the vein twitch in tiny, irregular spasms. She isn't sure if he is angry or simply overcome by what he has seen.

"That shouldn't be possible," David's words are steady, his emotions tightly controlled. "It just shouldn't work."

Joanne looks down, restraining herself from saying, *But it does work*. The words do not need to be said. The truth of it is already ricocheting through his brain and she knows how it feels to try to reconcile that realization with the world he already knows.

After looking back over the first page of notes, David stands up and starts gathering the notebooks together. He wants to take them back to the lab where he has more resources to reference, but Joanne stops him.

"Look, I don't know what to do with all this, and you might, but it's still my property." Her eyes dare David to bring up the stolen equipment, but he doesn't say a word.

"You can work on it," she tells him. "You can try to figure it out and then we'll go from there. But while you do, I want everything to stay here. With me. Can we agree on that?"

Tension flickers between them and David hesitates. The notebooks are still in his arms, but he knows that he won't be able to keep them private if he takes them back to the lab. He holds her steady gaze and considers the possibilities before carefully setting the stack back on the table.

"All right. For now."

Joanne winces and something turns in David's chest. None of this is her fault, he tells himself. For the first time, he imagines how it must have felt for her to discover all of this. He thinks it was likely easier for her, in a way, not really understanding the true improbability of this machine. But then he remembers that this machine was built by her husband, now dead, and populated with his memories. Of her. He cannot imagine how she must be feeling.

"I'll have to get some things from the lab," he tells her, more gently, while creating a running list in his mind. Items that might help. Resources. "But then, I want to come back later this afternoon. Can I get started then? Today?"

"Of course."

The girls are still at Eleanor's house, but Joanne knows that they can't stay there all night. She knows that this won't be solved in a single evening and that she will have to come up with something to explain David's presence. Something that seems natural and won't raise questions if they mention it to someone at school. Or, rather, something that won't raise questions she can't plausibly answer.

The idea is exhausting.

When David leaves the house, he isn't surprised to find Andy waiting for him outside. David glares at him, feeling a surge of anger spreading through his chest, but tries to walk by without a confrontation.

"Hey!" Andy reaches out a hand to stop him and David jerks away before spinning to face him.

"What the hell did you think you were doing?" His voice is low, but menacing, channeling all the emotion he had suppressed while talking to Joanne. "One phone call and I could have you arrested. Do you have any idea how expensive that equipment is? Do you have any idea what you've done?"

Andy meets him squarely, shorter but broader, knowing that he has both the brawn and the willingness to back it up.

"You're not going to do that though, are you, doc?" It's not really a question. "You don't want to turn in the poor, grieving widow and you definitely don't want to give up a chance to figure this thing out. Not something this big."

"You don't know me."

"Yeah, I think I do." Andy drops his aggressive stance, fishes out another cigarette and lights up. "See, I listen when I'm fixing all those little things that are beneath you. I watch the way all of you lab guys scramble around trying to impress whoever's in charge of your particular little world. All trying to be the big man with the big idea. And this is one fucking big ass idea."

They stare each other down. David leaning slightly forward with barely contained energy. Andy merely standing his ground. David is the first to drop his eyes. He lifts his chin and looks off into the distance, past Joanne's house, past the neighborhood, and all the way to the far-off lab where he works with two other research assistants, all jockeying for attention and opportunities.

Andy isn't wrong, as much as David wants him to be.

"So, what's in it for you?"

Andy's eyes widen and he flashes a surprised smile.

"What's in it for me?" He laughs, opening his arms to the heavens. "Fame and glory, man, same as you. And money. You know what people would pay for something like this?" He drops his voice to an intense whisper. "For a machine that lets you watch other people's thoughts? That's fucking huge, doc."

"So, you think you can-- What? Sell this to people?" David lips curve into a bemused smile. "As a service?"

"It's the invention of the century, right?" Andy takes a long drag off his cigarette, determined to stay on the same level, showing that they aren't at the lab now. "You gotta start thinking big, man. It could be like eye witness testimony for the police, but better, and a way to pass on memories to your kids and, like, I don't know, like the fucking ultimate reality TV show. You should be more excited, doc. We're making history here!"

But David doesn't feel excited while driving to the lab. When he remembers the look on Andy's face, the smell of his cigarettes, the sheer greed, he feels dirty. Compromised. Andy's ideas, his plans, are so ludicrous that David can barely wrap his mind around them. Yet he knows that there are others who would see this the same way. Even those with the means to try to make it happen. And if it did...

In that moment, David feels like he is standing at the edge of a cliff. Standing at the threshold of a line that could separate science fiction from reality. A line that, once crossed, could lead them into an actual dystopian society where people would have to protect their minds from invasion and be prepared to explain away thoughts which might be pulled out of context and put on display for the world to judge.

But that's crazy, he tells himself. *Or is it?*

He could be the person, David realizes. He could be the person who brings about the horror and loss of privacy that could come with real mind reading. Not in the baby steps that he's been researching at the lab, but with a sudden revelation that the world is in no way prepared to receive.

He doesn't want that responsibility.

He doesn't want to be the one who has to decide whether to bury a scientific breakthrough of this magnitude or bring it into the light and explore whatever path may follow. It's too big, too complex. It's so much more than Andy or Joanne, or even Jeff, imagined.

David sits at a red light and runs through his options. He could turn Andy in and have the equipment recovered. He could wipe the computer's memory and burn the notebooks, destroying Jeff's monster.

But then he imagines what someone else might do and realizes that Andy didn't have to come to him. Andy could have approached Fletcher or Madeline or even Dr. Keller himself. He still could.

Besides, if Jeff figured this out than someone else could, too. Maybe not at their lab, or even in this country, but someone, somewhere could hit upon the same discovery. That someone could be anyone. It could be someone less scrupulous than David. Someone with no qualms about exploiting this in exactly the way Andy has suggested.

But, David tells himself, *he* would be different. He would be responsible about his research. He would take steps to understand it, fully, and come up with a careful way to present his findings. A way to protect society, while still using this discovery to further their understanding of memory formation and retrieval.

As his thoughts begin to settle, David realizes that, whether he wanted it or not, Jeff's project is now his own.

CHAPTER FOURTEEN

Sunlight filters in from the wide windows on their left and from the entryway windows on their right, leaving Sarah and Ruthie centered in a square of cool, shadowy carpet. They are acting out a scene with their favorite dolls, while Nolan spins lazy circles in front of the nearby TV. He periodically stops his twirling to make his Spiderman action figure swoop into the middle of the girls' play, then fly away with slobbering, sputtering sound effects.

The frequent interruptions are too much for Sarah, who is already irritated by being shooed away from the grown-ups. On his next approach, she shoves Nolan hard enough that he stumbles, drops Spiderman and plops onto his diapered bottom. Even Ruthie, Nolan's usual protector, loses her patience and orders him to stay on the other side of the room. She doesn't know why she's so short with him, or why it's so much harder than usual to escape into their dolls' make-believe world, but the feeling bothers her.

While Nolan pouts with his back to the couch, Ruthie rubs the bridge of her nose, subconsciously imitating their mother, and Sarah vigorously smashes her doll's feet into the worn carpet. Below them lies the basement. The forbidden place where only the grown-ups are allowed to go. The mysterious place which draws back this new visitor, this Dr. Tyler, day after day.

The girls share an innate distrust of doctors. They become clingy at visits to the pediatrician, holding hands and wanting to sit side-by-side on the exam table instead of taking turns, no matter how firmly Joanne tells them that they are too old to behave that way.

To Sarah and Ruthie, doctors mean poking, prodding, and shots that aren't worth the glossy stickers they get on the way out of the office. But this is different and the girls are perplexed by Dr. Tyler's visits. They attempt to play in the living room while he talks with their mother in the kitchen or basement, but the house changes whenever he is there. The living room, with its buckets of toys and small play table, takes on the feel of an office waiting room and its transformation leaves the girls on edge, half-listening to be called in for their exam.

Unaware of their worry, Joanne unloads the dishwasher with quick, jerking motions.

"I just don't get what he's doing," Andy says from his spot by the kitchen door. He has an unlit cigarette in one hand and a half-empty pack in the other. Joanne shakes her head mutely and adds two clean plates to the stack in the cupboard. She's beyond tired of Andy's impatience and never-ending complaints.

"It's been two weeks," Andy continues. "Two weeks!

And he hasn't figured out how to record a single fucking memory. Even though it's all right there. All figured out. It's not like it's something new. Jeff already figured it out, so why the fuck can't Dr. PhD?"

He paces the floor, then drops his voice to a near whisper.

"You know what's going on here. The fucker's holding out on us. Trying to cut us out."

"Andy--" Joanne sighs, not knowing what else she can add to the reassurances she and Eleanor have been offering all week.

"No. I don't want to hear any more about how complicated this thing is. And, I tell you what, if he says that goddamn record thing one more fucking time, I'm going to break his goddamn jaw."

Joanne knows better than to tell him that she likes David's record analogy. That listening to a record *is* much easier than making one. Especially if you don't know how it was made. But she knows that Andy doesn't believe him. He's sure that Jeff left instructions in his notes, or in the computer code, and that David is either choosing to ignore them or hiding what he's learned.

Andy taps his cigarette against the pack, itching to light it but not ready to go outside. The cigarettes are a point of contention between Andy and Eleanor now. He gave them up when Nolan was born, but started smoking again when Jeff died. Joanne thinks he must be back to a pack a day now. At least.

"And all this shit about memory integrity? It's bullshit."

"He wants to understand how it works," Joanne

repeats for the umpteenth time. "What's actually happening in our heads."

"He's wasting time."

"He's being careful," Joanne counters. "You know these are our brains we're messing around with? I'd kind of like to avoid damaging mine."

"Damn it, Jo." Andy stops pacing, slams the half-crushed cigarette pack on the counter and turns to face her head on. "You and El are always treating me like the village idiot, but I'm not stupid. And he's not a fucking god, just because he knows some science. This thing is valuable and we have to stay on top of him. Keep him from cutting us out."

Joanne closes the dishwasher with a frown and crosses to the doorway where she can look in on the kids. Nolan lies on the couch, yawning. The girls freeze, stopping their whispered conversation to present stoic faces and eyes filled with questions. Joanne hasn't known how to explain any of this to them, so she's said nothing. She tells herself that there's time to answer their questions later, when they're older. When something actually comes of this. When they will understand.

"He's not even trying to record more," Andy rants on. "Just wasting our fucking time."

Joanne doesn't bother to reply.

"What he needs to do is, he needs to get the recording bit figured out first. At least enough to have a business plan, you know? Enough to take to investors and show them what we'll be able to do. Get a patent and whatever. Because people will go ape shit over this and we need to own it first."

The basement door opens as Eleanor climbs the last step into the kitchen. She sees the cigarette in Andy's hand, the pack on the counter, and scowls. "Don't even think about smoking that in here."

Andy thrusts the cigarette forward, inches from Eleanor's face.

"Does it look lit?"

Eleanor's body tenses, but she refuses to flinch as Andy's fingers nearly brush the tip of her nose. Across the room, Joanne bites her lip, makes two tight fists and presses the tips of her fingernails into her palms to keep from getting between them.

"It better not be," Eleanor snaps. "There are children here."

"Yeah," Andy sneers and takes a step away. "I wouldn't want to be a bad example. Speaking of, maybe you should start drinking your afternoon wine out of a coffee cup, like a proper drunk."

Joanne turns her back then, drifting away from their insults and into the living room where all three kids are now sitting in a row on the couch, absorbed in a noisy, hectic cartoon. She lets her mind focus on the colorful world. The patterns shift and swirl before her eyes, but she takes no notice of the story unfolding. Instead, Joanne feels the unlit cigarette held inches from her own face. She feels the tension in her muscles as a larger, stronger, angrier body looms close above. She feels the helplessness beneath a brave face and the anger that keeps her from backing down.

And then she forcefully shakes the thoughts away.

Joanne tries to remember a time when Eleanor and

Andy were happy. They were an on-again off-again couple throughout high school, and in the years after. They'd never last long, but would nearly always stumbled back together for the big moments. For prom, for graduation, for Jeff and Joanne's wedding. After a while they settled in, for the most part. Breaking up when Eleanor didn't get the ring she expected for her 21st birthday, only to get back together with a dramatic proposal a few months later.

They were happy when Eleanor was pregnant, Joanne decides, and when they brought Nolan home. They were happy and proud and full of plans. And that lasted until the sleep-deprivation and mounting bills began to take their toll. Until they slipped back into communicating by criticism and found it was less charming as parents than when they were teenagers or playfully bickering newlyweds.

As Joanne stands, staring blankly at the TV, her daughters look up at her with pleading eyes that she doesn't see. Ruthie presses her shoulder carefully against her sister and Sarah doesn't pull away. They are used to these moody reveries, though they've begun to notice that other adults don't seem to have them.

The credits begin to scroll up the screen and Joanne notices that the muffled voices in the kitchen have gone silent. She turns, without looking down at the girls huddled on the couch, and walks away.

In the kitchen, Eleanor leans her forehead against Andy's chest. His arms wrap around her back. They're rocking gently, side to side, and Andy's distant gaze stares across the kitchen over Eleanor's bent head. The sight stops Joanne short and sends a lurching jolt through her stomach.

"I should get the kids lunch," she tells them and begins bustling around the kitchen. There are unshed tears Joanne blinks away and a sudden heat that spreads through her stomach. She pulls a box of macaroni and cheese from the cabinet as Eleanor extracts herself from Andy's arms.

"I'll do that." Eleanor takes the box from Joanne's hand. "David wants you downstairs now anyway."

Joanne nods, looking toward the closed basement door. In the blur of her periphery, she sees Andy kiss Eleanor's temple, scoop up his pack of cigarettes and head outside. She tamps down her anger and releases a long, shaky breath. It's Eleanor's choice to stay with him, she tells herself. Eleanor can decide if she wants to be with someone who tears her down, then casually kisses the hurt away. And maybe that's reasonable, because not everyone can be Jeff. And because fatal accidents aren't always fair.

"Are you okay?" Eleanor holds a pan in the sink and has one hand poised on the faucet to fill it with water. Joanne opens her mouth to speak, but pauses. She can see Andy lighting up in the backyard, pacing more leisurely, yet still restless. Still breathing.

"Yeah," she tells Eleanor with several short nods. "I'm fine."

CHAPTER FIFTEEN

The video camera captures every expression that passes over Joanne's face. She had resisted the camera at first, not wanting this close digital scrutiny, but eventually agreed on the condition that the camera, and its footage, stay in the basement. Today, its flat eye and small red light fade into the background, along with the rest of the now-familiar equipment and the scientist scribbling notes on a yellow legal pad.

David's eyes stray from Joanne's face to the small monitor, then back again, watching for minute signs of what is happening inside her mind as she relates the memory she is viewing. His eyes are bloodshot and ringed with dark circles, showing the strain of working long hours at the lab while spending his nights and weekends poring over Jeff's work.

"I'm-- I mean, *Jeff* is backing out of the room," Joanne narrates, half in the memory and half aware of David watching her. "His mother is on the bed, thin, barely visible under the blanket, except for her pale face... He looks away, looking at everything but her face, and there's a nurse--" Joanne breaks off. She holds up one hand, their signal for a quote from Jeff's infrequent narration. "*I'm glad she's here.*"

David watches the rapid, shifty movements beneath Joanne's closed eyelids, while Joanne remembers how kind Isabella had been to them all. How grateful they'd been to have a caring, compassionate nurse with them at the end. It's a struggle not to drift into her own thoughts this way, to stay within Jeff's memory alone. Her lips press together in frustration and she focuses more on the details of the room. Pale blue privacy curtains are drawn back from around the bed and a bowl of pink carnations decorates the ledge by the window. A yellow, plastic pitcher sits on the rolling bedside table, beside a cardboard box of tissues, a black ballpoint pen, and a card for ordering the day's meals. She realizes that they won't be ordering any more meals, but isn't sure if the thought is Jeff's or her own.

Back in the basement, in the real world, a wheeled cart holds two additional pieces of equipment: a second computer monitor and something that spits out a paper print-out. A document stand displays David's meticulously drawn flow-chart for this memory, propped beside a master outline that he has been compiling over the last two weeks. He glances toward the charts before making another note on his legal pad.

"Out in the hall now," Joanne continues, sliding deeper into the memory. "It's bright, colorful now, almost hurts, here," she lifts her hand quickly to tap a spot at the top left of her forehead before dropping her hand back to her lap. "I'm there—Joanne is there—on the chair, alone, looking at my hands... or at her hands..." Joanne's voice stumbles, her head shakes slightly from side to side, showing the continued strain of seeing herself from an outside view.

"And now?" David prompts, knowing from previous sessions how difficult, how emotional, the rest of this memory will be.

"I look up and... and..." Her face contorts, sudden tears flowing freely, while her arms cross tightly over her stomach. She stops talking. David stops writing. His eyes linger over the play of emotion on Joanne's face. The sorrow. He's about to stop the memory and pull her out when a deep breath relaxes her features.

"I'm on the floor in front of Joanne," she speaks in a soft, but steady tone. David notes the change in perspective, and the tears still rolling slowly down her cheeks. She is deep in the memory.

"My face is in her lap and the... pain... the sadness... and the relief. I tell her: *Jo, she's gone*. And I'm glad that it's finally over. And Joanne is stroking my hair, and my eyes are closed. Everything is dark, but I can feel her hands and her jeans against my cheek. She says, *Now she's at peace*. And I know that she's right and there's nothing more we can do."

The room is quiet. David knows that the memory has ended, but Joanne's eyes remain closed. He leans forward and puts his hand on her arm, gently reminding Joanne of her presence in the basement, of her physical location. He doesn't want to rush her, but he wants her to open her eyes. He wants to see that she is okay, unharmed from reliving this memory again and again.

"It's only a memory," he reminds her softly, leaning close. "It was years ago. Only a memory."

His hand moves on her arm, grazing the soft skin. Her chest rises with an inhale, slow and deep.

"That's right," he soothes. "Deep breaths."

David's fingers slip to the inside of her wrist, feeling her pulse, lingering at the base of her palm. His gaze stays on her face and he smiles gently when her eyes finally open.

"Welcome back."

She returns the smile, but self-consciously.

"I lost it again."

David shakes his head.

"No, you did great."

His fingers are still resting on Joanne's wrist and it feels natural to curl them around her hand. Her fingers bend in response, accepting his comfort as her eyes drift shut. They sit together, Joanne lying back on the worn recliner and David perched on the edge of the wheeled chair. Her expression is composed. Her breathing is soft and easy. Behind her, a jagged line scrolls across the small monitor.

As the moment stretches, they both become aware of their hands clasped together. Joanne's eyes open, wary, and David releases her hand the moment her fingers uncurl. They both speak at the same time.

"I, uh--"

"Well--"

"Oh," David wheels back as Joanne sits up in the chair.

"Go ahead."

"No, you first."

Joanne begins peeling off the electrodes while David shuffles through his notes. She winds the wires carefully around one hand, creating a neat coil.

"I'm sorry," he says, then shakes his head at her look of confusion. "This memory," he clarifies, "I know it's a hard one. Emotionally."

"Oh," Joanne looks back down at the wires, remembering the feel of his hand over her own.

"I don't like putting you through that," he continues, standing to put his notepad on the table.

She hands him the bundle of electrodes, hesitating over her response. She wants to tell him that she doesn't mind, but that isn't quite right. She almost tells him that she likes watching the memories. Or needs to watch them. But that doesn't capture the feeling either, because now it's only partially about the memories themselves. It's become partially about working with David, about having a reason to get out of bed and having something to do with her time, besides simply breathing through each day.

But she can't say that either, because without these memories she would still have a reason to get up each day. She would get up for the girls. To take care of them, to mother them and watch them grow. Though somehow that isn't the same.

"They're all hard," she says at last. "Emotionally."

Their eyes meet again and David swallows, feeling his cheeks flush.

"Of course," he stammers. "I can't begin to imagine how--"

"Right, I didn't mean--" Joanne twists her fingers in her lap, looking away to give his embarrassment space. "You've been very... considerate."

The room is quiet again until a muffled thud overhead is followed by the sound of Nolan wailing. David looks up at the bare rafters.

"I'm going to get out of here for a while," he tells Joanne. "I've been here too much and you need some time with your girls."

"Oh, that's--" Joanne is about to disagree, but she stops herself, wondering if he's right and whether she might be afraid to have some time alone with her girls.

"But I do want to come back tonight," David adds. "Later. Maybe after they're in bed?"

Joanne looks up sharply and David pales.

"I mean, I need to talk to you. And Andy, and Eleanor."

"Oh," Joanne nods, but narrows her eyes. "Is there something wrong?"

"Well," David purses his lips and presses his hands into his pockets. "I don't know if you'd call it wrong. There are just some things I'd like to discuss about my findings so far, but, later. Say around eight?"

"Yeah, that's fine, but," Joanne glances back toward the clutter of equipment. "I thought we were going to go over the third memory again, too." *I was counting on it*, she doesn't add.

"We were but, it's not necessary right now. Unless you...?"

"Oh, no. That's fine." Joanne laughs, trying to joke. "I've seen it before."

"Yeah," David smiles. "I'm sure that's a vivid one for you."

The third memory is also in the hospital, right after the girls' birth. As Joanne thinks of it, she nearly stops David from leaving. She wants to ask him why Jeff chose these memories to record. The death of his mother, the birth of their daughters, and a moment in a park. All transitions, in a way. But they've discussed it before, indirectly, and she knows that David doesn't really have the answers. That anything he says will just be speculation.

"I'll walk you out," she says instead.

CHAPTER SIXTEEN

They gather around the kitchen table after the kids are asleep, the girls upstairs and Nolan in his bedroom next door. The ever-present baby monitor sits on the table between Eleanor and Joanne, transmitting the sounds of Nolan's deep and fretless sleep, while the worn cabinets create an enclosing background of wood panels and brass pulls. Andy leans back in his chair, its front legs off the floor and its back legs at an angle that would have distressed Joanne's grandmother. David has pulled his chair to the head of the table, a stack of papers neatly placed in front of him.

From her seat, Joanne can see out of the kitchen and into the dark dining room. The sight brings a flash of past holidays when she ate in the kitchen and stole glimpses of the grown-ups' table in the fancy room beyond. She wonders if she will ever really feel like one of the grown-ups.

David clears his throat, rustles his papers, and begins.

"As you know, Jeff's project is truly amazing," he pronounces his words slowly, looking at each of them in turn. "It's beyond amazing, actually. I've only begun to scratch the surface of what he's discovered and his work will have a profound impact on the scientific community.

"However," he pauses. Andy's chair creaks in the silence. "I need to, uh, explain some things I've discovered about Jeff's work. Especially given that, well, I believe you have some-- that there may need to be an adjustment of expectations."

Andy leans forward. The chair legs hit the linoleum floor with a soft thud.

"What does that mean?" There's a touch of menace in his voice, but David ignores Andy. Instead, his response is directed toward Joanne.

"The recorded memories aren't as complete as they may seem," his words are carefully chosen, his tone steady. "In each case, the playback covers the same broad strokes. There's the day in the park, the last moments with Jeff's mother, and the birth of the twins. When each of us views the memories, we see those same basic facts. Yet, the details, the sights and sounds, are more fluid, more influenced by our own perceptions."

"Meaning?" Eleanor has placed her right hand over Joanne's left.

"Meaning memories are more complicated than we are typically led to believe in books and movies. They aren't like video recordings or snapshots. Even the clearest memories are never going to accurately capture the events that actually happened. Not completely."

Andy drops his elbows to his knees, leaning forward

until his chin rests on his clasped fingers. Joanne sits more upright in her chair. Her eyes look beyond David, but he knows she is listening intently to every word he says. He tamps down a sense of nervous dread and pushes forward.

"You see, our brains are very efficient. They use shortcuts and tricks to quickly sift and process the massive amounts of information that our senses observe in any given moment."

"So, Jeff's memories aren't necessarily real." Joanne's words are hollow, her gaze is still an unfocused stare.

Eleanor and David study Joanne with concern, not seeing the way Andy has sat up with an alert gleam and a clenched jaw.

"Let's back up," David regroups. "You need to understand a few basic points about what goes into creating new memories. I mean, not the way Jeff created his recordings, but in the way our brains actually create them. And in the way we recall them."

Joanne's focus comes back to David's face, but now he's the one who can't bring himself to meet her glistening eyes.

"Basically, various sensory areas of our brains perceive signals which may be visual, auditory, tactile, et cetera. Then, a special portion of the brain, the hippocampus, combines those signals into a construct which can be held in long-term memory and accessed at a later time. And, well, the hippocampus does its best, but it's a selective process. It can't include every sense we perceive, because there is entirely too much raw data."

"Geez, doc," Andy shakes his head at the floor. "In English?"

"I'm making this as simple as I can--"

"It's not that difficult," Eleanor cuts in, speaking through partially gritted teeth. "He's just saying that our brains don't record every single detail of what's happening around us. Right?"

"Pretty much," David frowns. "Or, I guess that's enough for our purposes."

"So, there are holes in the memories?" Andy presses. "But the things that are there are still true?"

"Uh," David glances at each face, weighing pith against accuracy. "Sort of. But there's a little more to it than that."

"Doc--"

David holds up a hand to stop Andy's interruption.

"Okay, the first thing you need to know is that our brains don't process, or record, every bit of sensory input. So, yes, you could say there are holes in our memory. But, the second thing you need to know is that our memories are largely associative. Which means that they rely on earlier memories, or learned information, when processing and encoding new experiences."

He's met with silence.

"So, uh-- Okay. An example: you don't relearn the basic properties of a ball every time you see one." David stands up, miming the shape of a ball under his hands. "If there were a basketball sitting on this table, right now, your brain would instantly pull up past experiences to make assumptions about that ball.

"You'd assume it's an air-filled sphere which bounces when it's dropped or thrown at a surface. You would know what it feels like, without touching it, because you've handled a basketball before. You may also know its rubbery smell, and the echoing sound of its bounce on a gym floor, even though *this* experience, of *this* ball, is of it simply sitting on the table."

"So those are the shortcuts you mentioned earlier?" Eleanor squints to make sense of it.

"Yes!" David answers with excitement. "You can think of memories as a sort of construct, a framework, like a, uh, skeleton sketch of something that happened. And that skeleton is filled in, or fleshed out, by assumptions based on past experiences."

"All right, enough!" Andy stops Eleanor before she can ask another question. "Are Jeff's memories true or not?"

"They're the way he remembers things," Eleanor spells out with annoyance. "It's what he remembers, but maybe not to what actually happened. Right?"

David hesitates again, wanting to explain with more nuance, but not wanting to belabor the point.

"Essentially," he glances at Joanne, but cannot read her neutral expression. He hesitates, knowing that he has to continue. "Yet, there's another layer here as well."

All eyes turn back to him. Waiting.

"Normally, a memory is a construct built from selective perceptions of that experience. And, then, when we recall a memory, our brains kind of pull sensations from different storage areas to recreate that experience to the best of our ability.

"But, in this case, I believe that the constructs of Jeff's memories are being filled in by our own minds. In other words, our own personal experiences are influencing the way we see Jeff's recorded memories."

"Wait," Joanne shakes her head, as if clearing space for the idea. "Are you saying, we actually see different things when we watch the same memory?"

"No," Eleanor jumps in, looking from Joanne to David. "We've talked about them. We've all seen the same things."

"In a broad sense," David agrees, before resuming his seat and running a hand over his mouth. He rubs his chin for a moment. Thinking.

"Okay," he tries again. "I know this is hard to understand. But, here goes. You see the same general events. As in the first memory, where you all see Joanne and Jeff having a picnic in the park. You all hear him playing the guitar, singing, talking with Joanne--"

"We know what we've seen," Andy's fists are clenched, his eyes back on the floor between his feet.

"Right, yes," David nods. "The differences, though, are in the details. When I've asked each of you to describe the park, you offer different descriptions. There's a stream nearby, or not. There are children playing, or not. My own view of the park seemed to be entirely different from all of your descriptions, but when I searched online, I found that it matched pictures of a park near the house where I grew up. And these differences go on and on. Even the clothing Joanne is wearing, the color of the blanket, and the type of picnic basket all varied in each of your descriptions."

Andy raises his head, remembering something about his last session with David.

"This is the thing with the birds?"

"Yes, the birds!" David flips through the papers in

front of him and holds a chart out toward Andy. "In all of your descriptions, not one of you mentioned seeing birds. I didn't see any either. But when I asked you to describe the birds, as if I knew they were there, you each saw them. Eleanor saw two small birds walking around in the grass near the blanket, Joanne saw cardinals perched on the branches of a nearby tree and, Andy, you saw a flock of geese flying overhead.

"But only *after* I planted the idea. All I had to do was ask about birds, as if they were there, and your own brains inserted them into the memory."

The idea excites David. He's on his feet again, holding the chart out for them all to see, eager for a reaction that doesn't come. Joanne stares back into the void behind him, while Eleanor grips her slack hand. Andy shakes his head at the floor. There's something happening that David doesn't understand.

After a moment of silence, Andy sits up, bracing his hands on his thighs.

"So, you've been fucking around with our heads then?"

David pales.

"What? No, I-- I'm showing you how malleable our memories can be. That these recordings are more like triggers or suggestions," he casts around for the right words.

"But you *put* that memory, those birds, into our heads," Eleanor spits the words at him, glaring.

"David, you have to see how unsettling this is for us?" Joanne carries her argument more gently.

It's a question, but Eleanor doesn't wait for his response.

"What gives you the right to violate our thoughts like that? To just plant ideas in our minds?"

"Now, hold on," David's voice begins to shake as he looks from Eleanor to Joanne and back again. "I've been clear with you all from the beginning. This entire project *is* manipulating our minds, all of our minds, that's just the nature of viewing these memories. Of sending signals recorded from someone else's mind into our own."

Eleanor opens her mouth to speak, but David continues quickly, his own anger building.

"If you didn't understand it before, you need to understand this now. We are not watching a realistic, immersive video. We are inputting signals that mix with our own memories, and our own experiences of the world, to create new memories that we did not previously have. I don't know what the long-term effects of this is going to be. On any of us. Myself included. This isn't the sort of a thing a-- a professional scientist would do. But we're here, and this isn't what I would call-- Well. It's not professional. To say the least.

"Furthermore, as real as these imported memories seem, they are still only constructs. We can't entirely--"

He stops short, turning toward Joanne, but she already knows where this idea is headed.

"We can't entirely trust them," she finishes. "Jeff's memories aren't real."

There's quiet around the room as Joanne's words sink in. Eleanor reaches for her hand, but Joanne flinches away. Andy is now lost in thoughts, staring at the closed basement door.

David takes a deep breath.

"I am not saying whether Jeff's memories are true or not true," he speaks slowly, each word a penance for his earlier loss of control. "I'm not *able* to tell you that. The best I can speculate, is that they are the way Jeff's mind chose to remember those moments."

Joanne nods, quickly wiping a single tear from her cheek.

"What are the differences?" Eleanor asks. "Other than the birds? Are they small things? Big things? Do they change anything?"

"Both," David answers honestly, before shuffling through his papers for a particular set of notes.

"You know what? Fuck this." Andy shoves the table as he stands, nudging it toward David and rattling the dishes.

"Andy," Eleanor sighs, looking away.

"No. I'm done hearing this tonight. We had a simple thing here, and he," his arm reaches to point at David accusingly, "he comes in here just looking for ways to fuck it all up."

"Andy, that's not what--"

"No, you've said enough. I don't need to hear about the brain, and the hippowhatsit, and fucking constructs. Whatever the fuck that means. We're seeing Jeff's version of events. Period. So, yeah, maybe he didn't get it all perfect and maybe we don't use it for court testimony, but, fuck, man. You're making it sound like this is all just bullshit."

With a pivot, Andy paces the kitchen, toward the dark dining room and back again. Both hands run over the back of his head, elbows out to the side. For several moments, no one responds.

"There's a nurse," David interjects. "In the second memory."

Joanne and Eleanor look up sharply.

"The fuck are you talking about?" Andy is still angry, but he's stopped pacing.

"Isabella," David answers calmly. "The nurse who is at the hospital with Jeff's mother."

He has their attention and makes the most of it. His shoulders drop back, his head lifts, and his eyes stay locked on Andy.

"We all seemed to see Isabella the same way. Even me. So that told me the way she looked likely came from Jeff's memory construct, not from each of us filling in our own pictures of a nurse. And it seemed like something I might be able to corroborate.

"So, I found out when Jeff's mother died, called a friend at the hospital and made up a story about trying to remember a nurse I'd met who worked there around that time."

"You what?" Eleanor's mouth falls open in disbelief, but David simply continues his story.

"It turns out there was a nurse named Isabella who worked there, and she did fit my description. But," he pauses dramatically, "she stopped working there about six months before Jeff's mother was admitted. And you know where she did work, when she was there? The maternity ward. She worked in the maternity ward during the time when Sarah and Ruthie were born. My guess: that's where Jeff met her."

"Your point?" Andy practically hisses.

"My point," David sighs, "is that this isn't bullshit. It

isn't a worthless project, not by a long shot. In fact, this is a ground-breaking, game-changing accomplishment. But we still need to be aware that human memory is not a video tape. It has limitations and failings, and we are responsible for how something like this machine is used, or misused, in the future."

Andy's right eye begins to twitch and David notices that his chest is shaking with an effort to breathe evenly. Something seems to be fading inside Andy, pulling him inward and away from the conversation. But before David can question him, Eleanor steps between them.

"Maybe we agreed to have ideas put in our heads, but none of us gave you permission to dig into our private lives."

"What?"

"You talked to a friend at the hospital?" Eleanor repeats pointedly. "You talked to a friend at the hospital to look into something that happened in *our* lives?"

"Oh, well--" David looks toward Joanne, but she is watching her fingers, now interlaced on the table.

"I'm done," Andy announces abruptly. "I need a fucking drink."

Only David looks his way, but Andy is already out the door. A minute later they hear the sound of his truck spitting gravel as it roars away. They pause, frozen in his wake.

"This is hard on him," Joanne offers gently. Her eyes lift toward David. "He's out of his depth, and he isn't good at seeing big pictures."

David nods, reclaiming his chair as he looks across the scattered pile of papers in front of him.

"I'm sorry," David looks up at Eleanor. "I'm sorry I provoked him and that I pried into your personal lives. That wasn't my intention."

Eleanor nods in return, but stays standing.

"You shouldn't have done that," Joanne agrees. Then clarifies, "If you have questions you should ask me, or El, not poke around and talk to strangers."

"All right, I can do that." David notices that she didn't include Andy as a resource, but he doesn't comment on it.

"This is a small town," Joanne continues. "It will be hard enough to explain why you're here without you also asking strange questions everywhere you go."

"Right," David flushes. The mention of other people, noticing him, here, raises concerns of his own. The lab is thirty minutes away, yet he knows many locals work there in some capacity. If they start to notice… or if Andy says something…

"Maybe I should smooth things over with Andy," David ventures, trying to sound calm. "Make more of an effort."

"Maybe," Joanne agrees, while Eleanor frowns.

"Any idea where he went?"

CHAPTER SEVENTEEN

The bar is dark and smoky. A small-town dive where regulars come to drink on weeknights, in relative peace, and to mingle with friends when the weekend rolls around. Customers sit alone, or in loose groups, along the long counter of an L-shaped bar and in the dark booths that line the opposite wall. A single touchscreen game station sits in the center of the bar's shorter run and a group of twenty-somethings gather around it, occasionally cheering or chiding the players.

It doesn't take long for David to find Andy. He's sitting at the long edge of the bar, alone, as far from the laughing twenty-somethings as he can get. Despite being the same age, he seems much older as he smokes a cigarette and stares at the range of bottles behind the bar. There's a half-full beer and an empty shot glass sitting in front of him. This bar still allows smoking indoors and the smell of it clings to the air, contributing to a distinct aroma of tobacco, beer, and fried food.

David takes the empty seat beside Andy just as the bartender closes in. He orders a beer. Andy ignores him, continuing to stare at the bottles. Joining his gaze, David sees a motley assortment of rail liquors and call brands, mainly blended malts and mid-range vodka. A few brightly colored liqueurs round out the selection. One half-full bottle of David's favorite cognac gathers dust on an upper shelf. The bartender sloshes over a smeary pint of beer, and David passes across his credit card. He tells the bartender to start a tab and to bring Andy another round, but Andy still doesn't acknowledge his presence.

"I'm not going to apologize," David tells Andy without looking his way.

"Okay," Andy sips his beer.

"You probably think I should," David pauses for a reply that doesn't come. "You're probably pissed at me. Probably think that I'm taking over. That I think I'm better than you."

"And?"

David frowns and drinks his beer.

"And I am better than you," he answers at last.

"Great," Andy tips his empty shot glass, watching it balance on one fine edge. "Glad you tracked me down to clear that up."

"You can be pissed all you want. I'm pissed that you and Jeff started this whole damn thing. But we both know that I am vastly more qualified than you when it comes to the science of this. It's not even close. And I'm not going to pretend otherwise."

Andy stays quiet, waiting to hear more.

The bartender comes by with Andy's next round and

leaves the drinks without interrupting. He continues to surreptitiously eye them from the other end of the bar, wary of any trouble that might be brewing.

"Look," David decides to lay his cards on the table. "I could have turned you in the moment I found out about this mess. But I didn't. You could turn me in now. People at the lab are more likely to believe that it was Jeff and me who started this scheme, and you know that. But then you'd lose out, too. So, we're stuck together. And the only way this works is if, one, you let me lead the research and, two, we both work to keep this secret."

"Then what?" Andy's empty glass continues to rock precariously, while the drinks David ordered for him go ignored. "You don't think this is something we can sell."

"No," David watches Andy in the tinted mirror behind the bar. "I don't."

"You'll want to go public with this though," Andy ventures. "When you've got it figured out. Promote it as your big-- What did you call it? Game-changing research? So, how the fuck does that help me?"

"I'll need a subject," David studies Andy's tense profile. "I'll need test memories to show that it works. And I think it would be better if I was the one who recorded them. And if that subject was alive. To answer questions and be part of future studies."

Andy frowns, but his shoulders soften.

"For you, that could mean a lot of attention," David continues. "Interviews. Maybe a book deal. A movie. People will want to know what it was like. For you. To be the first person to have his memories recorded."

Andy turns to face David now, his expression

carefully blank.

"So, you'd just throw out Jeff's memories? Pretend he was never a part of this?"

"Not exactly," David drinks his beer, stalling to find the right words. "It wasn't a secret that Jeff and I often met over lunch, or that we enjoyed discussing things like this. I can still credit Jeff with the idea, but present it as more of a, uh, collaboration. Something that I decided to pursue more seriously after his death, but that I kept as a side project because I wasn't sure it would ever work."

"And you brought me in as your lab rat?"

"Because I knew you'd want to see if something could come of Jeff's idea, too."

"And what? You borrowed equipment?"

David looks sharply around before admitting that they would have to find a way to bring it back to the lab by then. Rebuild the whole system in a controlled space that David could justify as an off-shoot of his current research.

"But first, I need time to figure out how it all works."

There's a full thirty seconds of silence as they mentally size each other up. They need each other for the project to move forward. Neither of them likes it, but they both know it's true.

"What about Jo?"

David is surprised by the question.

"You're going to just erase Jeff's memories? Take them away from her?"

David considers.

"Publicly, they won't exist," he agrees slowly. "Privately, we can work something out. I think that would be better for her. And for the girls."

"Yeah," Andy nods, "that makes sense."

Andy finishes his first beer, then points to his untouched shot of whisky and calls to the bartender, "Hey, Mike, one for my friend."

"And that means?" David leans in, asking before the bartender makes his way to them.

"It means... I guess we have a deal."

Mike steps in front of them, depositing a shot glass filled with a dark liquor, then retreats just as quickly. The place is filling up now, people grouping together between the bar and the booths. David lifts his glass, surprising Andy by tossing it back with a practiced movement, then waves to order another round.

Andy downs his own shot, and shakes his head at David, but there's a smile creeping in when he says, "You're picking up the tab tonight."

The next shots are slow to come. Mike is busy mixing some colorful concoctions for the touchscreen crowd, but Andy and David are content to sip their remaining beer and wait. The tension has lessened between them. It's mellowed into an uneasiness. A sense of reluctant trust. They are bound now in a way they weren't before. Finally finding common ground.

"I forget sometimes," David confides, after a few minutes of quiet contemplation. "I get so caught up in the science of it that I forget about Jeff as a person. You know, as your friend and Joanne's-- I can be a dick like that sometimes. When the science is good."

Andy nods, feeling himself really relaxing for the first time in David's presence.

"It's a dick thing to do," he agrees, and David is the

first to laugh. Mike brings their next shots and the room softens around them.

As the night wears on, and the whisky continues to flow, the nearby conversations take on a familiar, rhythmic murmur. Everything beyond David and Andy begins to fade into a fuzzy haze of movement. David turns his focus back from the bleary crowd and realizes that Andy is talking about Jeff now. He's talking about how strange it is to know that Jeff's really gone for good.

"Yeah, well, he was your best friend," David contributes. "It's a hell of a thing."

Andy shakes his head, brushing off the comment.

"Not like it's the first time," he says, before draining the last of another beer and waving for Mike's attention.

David holds his own beer an inch from his lips, then stops without taking a sip.

"What?" He genuinely thinks he misheard Andy. The room seems to be getting louder. More people narrow the space around them. Someone turns on the jukebox and there are shrieks of laughter as two girls drag their dates toward an improvised dance floor. David remembers that it's a Saturday night.

"Jeff wasn't my best friend anyway," Andy adds with a frown. "Mark. Mark was my best friend."

"Mark?" The name means nothing to David.

"He was like my fucking brother, man. We grew up together, you know? Two doors down since birth. Womb to tomb and all that shit. Jeff didn't show up until like, I don't know, the end of junior year, and when he did-- Man, I couldn't stand that fucker!"

"Really?" David counts back, knowing from Jeff's

obituary that he was 27 when he died. "But then you were friends for what? Ten years? Was that just because he was with Joanne?"

Andy laughs and shakes his head. He stacks their empty shot glasses, still chuckling.

"You don't know how fucking hilarious that is, man."

"So, tell me."

The bartender drops off another round of beer, his eyes trained on two girls further down the bar. David ignores him, leaning in to hear Andy over the man on his right who's loudly telling jokes to whoever will listen.

"Well, yeah, I mean, I guess we did meet Jeff through Joanne. In a way. She was failing math, or science, or something, and some teacher got Jeff to help her out. And Mark did not like that shit."

"Mark?" Andy hands David another shot but he mindlessly sets it on the bar, still focusing on what this Mark person had to do with Jeff and Joanne.

"Yeah, Mark didn't like any guy around Joanne. So, we had to explain that to Jeff, you know? Which I thought would be the end of it. For Jeff hanging around. But, well... Fuck."

"So, wait, so," David reaches for his beer, considering. "So, Mark was dating Joanne?"

"Well, yeah," Andy seems genuinely surprised that David wouldn't know that. "It was always Mark and Joanne. Would have been fucking forever."

"But then... she left him for Jeff?"

"What?" Andy spins on his stool, bristling, then relaxes when he sees David's utter confusion. He sighs. "No, man. Mark and Jo were solid. They just, I don't know, they just had that drama thing going on. You know all Sid and Nancy or whatever. But then they got in this fight and Mark was out drinking and-- Fuck. It was just a stupid, fucking accident, you know? Like Jeff and his stupid, fucking accident. Fucking fate, man. It's a fucking bitch."

David tries to make sense of the story, but he realizes that the whisky and beer have caught up with him faster than they would have in his college days. He tries to flag the bartender to get some water, but a new crowd of young drinkers is keeping Mike busy.

"So, you became friends with Jeff after high school?" David persists. "When Joanne started dating him?"

"No, dude," Andy holds up both hands in frustration. "You're getting it all wrong."

Mike appears out of nowhere with a plate of wings and a basket of shoestring fries, making David wonder when Andy had ordered them. Andy grabs a wing, pushes the plate toward David and tries to untangle the timeline.

"Okay, back to junior year, when Jeff moved to town--"

"When you and Mark beat him up?"

"No, geez," Andy frowns, gesturing with the wing as he talks. "*Beat him up*. Fuck. No, we just *explained* things to him. But then there was this thing in class. Like, I don't know, a few days later.

"Okay, see Mark dropped this cheat sheet during a test, like right in front of the fucking teacher, you know? But she only saw it on the floor in the aisle between Mark and Jeff.

"Well, so, she knew it was Mark's and she starts to bitch at him, but then Jeff says, *'It's not his, Mrs. Hillard,'* in his whiny-ass little teacher's pet voice. And she's like, '*what the fuck*,' and he asks to talk to her privately. Privately! Right?

"So, they go to the front of the room and he starts telling her some bullshit and then she starts looking sad and patting him on the arm and shit, and that's that. So, I don't know, that like impressed Mark, I guess, and next thing he wants to start bringing Jeff along. Like every-fucking-where."

Andy tears into the wing, still shaking his head over the memory, while David squints at him, waiting.

"Well?" David prompts, when Andy reaches for a handful of fries. "What did Jeff say to the teacher?"

"What? Oh, I don't know. It was some bullshit about a study guide." Andy laughs again, remembering. "Oh, yeah, he said it was that small just so he could hide it and people wouldn't make fun of him for studying all the time. Only Jeff could get away with shit like that! Teachers fucking loved him. Funny thing is, I don't think the dude ever studied a day of school. I know he fucking didn't when he was rolling with us. He just kinda knew everything, you know? Scary smart."

"Yeah," David agrees, deadpan. "So, I've noticed."

CHAPTER EIGHTEEN

Joanne flips through the papers slowly. They make a soft *fwip-fwip* sound on their descent to the worn kitchen table, meeting to form an uneven stack beneath her restless hands. The motion stops when she reaches a packet of color-coded spreadsheets held together with a single bent staple. She pulls the packet out and chews her lip while studying the data. There are columns for each of them, everyone who has watched Jeff's memories: Joanne, Eleanor, Andy, and David.

Rows below the names list details from each of their experiences, grouped by the corresponding memory. Items that David had mentioned in their meeting jump out at Joanne. There's the stream, Joanne's clothing, the blanket, and the picnic basket. But there are many other items as well. There are flowers, foods, expressions, the sky, scents, textures, emotions, and bodily sensations. Everything that David had thought to question. Birds are in the last row.

Sliding her eyes across the paper, Joanne sees the

differences that David had explained, but also the similarities. Some rows show four different descriptions, others show that two or three people had shared the same experience, and any row with matching descriptions across all four columns has been highlighted in yellow. It's the yellow rows that Joanne cares about. It's those details, she assumes, that are more likely to have come from Jeff's own memory. From his *construct* of the experience, she tells herself, trying to internalize David's explanation.

After several minutes, the rows and columns begin to blur under Joanne's intense stare, fading together into a mass of black lines and yellow streaks. She sets the paper down and rubs the bridge of her nose.

Is this what you've become? She addresses Jeff in her mind. *You're yellow lines on a spreadsheet now? A stack of paper?* And then she thinks of the machine sitting in the basement below her feet. *Are you in there?* She wonders, not for the first time. *Has the computer become you? All I have left of you?*

The kitchen is quiet around Joanne, except for its familiar creaks and hums. She pictures Sarah and Ruthie, asleep upstairs, and has an urge to go sit in the dark between their beds. It's become a favorite place at night. A space to sit and listen to her daughters' rhythmic breath. To imagine that she's only lonely because Jeff is working a night shift and that she will hear the sound of his truck crunching into the gravel driveway any moment. But she can't bring herself to play out that fantasy tonight. Not when her mind is overflowing with the ideas that David had explained this evening.

Reaching for the spreadsheet packet, Joanne flips pages until she finds a line item marked *Isabella*. There are several rows describing the nurse: Hair, face, clothes, voice, age. Each row is highlighted in yellow while scribbled notes in the margin show her full name—*Isabella Montanari*—as well as her years of employment at the hospital and her time in the maternity ward. Joanne closes her eyes to better picture Isabella. She remembers her from the girls' birth. She remembers her offering ice chips and helping with the epidural. But she also remembers Isabella being with Jeff's mother at the end. She can see her there, in the room, and can remember how kind she had been to them. Unless…

David's explanation doesn't seem possible. Joanne remembers Isabella being in that room. In her own memory. But when she tries to picture that day, the image matches Jeff's recording so well that she doesn't know whether it's corroboration or a sign that watching Jeff's recording had actually changed her own memories of the event. Could it be that easy to replace her memory? Did Jeff know it would work that way?

A prickling sensation begins under Joanne's ribs. A suspicion that she can't quite grasp. Joanne turns to face the table, dropping the packet on top of the other papers and pressing her palms into its wooden surface as she closes her eyes. She forces herself to think through Jeff's memory of that day in the hospital. She closes her eyes and pictures the room. She pictures Rachel lying in the bed, pale and still, but tries to focus on the other details. On the privacy curtains, the monitors, the wheeled cart with its box of tissues, the meal card, the pen, and the yellow water pitcher.

It feels almost like being back in the chair downstairs, but different. Simultaneously less and more vivid. With a slow exhale, Joanne turns her focus to the place where Isabella sits in the corner, trying to tap into her own memory of the moment. She sees Isabella's long dark hair, braided, her pink scrubs and her thin gold necklace. It's just as they appear when watching Jeff's recording. But then, the nurse stands, bending to check Rachel's IV, and everything shifts.

Her hips begin to spread beneath the fabric, and the scrubs darken to a deep red. When she straightens up, her hair is short and curly. Dirty blonde. Her dark eyes peer at Joanne through thin-rimmed glasses, and she offers a sympathetic pat on the arm while leaving the room.

Joanne shakes her head against the image, but a new name rises in her mind: *Bethany*. Bethany was there with them that day. Bethany sat with her mother-in-law. Bethany was the one who came out to talk to them later, after the doctor had come and gone. Joanne knows it just as surely as she knows that Isabella was the one who did those things. Except they couldn't have both been there in those final moments. There was only one nurse there and, with every passing moment, Joanne becomes increasingly unsure whether which, or either, was there at all.

When she opens her eyes, Joanne's heart is racing and the room appears to be receding, pulling away from her. Objects blur as she inhales in short, fast gasps. *Breathe. Breathe.* She hears Jeff's voice, calming her panic, pulling her back toward solid ground. Except this time, he isn't here to steady her.

The avalanche of memories begins. Splintered fragments. Her parents, a hospital hallway, her fourth-grade teacher, a pair of striped shorts barely covering tan legs, a dark car, flowers in the rain, the stench of cheap beer, Mark's eyes, her grandmother's hands, the crash of breaking glass. The pieces move too fast, too loud, buzzing by without meaning or purpose, and Joanne waits them out, feeling her breath, feeling the table under her hands. The wood is hard, slick against her palms. Her fingertips press into the scattered papers, feeling uneven layers and crisp edges above the smooth wood.

The table draws her back. Its material feel lets her reel in her breath, slowing the effort, bringing the room back into gradual focus. And, when her thoughts clear, the two nurses remain. Two women who seem equally in place, and out of place, in her memory of that day.

Taking a seat at the table, Joanne ignores David's stacks of meticulous research. She drops her head into her hands, raking fingers through her hair, and stares into the darkened dining room.

She wonders what else she actually remembers about her life. Did she really eat in the kitchen, separate from the grownups, during holiday meals? Or is that an amalgam of TV shows and holiday movies? She tries to remember who came to those dinners. Her cousins? Her aunt and uncle? The images are muddled.

There were holidays when they were the visitors and holidays after they moved to town. There were holidays with other visiting relatives and some years with Eleanor's family joining them as well. But were those actually holiday meals or just a jumble of other shared dinners? Random Friday nights followed by a round of cards?

Closing her eyes, despite the buzz at the back of her skull, Joanne forgets the people and conjures her grandmother's good china. The dishes and glassware that came out of storage for every holiday meal. She sees the dishes' creamy surfaces and scalloped edges, trimmed in gold. She feels her fingers running over the intricate facets on the cut-crystal goblets. And then, her grandmother's face swims before her closed eyes. The soft waves of her silver hair, the pale hue of her purple-framed glasses, and the pink lipstick that always ended up with lopsided lines.

A voice floats behind the face, just out of hearing. Joanne can't make out the words, but her ears and chest react to the not-quite-heard sound. It's almost like a vibration. She can register the timbre of her grandmother's voice. Its inflections. The sensation brings a stinging sensation to her inner ears and a hollow slash of longing through her gut.

With a deep sigh, Joanne opens her eyes to the dim kitchen and the dark dining room beyond. She pulls the papers together, tapping them into a neat pile. These splintered memories, panic attacks, and deep reveries aren't new to her. They weren't new to Jeff. But, for the first time, she openly considers the truth behind them.

Joanne walks to the basement door, as if in a trance, and makes her way down to the rough wooden bookshelves at the back of Jeff's room. There are books on neuroscience, on computers, and on psychology. And, on a lower shelf, the two books that Jeff had asked Joanne to read. Books on trauma and PTSD.

Joanne runs her fingers across their spines, remembering how Jeff would read passages aloud, asking if anything sounded familiar. They had argued about that. About whether talking about it could help or whether it was something that would just get better with time. About whether they should pay for therapy.

Joanne's stomach turns at the sight of those books. They make her feel broken. And they remind her that no matter how close they had been, there had always been secrets between them.

CHAPTER NINETEEN

"Absolutely not."

Eleanor is leaning against the kitchen cabinets, her hands braced on the Formica countertop behind her as if she's about to push off and resume pacing at any moment. Her eyes shift from David to Andy, skimming past Joanne entirely. "I've tried to get on board. I've tried to see the good in it. But I think it's wrong. And this…? No. This is exactly what's wrong with this whole thing."

They are back in Joanne's kitchen, twenty-four hours after their last group meeting. The people are the same, but the energy has changed. David and Andy are on the same page now. They want to record new memories and document the process. They want to legitimize the project and devise a plan to get it back into the lab. They're ready to move forward. They're working together.

Joanne and Eleanor have listened, but barely spoken. Not to the group or to each other. Until now.

Andy opens his mouth to respond, but David

intervenes with a simple raised hand and a shake of his head.

"Let's not throw the whole project out over one point," he tells Eleanor. "We can discuss this."

"The hell we can!" Andy interjects, turning on David.

"Andy," David pleads, "Eleanor. We can discuss this. Nothing is set in stone."

"I'm the lab rat here," Andy reminds them. "Don't I get to think about whatever I want? Jeff did."

"Now, that's--" David tries to get between Andy and Eleanor, but they are both on their feet now, talking over each other in a jumble of angry, half-formed thoughts and narrowing their distance menacingly.

"Enough."

Joanne has kept her seat, hands crossed on the table before her, knuckles white, but the tone of her single word cuts through the argument and brings quiet back to the kitchen.

"All right, look," Andy takes a deep breath, "I know it's a hard thing, a bad time, but he was my best friend."

There are tears in Joanne's eyes that do not fall.

"So, remember something happy about him," Eleanor counters. "When you were kids or something. Why would you want to record that night?"

Andy's arms hang by his sides and his face softens.

"Because it was the last night I saw Mark alive."

Eleanor spins on her heel and runs both hands over her face. David presses his lips together, considering his position.

In that moment, Joanne slowly uncurls her fingers, pressing her palms flat on the table. Seeing her slight movement, Eleanor steps forward to sit by Joanne's side, turning to the one person whose opinion matters the most. There's tension in the air and silence expanding around them.

Joanne gradually lifts her eyes to meet Eleanor's unwavering stare. Her breath shakes. She closes her eyes. She exhales. Slowly. As her eyes open, her shoulders roll back and her chin lifts. David is reminded of a computer rebooting after a crash and he wonders what messages are playing through Joanne's mind, or have played through her mind, to bring about this transformation.

Andy cracks his knuckles, loudly, but David cannot pull his eyes from the wordless conversation that is happening between Eleanor and Joanne. The long, meaningful look between them that somehow unravels Eleanor's remaining anger and fear. She nods once, swallowing hard.

There is a poignant pause around the room, a distinct shift, before Andy clears his throat.

"It's not like we have to keep it anyway."

His voice is thick with emotion.

"I mean, it doesn't have to be one that goes public," he amends. "It's just-- It's just something I want to see again. You know?"

"You mean," David blinks quickly, pulling himself back into the conversation. "It could be a test memory?"

"Yeah, I guess." It's Andy's turn to nod agreement. "We can always make more and erase this one. Once we figure it out."

A question occurs to David, but Eleanor is the first to ask it.

"Were there more memories? That Jeff erased?"

Andy shrugs, looking flustered.

"I don't know. I guess there could be. Not like Jeff told me everything."

Eleanor's eyes narrow, Joanne's widen.

"Are you looking for others?" The tremor in Joanne's voice sends a wave of anxiety across David's heart.

"I haven't been, but I could look. Although, I've taken a pretty good inventory of what's on the computer already. I doubt there's anything I've missed."

"Maybe you should look again." Andy's words are heavy, spoken as he's staring at the ground between his feet. David feels compelled to agree, although he doubts there is anything else to find.

To break the tension, David reaches for the half-empty coffee pot and offers it around before refilling his own mug.

"So where do we go from here? What's next?" Joanne asks the inevitable question and David begins to explain that he'll need to figure some things out before they record anything. He confirms that Jeff did not leave instructions for making new recordings, but he doesn't seem overly concerned about that point.

"Now that I'm ready to move forward, it shouldn't be too hard to decode his process. The tools are there, even if they aren't documented."

"Well, I'm ready when you are," Andy swings into his seat and checks to see if there's anything left in his cup. "Whatever you need, doc."

"Good. I have some ideas I'd like to try, but first-- It's just, let's be aware that we may not have as much control as we think when it comes to what gets recorded."

"What?" The question comes from Andy, but Eleanor looks up in alarm. "Why not?"

David sees the expression on Joanne's face and knows that she already understands.

"We can try to choose a specific memory," David begins hesitantly.

"But we can't always control our thoughts," Joanne finishes.

"That's right," David confirms. "The mind has a way of thinking about whatever it wants, even when we don't want it to."

"Oh. Well--"

Eleanor doesn't wait for Andy to respond. She stands up, palms pressing into the tabletop.

"You know what?" Her eyes are glittering and her voice shakes. "I think it's my turn to make a dramatic exit. I'm trying here, but I need a break."

"El," Andy reaches across the table, but she pulls her hands away. David interjects, again, this time agreeing that it's probably best to call it a night.

"It's late," he reminds them. "We're all tired, and we can pick this up tomorrow."

Without another word, Joanne stands and starts gathering up the nearest coffee cups. David quickly begins to help. As they move to the sink, rinsing and stacking cups in the dishwasher, the situation takes on a surreal feeling for Eleanor. The parody of a casual dinner party. Two couples saying their goodbyes after a final cup of coffee.

It's gruesome, Eleanor decides. With David here. Without Jeff. But it's the new reality, she tells herself. The new now that needs to be survived.

With a deft movement, Eleanor grabs the baby monitor and gives Joanne a brief hug before leading Andy out the kitchen door. The night air hits them with a coolness that isn't expected in early summer, but, while Andy pauses to breathe it in, Eleanor doesn't seem to notice. She turns on him the moment they are alone.

"The night Mark-- Really?"

He shrugs and pulls out a pack of cigarettes. Eleanor has stopped walking halfway across the wide, shared driveway and stands now with her arms tightly crossed, staring at Andy's broad back. When he finally turns back to her, smoke streams out of his nose and she can see the glow of the cigarette dangling from his lip.

"Yeah, El. The night Mark fucking died."

The weariness in his voice spreads over Eleanor and her indignation slips away. She wonders if marriage is always like this, for everyone, or if their combative nature means something more. With effort, she pushes aside her own feelings and looks for common ground.

"You don't think that might be a difficult memory for the rest of us?" Eleanor tempers her tone. "You don't think that memory might upset a lot of people? Me? Joanne? To bring it up again?"

"Nope," Andy is unmoved by Eleanor's new tack. He takes a long drag off the cigarette, filling his lungs with smoke and letting it back out in a slow plume, just to annoy her. "It happened. It sucked. And you know what the hardest thing about it is? For Me? For Dee? It's that everyone acts like he never lived at all."

"You still talk to Dee?"

"Yeah, somebody has to." The words are short, his

expression firm. Another smoky exhale, a look into Eleanor's searching eyes. "She's alone now that their mom's gone. I mean, she has friends and that boyfriend, but not people who really knew Mark. She'd want him remembered. Hell, I want him remembered.

"And, you know," he continues more thoughtfully. "I felt things when watching Jeff's memories. Like, I felt the way he did about Joanne. At least for a minute. Probably not the same as he did, but I could feel that it was this big feeling, you know? And I see her different after knowing how much Jeff felt. In a way. So maybe people watching my memories would get a bit of that about Mark, you know? See what was good under that punkass image he had back in the day. At least, that's what I hope."

Eleanor has nothing to say to that, because she rarely sees this side of Andy. The softness. When it appears, she remembers why she married him. Why she hasn't left him. It's as if she's married to two people and she's afraid to say something that will scare this one away. She cautiously opens her arms to him, ignoring the hot tip of his cigarette as he pulls her against her chest.

Back in the house, David is feeling vulnerable in his own way. He's not used to the tense, emotional moments that have now become a regular part of his life. He's not used to staring down a widow or asking people to reveal their deepest secrets. For the hundredth time, he wonders why he was brought into this mess and what he would be doing right now if Andy had turned to anyone but him.

"I was hoping it would help," David says softly, one hand on the doorknob, but not quite ready to leave. "All of this, in general."

"I know," Joanne tells him with a small smile.

"But I guess I've just traded one bad memory for another." And then he regrets his words, not meaning to call Jeff a bad memory or to compare the two men in her life. The two men who had both died so young.

Joanne looks down at her baggy socks. She swivels her right toes against the wood floor and the wool twists around her foot. Her fingers twine together in a nervous tangle and David knows that there is something she is preparing to say, yet it startles him when she looks up. Directly into his eyes.

"What did Andy tell you about Mark?"

"I, uh," David racks his brain to remember what Andy had said, but the stories tumble together in a haze of whisky, music, and the buzz of surrounding conversations. "Well, he said that they were friends. Best friends," he manages to pull a few facts together. "That you and Mark, uh, dated in high school. That Mark had an accident--"

"An accident?" Joanne gently bites her bottom lip and, to David, the foyer suddenly feels too small for them both. He swallows.

"He didn't explain--"

"It wasn't exactly--"

They both stop. Joanne drops her gaze to the floor and David watches her hair drape forward, over her shoulders. It's always her hair, he thinks absently, noticing the way the light shines off its soft waves. *What is it about her hair?*

Joanne looks back up, without fully meeting his eyes. "It was reported as an accident, officially. But there are people who think it wasn't."

"If it wasn't an accident..." David trails off, feeling like he should already suspect what happened. That he should be reading between the lines, but he can't seem to focus on a long-dead teenager or whatever may have happened so many years ago. He's too aware of the woman standing in front of him, her sleeping children upstairs, and the general strangeness of this situation.

"He was out on a bridge," Joanne tells him, with wide, dry eyes. "He was out late at night. Drinking. Alone. And he was-- He was upset."

Realization dawns with a sinking, cold sensation.

"You think he jumped?"

Joanne meets his eyes, then lowers her gaze to the floor.

"Some people may still have questions," she answers cautiously. "And maybe it's safer not to stir that up."

David watches her, watching the floor, and feels torn between too many reactions. Before he can settle on a response, Joanne looks up with him with sadly smiling eyes.

"It's okay," she tells him. "I trust you to do what's right."

CHAPTER TWENTY

It doesn't matter, David tells himself. Over ten years ago, some kid he didn't know died. It doesn't matter whether he slipped on the ice or did a swan dive onto the rocks below. It happened and now it's nothing more than a memory. Just data to be captured and stored, analyzed and understood. Yet there's something in the idea of it that disturbs him. Something that disturbs him even more than dealing with the self-recorded memories of a dead man.

And that's when he has to stop thinking.

David runs his hands through his hair and looks around the cluttered room. The space is larger than Dr. Keller's adjacent office, but crowded with several small desks and large bookshelves. Fletcher hunches behind a monitor near the door. His lips move silently as he counts something on the screen, his right hand hovering in front of him, index finger tapping the air with each count. Madeleine sits closer, at a desk about six feet away from David, watching him intently. The realization, that she is watching him, causes David to visibly startle, and she smiles at the response. Before he can consider what that smile means, she is on her feet and crossing over to him.

"You've been quiet all morning." It's the first thing she's said to him today.

"Have I?" He knows he has but doesn't know what else to say.

Madeleine peers at him through thick-rimmed glasses and the moment stretches. Uncomfortably for David. Amusingly for Madeleine. A grin plays across her face and her left shoulder lifts in a half-shrug.

"Not that that makes today any different than the last few weeks."

David looks down at his notebook—a step-by-step plan for how to record Andy's memory—then shuts it quickly. Quickly enough to make Madeleine drop her eyes and raise an eyebrow at its plain tan cover.

"Secrets?"

"Oh, uh, no," David's chest constricts, and he tries to release the sensation with a deep sigh. "Just working through an idea."

"More on how to incorporate acoustic and tactile encoding to our visualizations?"

"Uh, no," David feels the tightness move into his jaw. "Keller was clear about that."

Over the last few weeks, David's attempts to work Jeff's proven, yet secret, ideas into their research have been mocked by Fletcher and shot down by Keller at every turn. During their last group meeting, Keller had given him a stinging lecture on the difference between science fiction and actual research. Now, in the too-fresh memory, David can still hear the scorn in Keller's final words: *Stick to the parameters given or you can turn in your resignation and go write your screenplay.* Madeleine watches the play of emotion on David's face, then reaches out to lightly touch his hand, regaining his attention.

"Come on," she glances at Fletcher, dropping her voice so he won't overhear. "Let's go get some lunch."

As they walk to the cafeteria, David steals side glances at Madeleine. Considering. Despite some mild flirtations when she was first hired, they haven't spent much time together. They've never seen each other outside of work or even walked through the parking lot together. Not for the first time, he wonders if her distance came about as an effort to maintain professional boundaries. Or whether she'd rapidly lost interest. Or whether he'd only imagined her possible interest in those first few weeks.

Their short walk to the cafeteria is quiet, but not entirely uncomfortable. David listens to the clack of her thick heels on the stone floor and tries to think of something neutral, something friendly, to say. Nothing comes to mind.

When they reach the sunny cafeteria, in the building's central atrium, David steps back to let Madeleine pick up a tray and join the queue ahead of him. Her dark red hair hangs down her back in a thick braid and her knit skirt softly hugs her hips before falling into a wide, modest hem. She picks up a salad, a club sandwich, and a tray of fries. He does the same, absently, still wondering why today, of all days, she asked him to join her for lunch.

"Keller doesn't have much imagination," Madeleine

says, once they're seated at an empty table. She sets down her tray and begins rearranging its contents, lining up the silverware and separating dishes more precisely. "He's too cautious."

"Maybe," David hedges. For a fleeting moment, he wonders how much of what he says to Madeleine will get back to Fletcher or to Dr. Keller himself. He remembers what Andy said about the competition on their team and knows that jockeying for favor, or to make a breakthrough, is a real part of the research environment. But he doesn't want to believe that Madeleine would try to use him in that way. Fletcher, definitely. But Madeleine...? The thought trails off, not wanting to be resolved.

Madeleine chews her first bite of sandwich and studies David intently.

"You know, I spent some time with Jeff, too."

David chokes on his coffee.

"Not as much as you did," Madeleine continues smoothly. "But enough to know that his ideas might not have been as farfetched as they seemed on the surface."

David takes another bite of his sandwich, telling himself to go slow, to take his time. Distant conversations rise around them. There is a burst of laughter from a nearby table. A clatter of silverware as a group of men prepare to leave. David wonders how many times he and Jeff had sat at one of these tables, sharing lunch and trading ideas, defiantly ignoring the questioning glances from other scientists.

Or maybe, David tells himself now, maybe he only imagined those questioning glances. Maybe no one had really cared if he had struck up a friendship with a friendly maintenance man who liked to talk science. Maybe, like Madeleine, many of them spent some time with Jeff, too. Hearing his ideas and seeing that he should be doing more than repairing their labs. David feels himself nodding, thoughtfully, before consciously deciding how to respond.

"Jeff was a smart man," he says, after his next swallow, and reaches for more coffee. Madeleine cocks her head to one side, then looks down to pick through her tray of fries. David has the distinct impression that she is disappointed in his response, but he doesn't know why or what she might have expected. He waits for her to pick up the conversation, which she does after a quiet moment.

"Do you know much about Hedy Lamarr?" David says yes, but Madeleine continues as if he'd said nothing at all. "During World War II, Hedy Lamarr was a Hollywood actress who wanted to help with the war effort. She designed a frequency hopping system for radio-controlled torpedoes, to evade the enemy. That idea eventually became the basis for spread spectrum technology."

David tries to remember what he's heard of the story. "She partnered with someone to create that, didn't she?"

Madeleine frowns.

"Yes, George Antheil. A composer and inventor. They used a piano roll, from a player piano, to synchronize the transmitter and receiver. It would have kept the Nazis from locking onto our torpedoes, but it wasn't used during World War II. Do you know why?" David opens his mouth to speak, but Madeleine answers herself.

"The military didn't see the value of her invention," she pauses for effect. "Hedy Lamarr didn't fit their idea of an inventor or scientist—too beautiful, too female—so they dismissed her. They ignored her brilliance, her vision, her hard work. Because she didn't seem like someone they should take seriously. Because they didn't have much imagination."

Their gaze meets across the table and there is a gleam in Madeleine's eyes. David wants to tell her, something. But what? And how much? The moment feels large, as if taking up actual space around them, cutting them off from the rest of the cafeteria. David can feel that this is a pivotal moment. That he will look back on this, no matter what he says now, and always wonder about his response. It's a frightening thought. He could say anything. Everything. Or nothing. He could tell her about the machine, the memories, and his plan to move forward. He could take her to Joanne's, and they could work together on discovering the missing piece together. She would approach the project with fresh eyes, maybe see something new. Something he has overlooked.

But that's the problem.

"That's a shame," David responds at last, trying to hint at a deeper meaning, cracking the door just an inch without revealing too much. "We shouldn't overlook imaginative ideas just because they seem farfetched."

"Sometimes those ideas are simply ahead of their time," Madeleine offers in agreement, leaning forward with lightly squinting eyes. Waiting.

David picks up the second half of his sandwich. He feels the crumbling surface of the toast beneath his fingers. He weighs his options and knows that anything he does reveal can't be taken back. *Careful*, he tells himself.

He doesn't have to tell Madeleine anything concrete about the project to begin feeling out what her response might be. A picture of Joanne's living room comes to mind. Of sitting across the room from her without knowing the truth of why he was there. She had asked about his research that day. About what he would do, how he might help people, if he had the abilities she was about to offer. And he had never suspected the extent of what she was about to reveal.

They eat in silence for another minute as David tests Madeleine's patience. Tests her willingness to wait for whatever information he may offer. He feels a shift in their positions. A power that he now has over the conversation. It feels good after the weeks of being shunted aside by Fletcher and Dr. Keller. It feels right to remember that he controls something vital to their research. To the entire future of their field.

The trouble recording new memories is a setback, he tells himself. It's a problem that he will solve and when he does, he will be able to go public with the discovery. Form a team of his own. Possibly with Madeleine by his side.

"Hypothetically," David begins slowly, still searching for the best way to test the waters. "Do you ever consider the ethical ramifications of, uh, interfering with a person's memory?"

"Interfering?" Madeleine frowns and David shakes his head.

"Maybe that's not the right word." He presses his lips together. Thinks. "Say there was a way to artificially preserve and retrieve memories. Not just visualizations, but fully formed constructs pulled like movie clips from long-term memory. Would that be ethical?"

"I suppose it would depend on the memory." Madeleine continues eating, keeping her tone light and her eyes downcast, but David can see that her body is alert. Interested. "There are some experiences that people want to remember and others they'd rather forget."

"And some they'd rather not share," David adds knowingly.

"Share?" Madeleine lifts her gaze.

"Memories, and thoughts in general, are private," David continues. "But if we begin documenting them, externally, they are bound to lose a certain sense of privacy."

"I suppose," Madeleine shrugs the idea away. "But no more than when a person willingly writes in a journal or records in a video diary. Why would capturing thoughts or memories be any different?"

She sets down her last bit of sandwich and looks up for an answer, but something across the room has caught David's attention.

When Madeleine turns, she sees a young woman with long, dark hair and an older man in a suit ordering drinks from the standalone coffee cart at the front of the atrium. They're wearing guest badges, and he is carrying a leather briefcase. As she watches, the woman looks their way, freezes, then smiles, tentatively, before turning back to the older man. By the time Madeleine turns back toward David, a similar smile is fading from his face. He looks down at his nearly empty plate.

"Do you--?" Madeleine hesitates, sensing that she's stumbled onto something private in David's life. Before she can finish the thought, David crumples his napkin, stands up and suggests that they get back to work. He's halfway to the tray return before Madeleine rises to join him and she knows that the conversation is over.

For now.

CHAPTER TWENTY-ONE

There are only a handful of toddlers at the playground. They climb through the lowest rungs of the monkey bar ladder and chase each other between the empty swings. In a few days, when school lets out for summer, the playground will be overrun by older kids. The toddlers will be eager, but more leery as they navigate their place in the crowd. Today, mothers stand in small groups, chatting with one eye on their children and enjoying the last quiet days before summer vacation. Some sit on benches, holding babies or rummaging through overstuffed diaper bags.

Eleanor and Joanne have claimed their own bench in a sun-dappled spot beneath a spreading oak tree. They wear large sunglasses and keep their eyes on the playground as they watch Nolan wobble around between a group of small friends. The other neighborhood mothers give them space these days. No longer coming over to offer their condolences or even eyeing Joanne sympathetically. Not yet crashing in to act "normal" as if nothing has changed.

They're waiting now, for her to make the first move, but Joanne likes the quiet.

As she sits on the bench, feeling the warmth of the sun, Joanne's eyes drift over the distant jungle gym. Crisscrossed metal bars make wide triangles in a large domed shape. The bars remind her of the bridge at Landon's Hollow. They remind her of the way its tall trusses form large, open triangles. The metal green with flaked paint. The bridge was not designed for pedestrians and has no additional railing or fence. Not now or then. Not even after Mark.

Closing her eyes, Joanne can remember standing between two trusses, arms stretched wide, fingers gripping the rough, weathered metal, leaning forward to look down into the rocky river below. Her feet would brace on the very edge of the bridge, with nothing but her fingers holding her back. She never fully realized the danger of that position. Then. Only enjoying the sun on her face, the wind in her hair, the sound of her friends, laughing and talking on either side. She pictures the bridge at night. Ghostly green in the glare of headlights. Cold and dark. Her footsteps echoing with nowhere to run. A wide truss rough against her back, snagging her shirt, and Mark pinning her in place, wrists bruising in his iron grip.

"The girls will be home soon," Eleanor breaks into Joanne's reverie. "For the summer."

"Yes," Joanne swallows, inhales slowly.

"Do you think they'll ask more questions? When they're home all day?"

"I don't see why they would," Joanne hasn't thought beyond today. She doesn't want to consider next week or next month. "David will only come over nights and weekends."

"Still," Eleanor pauses, giving Joanne time to catch up. "They must wonder what's going on."

They've had this discussion before and Joanne doesn't want to have it again. Her daughters are separate, in her mind, from the revelation of Jeff's project, and she wants to keep it that way. She wants to think that she can protect them from this. That she can create a new normal. A new life where they can simply grow and play and find their own way in a world where they now know that people can disappear without warning. A world where there are no easy answers, other than breathing and moving and going on, no matter what.

She doesn't know how she will survive the summer.

"So, you've signed the papers," Eleanor changes the subject and Joanne nods, confirming that the settlement is done. She doesn't want to talk about this either. About reducing Jeff's life to a number. To an amount transferred into a trust in her name. She doesn't want to tell Eleanor about seeing David at the lab or the way it felt to catch a glimpse of him in his other world, having lunch with a pretty, stylish redhead.

"Now that you have the money, we don't really need--" Joanne cuts Eleanor off, knowing exactly what she is going to say. Again.

"Do you ever think about how things could be different?" Joanne feels Eleanor look her way, but her own shaded eyes stay on the playing children. "About where we would be if certain things hadn't happened? If Jeff hadn't died? If I hadn't gotten pregnant? If Mark hadn't...? If my parents hadn't...? Sometimes I wonder how far back I would have to go to really reset it. To make a real difference."

Eleanor doesn't have anything to say. She turns back toward the playground and lets her eyes follow her roaming son.

"Doug thinks I should use the settlement money to go back to school," Joanne continues. "He says I could study whatever I want. Get a good job when the girls are older. And it's a nice idea, but... How would I ever know what to study? What I'd want to be?

"I never had a dream job," Joanne continues with a sigh. "Nothing I wanted to be. Not that I remember, at least. I never thought I would live this long. Past high school or past the next year, or month, or week. I never thought my life would be this, I don't know, this permanent. Not when it's so temporary for other people. So why, or how, would I go to school? How would I make a plan?"

Across the playground, Nolan trips, falling onto his diaper-padded bottom with a thump. For a moment, his face crumples and his eyes dart toward his mother. Eleanor forces herself to smile at him, making their *uh-oh* gesture, and he laughs. He gets back to his feet and chases after a little girl with blond ponytails.

"We can't change the past," Eleanor begins cautiously, knowing exactly what she needs to say. "We can't change the past, but we can start over. Every day. Every hour. We can put aside the past, the things we've done, and move on. Reinvent ourselves and try again, and again."

"Can we?" For the first time this afternoon, Joanne

turns to face Eleanor. Their eyes struggle to meet through their tinted lenses. There's an unspoken question in her tone. *Should we?* She doesn't say it.

"Isn't that what we decided?" Eleanor counters. "Together?"

Joanne looks down at her hands. A bird lands a few inches from her feet, pecks in the grass, then flies away. Eleanor waits.

"Yeah," Joanne agrees softly. "I'm sorry, I didn't mean--"

"Of course you didn't," Eleanor assures her, placing a hand briefly on Joanne's thigh. "But I don't see how we can move on when they keep bringing it back."

"It isn't them bringing it back," Joanne brushes Eleanor's hand away and crosses her arms over her chest. There's a sharpness in Joanne's voice, but Eleanor knows it isn't directed at her. She waits, watching the kids stumbling around the playground in darting stops and starts.

"There are other things that bring it back. More," Joanne continues hesitatingly. "Triggers, or whatever. But even without that, the memories still come back. They're insistent like that. Always creeping in, taking over, or just-- I don't know, shading things.

"It's like that ball, you know?" Joanne turns back toward Eleanor, more animated now. "The example David gave of associated memories? There was that whole thing of how your brain uses its past experience of a ball to fill in more information the next time you see a ball. And maybe it's like that with everything. With other experiences. You know? Little details, little remembrances always coming back to the present."

"Jo," Eleanor tries to pause the conversation, giving herself time to think, but Joanne continues.

"All those memories just keep pushing their way in, insisting to be part of everything that happens next. Twining into everything and clinging, like weeds, or shadows, or--"

"Jo," Eleanor reaches for Joanne's gesturing hands, breaking her train of thought.

"El," Joanne levels her gaze, "What if we can't separate past memories because they're already here, mixing in with our thoughts and experiences, every single moment?"

Eleanor doesn't have an answer.

They watch Nolan and the other kids on the playground. Eleanor finds it impossible not to remember the feel of swing chains on soft palms, the skidding friction of a warm slide on bare legs, or the invading pinch of playground mulch on sandal-covered feet. Joanne wonders whether Jeff thought he could reshape the future, by replacing memories from the past.

"El," Joanne is quiet now, nearly whispering. "I found something. Of Jeff's."

Eleanor waits, too worn down to react, as Joanne continues in a hollow monotone. "The other night. I was looking at Jeff's books and there was-- I found a Salvador Dali book mixed in with the science and tech books. One that we bought at that museum, way back on that first day we ever left the girls alone with Gram. It was-- I loved that day, and--

"El, there were some pages from Jeff's notebooks tucked inside the book."

Eleanor gently bites her lip, letting her head bow forward.

"I think the pages might be important," Joanne clarifies needlessly.

"He hid them from Andy?" It's a question, but Eleanor has already made up her mind.

"I don't know," Joanne shakes her head. "Maybe. But maybe they're what David needs."

As they sit with this new information, Eleanor has the distinct impression that they're playing chicken with the past. Inching closer toward impact, but constantly wavering between either swerving or forcing their way to the finish. It's a thought she's had before, but this time she isn't entirely sure whether Joanne is sitting by her side or driving the oncoming car.

"You know Andy will end up recording that night," Eleanor begins carefully.

"Probably. But Andy doesn't know anything," Joanne counters.

"I suppose," Eleanor doesn't have to spell out her concerns. Again.

Joanne sits straighter, becoming defensive. "We already agreed to do this. To go forward."

"I know," Eleanor sighs. "It's just--"

"There was an investigation," Joanne reminds. "It was settled."

"It wasn't conclusive."

"It was conclusive enough," Joanne runs both of her hands over her face, rubbing her eyes and wishing she had more patience. "His blood alcohol was nearly 0.2 He was alone. Whether he slipped or jumped-- It was his fault."

They sit together, considering those facts. Stumbling over what they know and what they feel. Joanne tries not to remember why Mark was so drunk. Eleanor tells herself that no one made him drink that much. And if he hadn't...

"I know. It's just--" Eleanor searches for the right words. "I thought it was just us. I thought Andy had made peace with it."

"No," Joanne shakes her head. "He'll always blame me. A little."

"That's not fair." Eleanor reaches for Joanne's hand and Joanne nods, accepting the situation for what it will always be. After a moment, she releases Eleanor's hand and stands up, shakily.

"Are you ready to head back?"

"It was my fault," Eleanor says firmly from her place on the bench. Her words create a pang in Joanne's heart. She remembers Eleanor's fingers gripping her arms, her eyes pleading with Joanne to leave him. To get help. To tell someone. She remembers Eleanor's words, *"If you don't tell him you're through, then I will."* She remembers the feeling that she couldn't let Eleanor down. That she would be strong and end it. That she would stop listening to his apologies and tears. To his threats.

A warm breeze blows across the playground, rustling the leaves over their heads. Nolan's small voice yells, "Mommy!" and he plods across the grass holding up a smooth, striped rock. But Eleanor and Joanne barely notice his approach. They only hear the echo of Eleanor's last words, until the corners of Joanne's lips stretch into a sad smile.

"You were only trying to help."

And then Nolan is beside them, holding up his rock and rubbing a tired eye with his free hand. Eleanor scoops him up and gazes at Joanne over his downy head. Their eyes meet and they begin the motions of wrapping up a normal day at the playground. Eleanor bends to strap Nolan into his stroller. Joanne tucks his bag of snacks and small toys into its storage bin. A few women wave from the other side of the playground and Joanne returns the greeting, knowing that she can't hide forever.

CHAPTER TWENTY-TWO

They are back in the basement. David watches Andy's chest rise and fall with slow, steady breaths. The room is quiet, the lights are dim. Andy's body drapes across the leather recliner with his feet propped on the battered ottoman. David checks the monitor and raises an eyebrow at its falling line. He's about to speak when Andy's mouth falls open with a loud snore.

"Damn it, Andy!" David leans forward to shake Andy's arm. Again. Andy's eyes squint, then blink open.

"What?"

"What?" David sighs. "You're supposed to relax, meditate, not sleep." They've been at it for an hour and this is the third time David's relaxation techniques have put Andy to sleep.

"I'm telling you, man," Andy yawns. "You're going about this all wrong."

"We're not using illegal drugs." Andy shrugs. "Besides, you don't know that's what Jeff did."

"Nah," Andy agrees. "I don't *know*, but the only time he asked me for weed was right before he started getting results."

"And he also had books on self-hypnosis and meditation," David counters, not ready to concede the point.

"All right, doc," Andy raises his hands, then stretches them overhead. "I already said we'd try it your way. Again."

David frowns and looks down at his notes. Maybe Andy's right. Maybe he is going about this the wrong way, but he doesn't know what else to do. He looks at his own notes, feeling another flash of anger toward Jeff for not leaving more explicit instructions, then sighs out his frustration.

"Okay, maybe you're relaxed enough now," David tells Andy, trying to convince himself. "Let's give it another shot." He types a command at the prompt, but nothing appears to happen. He can tell that the recording process is running, but all he sees on the screen is the same blinking cursor.

"Lie back," he tells Andy anyway. "Shut your eyes. Good, and describe the memory in as much detail as you can. Ready? Okay. Where are you?"

"At a party."

"Okay," David pauses before prompting, "Can you picture the room?" He readies his pencil and paper. Waiting.

"Yeah." Andy's eyes are still beneath his closed lids, relaxed, but the second monitor's digital line is jerking its way across the screen in tall spikes.

"And?" David encourages through slightly clenched teeth. "Can you describe it?"

"Sure," Andy's eyelids crinkle slightly. "It's, uh, a living room. In a house. Couches and chairs and stuff. Music."

"Right," David sighs. "And who's there?"

"Oh, lots of people. Jeff. Others." Andy rattles off a few names quickly, ready for the next question.

"Wait," David glances over his hasty notes. "You didn't include Mark."

"I know," Andy peeks from one eye, then settles back into the chair. "He wasn't there yet. Obviously."

"Obviously--" David presses his lips together. Counts to five. "Okay, so you're standing at the party? With Jeff?"

"Yeah," Andy's jaw tightens. "He's there. Right next to me."

David peers over his notepad, studying the tension that's come over Andy. It's the first sign of emotion that has passed over Andy's face tonight and David locks in on it, trying to lead them into a deeper memory. Trying to get Andy to paint a fuller picture of the moment.

"You seem angry about that?" David prods carefully. "Angry with Jeff?"

"Yeah, or maybe not," Andy shakes his head, frowning. Then his eyes open and he sits up. "Look, doc, this isn't working for me."

David frowns, but has to admit that it doesn't feel like they are making progress. The failure hangs between them, feeding David's frustration as he taps out the command to stop the program and sees that the file it created is empty. He doesn't know what Andy is seeing behind his closed eyes. He doesn't know what Andy is feeling or whether there is any depth to this memory at all. Maybe Andy isn't in a deep enough state of reverie.

Maybe there simply isn't enough input for the program to capture.

"It's weird, okay?" Andy speaks so suddenly, so gruffly, that David looks up in surprise. "It's weird to have you asking me how I feel and shit. It's just fucking weird for me."

"Oh," David's eyes widen. "Yeah, I guess it's-- I mean, this is personal, and--"

Andy gets to his feet, heading out of the room and toward the basement stairs.

"You want a beer, doc?"

"Oh, uh," David sets his pencil and pad on his chair and follows Andy up to the kitchen where the side window shows a dim light on in Andy and Eleanor's house across the driveway. He pictures Joanne and the girls over there, curled in front of a movie with Eleanor while Nolan sleeps upstairs.

Andy sets the beer on the table, a six-pack that he'd stashed in Joanne's refrigerator before they began, and they each pick up a bottle. They take a few long, silent swallows before Andy drops into a seat at the table and David joins him. His thoughts turn to Jeff and how many times he may have sat here, with Andy, drinking and making plans. Talking about memories and the future. Or maybe talking sports, or parenting, or some other shared interest.

"I was mad at Jo, not Jeff."

It takes a moment for David to put Andy's words into context.

"That night? At the party?"

"Yeah," Andy agrees before quickly clarifying, "I mean, yeah maybe that night, but not really. I meant after that."

"After Mark died?"

"Yeah," Andy confirms. "I just-- Fuck, it's not like Mark needed an excuse to be drinking. But to be that shitfaced out alone was... Okay, maybe not that unusual. But still. They'd had this fight and, fuck, I don't know. He was really pissed, you know? Not thinking right. The way he'd get about her."

"So, if he hadn't fought with Joanne that night...?" David's thumb begins peeling at the edge of the beer label as he remembers the look on Joanne's face while talking about Mark. The regret. The guilt.

"Yeah." Andy pulls out a pack of cigarettes, looks toward the door, then shoves the pack back in his pocket. "Or, well, I don't know. I thought that back then. For a while."

"But now?"

"But now, I don't know. Maybe I was kinda pissed at myself," Andy squinches up his eyes and lips, looks to the ceiling, then shakes his head. "Man, I knew he was fucked up that night, but I stayed at that fucking party. Chasing this chick that wasn't gonna give it up anyway. It was fucking stupid."

David takes another long pull, giving Andy time to keep talking.

"I just didn't think he'd-- I mean, I know he didn't-- on purpose. No matter what anyone else thinks. I knew better. I knew him better." He looks up menacingly and David shrugs with a slow shake of his head.

"Hey, I'm not saying otherwise. I wasn't there."

"Yeah, okay," Andy pulls out the pack of cigarettes again, twirling them on the table. "But still it was icy and he was fucked up and-- Shit. I just shouldn't've let him leave that party alone. You know? I replay that moment over and over, but every time I know I just watched him walk away."

"You couldn't have known what would--" David stops, realizing what Andy just said. Replaying that moment. But what about the others? The moments leading up to it?

"So, that night," David turns the bottle between his hands, mentally noting the details of the story. He wants to get his notepad from downstairs, but is afraid to break Andy's reflective mood. "Mark and Joanne were at that party with you? Before their fight?"

"No, they were out. Somewhere. Jeff and I were at the party."

"And Eleanor?"

"Nah, El and I weren't together then. She was-- I don't know." He takes a swig of beer. "Oh, yeah, she was babysitting somewhere, 'cuz that's where Jo went. After the fight. I mean, I didn't know it then, but later. That night I just knew Mark was looking for her. That's why he came to the party. Something happened and she took off. And he was, well, pretty well on his way to being fucked up already and saying that he had to find her and shit.

"So, Jeff and I talked him down and said he should give it a night, you know? Let them both cool off. And he said, yeah, and he stayed a minute, but then he said he couldn't be there. With people, you know? But I was checking out that chick, and, fuck, I should've gone with him. But I just let him go.

"And you know what I did?" Andy's eyes film over as he goes on without waiting for an answer. "I looked Mark in the eye, right in the fucking eye, and said, '*Fuck it, you're better off without the bitch.*' And he gave me this look. Like I just didn't get it. And I guess I fucking didn't, right? And that was it. Last time I fucking saw him."

There is nothing then but the sound of drinking. Of David thoughtfully rocking his nearly full bottle on the table and Andy opening his second. Andy's hand is shaking when he picks up the pack of cigarettes and says he needs a smoke. David nearly lets him go, but calls out when he reaches the door.

"Hey, Andy," he takes a chance. "I think we're onto something with this one. Keep remembering the details, really picture them in your mind, all of them, and I'll figure out what's wrong on my end. We will get this."

Andy stares at David for a moment, then nods, looking into the dark yard.

"Yeah," his lips press together against a rising pain. "Okay."

CHAPTER TWENTY-THREE

Ruthie's pepperoni slices circle the pizza in an evenly spaced spiral, while Sarah's chopped peppers and olives scatter the surface in random clumps that dribble over the edge of the crust. They haven't made pizza, or helped Joanne with dinner, in months and they struggle to hold on to their recent reserve between glimpses of genuine smiles and the beginnings of laughter. They glance at each other periodically, doing their best to behave, as if sure that the wrong step will bring the evening of normalcy to an end.

They may be right to be wary, Joanne realizes while watching them over the rim of her wine glass. She hasn't sipped at wine while making dinner, or listened to music, or invited the girls to help, since before Jeff's accident. Doing all three now feels like an act. Like a game that could be called for rain at any moment. Especially with David in the basement, working alone in Jeff's private room.

"Are we going to the zoo this year?" Sarah asks while

brushing the last of the damp olive slices off of her fingertips. "Or the aquarium?"

Ruthie shoots a warning look, which Sarah ignores, and Joanne recognizes the importance of the question.

"Which do you want?" She reaches across the table to take a piece of bell pepper and makes a point to smile at them both. The family trip to either the zoo or aquarium is an annual tradition on the first weekend of summer, and Joanne doesn't want the girls to lose that. Not this year.

"Will it just be us?" Sarah asks in return. This time Ruthie doesn't try to censor her. They both look at Joanne with wide, wary eyes that make her frown. She knows who they are asking about.

"Yes, just us," She tells them, then clarifies. "Well, us, Aunt El and Nolan." That is part of the tradition, too. Both families going together to visit the animals and share a picnic lunch.

"And Uncle Andy?"

Joanne runs her index finger along the rim of her wine glass.

"Maybe," she answers slowly, drawing out the word. "If he isn't working."

She's been wondering whether Andy will come with them, now that Jeff won't be along, but she hasn't brought up the subject with him. Or with Eleanor.

"Did you always do things with Aunt El?" Ruthie asks before slapping Sarah's hand away from her neat circles of pepperoni. "I mean, before we were born." Joanne pushes the bag of extra pepperoni slices toward them both and stands up to set the pizza aside until the oven has finished heating.

"Pretty much," she tells them.

"Because she's your best friend forever?"

"Yes," Joanne has answered this question before. "More than that."

"Like your sister?"

Joanne is behind the girls now, taking out the makings for a salad, but she can hear the smirk in Sarah's question. It's a sign of the superiority they sometimes show toward Joanne's only-child status. A state that they cannot imagine.

"Yes," she replies simply and sets a large wooden bowl of clean spinach, mixed greens, and shredded carrots between the girls. She hands Sarah a box of croutons and Ruthie a bag of shredded cheese, before going back to the refrigerator for cherry tomatoes and a bottle of salad dressing. But when she opens the door, Joanne registers the near empty shelves. She had forgotten to buy salad dressing. And cherry tomatoes. And any food other than what she's already used for the pizza and salad. What she did buy had been dropped into her cart quickly, in a burst of confidence that had threatened to leave with each moment she spent in the brightly-lit grocery store. Before today's rushed trip, whatever food has been in the house over the last two months was brought in by Eleanor. Or by the neighbors who brought countless casseroles. Casseroles that Joanne had thrown away late one sleepless night.

"What makes someone a best friend forever?"

Joanne hears speaking—*Sarah? Ruthie?*—but not the words. She is staring at the almost empty shelves inside the refrigerator door. Shelves which were also ruthlessly cleaned out on one of those sleepless nights. Those shelves had never been empty before. They had been full, overflowing, with everyday staples. Butter, ketchup, relish, mustard. Garlic-stuffed olives, roasted red peppers, and salad dressing, along with one ancient jar of capers.

They had bought the capers after watching a cooking show late one night, Joanne remembers. She and Jeff. They'd driven to a gourmet store across town and paid a small fortune for them, only to later realize that their usual grocery store actually sold them for half the price. They'd used them exactly once, in a poached fish recipe that was a culinary failure, yet the capers had remained. For years. Floating in a suspiciously brownish-green fluid. While the capers were never opened again, Jeff and Joanne often joked that the jar added a touch of class to their refrigerator. Or they did. Until the capers were pitched angrily into a trash bag with every other nearly empty or rarely used bottle, jar, or tin.

"Mom?"

Hearing the voice, Joanne pulls away from the refrigerator and shuts the door. She stands for a moment, hands clutching the handle, eyes closed, and breathes. Salad dressing. She looks at the counter, sees a bottle of olive oil sitting next to the stove, and remembers that there may be a bottle of vinegar in the cupboard.

"Mom? What makes someone a best friend forever?"

This time the words sink in and Joanne lets go of the refrigerator door. She lifts her feet, one after the other, making her way toward the olive oil and trying to remember where she stashed the small glass cruet her grandmother had always used for salad dressing.

"Well," she pauses the search to take a sip of wine and consider the question. "We grew up together. We spent a lot of time together. Still do. We've been through a lot together."

"Like growing up stuff?"

Images of a dark night come into Joanne's mind. A cold bridge, a warm couch. Eleanor's fingers gripping her own. Eleanor's eyes reflecting her pain. She shakes them away, searching for other memories. She conjures school days and sleepovers, first dates, weddings, and pregnancies. But still feels the chill of snowy metal seeping through her body.

"Yes, lots of growing up stuff." She fishes the cruet out of a deep cabinet and begins washing it in the sink. "And other stuff, too."

"Like bad stuff?"

The soapy glass slips in her hands, but Joanne manages to keep the cruet from falling. She rinses it quickly, sets it on the drainboard and turns to face Sarah head on. Their eyes meet and Joanne sees her own mother's features staring her down. She blinks and draws in a slow, shaky breath.

"Yes."

"Like people dying?" Ruthie claps a hand over her mouth, then corrects herself quickly. "I mean your-- When you were little. Your…" She trails off and tears spring to the corners of her eyes.

Joanne abandons the salad dressing and takes a seat across from her daughters.

"Yes. Like my parents dying."

Both girls watch her, wide-eyed, waiting for the story to begin.

"I was thirteen when my parents died and I felt very

alone, even though I had Great-Gram to take me in. I didn't have a sister or brother to talk to or just be with, and I was very sad. But Aunt El was there and it helped me feel… connected. Like I wasn't so alone."

The girls don't look at each other, but they shift closer in their seats. So close that their arms are nearly touching. They know all of this. They've been told about their never-met grandparents. They've seen pictures of them and heard stories, but they haven't been able to fully imagine them as real people, any more than they could truly picture their mother or Aunt El as little girls.

"And then Great-Gram died, too."

"Yes, but not for a long time. First Great-Gram got to raise me. And Aunt El, too. In a way. We were both very close to Great-Gram and loved her very much. Which also made El more like a sister, I guess."

"Didn't she have her own grandma?" When Sarah speaks, Joanne notices a pilfered crouton hidden in her cheek, but she doesn't mention it.

"Not that she knew. Aunt El's grandparents died when she was little."

"Like ours," Ruthie nods, as if their grandparents and Joanne's parents weren't one and the same. In the quiet of the kitchen, Joanne can see them both tallying up the death around them. She wants to list the people who are still alive: Eleanor's parents, Andy's parents, so many other parents. But she doesn't. What does it matter how many other parents live to see their children grow into adults when they've already felt their own loss? Death doesn't take turns. Death doesn't pass by a family because they've already lost enough.

"We don't remember Great-Gram," Sarah confides, breaking the silence. "Not really."

Joanne looks from Sarah to Ruthie.

"You remember her sugar cookies though and her bedtime stories." She thinks of the other things the girls talk about sometimes. The memories they've surprised her with, despite being so young when her grandmother died.

"Not really," Ruthie confirms. "But it feels real. From the stories."

Joanne nods, swallowing a lump in her throat.

"Same with Nana," Sarah agrees, adding Jeff's mother to the list of their dead.

"Well, you were younger then," Joanne answers weakly, not knowing what else to say.

"We're not so old now," Ruthie tells her and Joanne knows where her mind is going. She glances to Sarah and sees the same fear looming behind her eyes. A fear she promptly puts into words.

"We'll forget Daddy, too."

Joanne's mouth opens, but no sounds come out. She can smell the heat of the oven. Past drips burn to ash as the fresh pizza waits on the counter for the temperature to be right. She hears a door close in the basement. David using the bathroom or going back into Jeff's room. She forces herself to think back. To remember being eight. To picture earlier family memories. Before moving here. Before knowing Eleanor.

There's a blur of images. Fuzzy, snapshot memories of a house with wood paneling, a bedroom with soft blue carpet. There's another friend, a little girl from her old home town. Natalie Brown. Red hair and freckles. Dolls and jacks and sidewalk chalk. Her parents from that time are hazier though. They're more sensation than clear image. The feel of their arms around her, the warmth in their voices. Fragments that could easily be recreations from her own imagination.

"No, you won't forget Daddy," Joanne says at last, nodding with a determined frown. "You're older now and you'll remember him. I'll help you remember him."

The girls squint at her, twin faces of skepticism.

"How?"

CHAPTER TWENTY-FOUR

David hears footsteps on the stairs before Joanne appears in the doorway. He glances her way, offering a quick hello, before jotting down one more idea. The main computer is on, but the other machines are silent. One of Jeff's notebooks lays open on the table as David makes his own notes on a yellow legal pad. When he looks up, he notices that Joanne is cradling a large book in both arms.

"Making progress?" Her words are light, but strained.

"Some," David's eyes flick toward the dark machines and Joanne sees a slight frown play over his features. "Slowly."

Joanne lingers in the doorway, even after David moves a few books from the other empty chair, making room for her. She's come down here for a reason, he assumes, but when she doesn't speak he starts to wonder. Maybe she just wanted a moment away from the girls. A moment with another adult. It feels odd to think she might see him that way. As someone to talk to. As someone to spend time with.

"Today was the girls' last day of school," Joanne volunteers the information from the doorway, leaning now against the frame. David nods, trying to think of what that may mean.

"That's, uh, nice," he smiles uncertainly, clarifying, "for them. Kids love summer vacation, right?"

"Yeah," Joanne responds with the same hesitant smile, holding back. "Summer is big to kids."

She rocks slightly on her heels, her arms tightening around the book, and David bites his lower lip. He looks toward the clock. He'd left the lab early today and come straight here to try another idea. An idea that didn't work. He rubs the bridge of his nose, glad for the distraction of Joanne's visit.

"They finished second grade?"

"Third," Joanne corrects. "They'll be in fourth next year."

"Fourth grade," David repeats inanely, then breaks into a genuine smile with the hint of a laugh. "I remember fourth grade."

"Do you?" Joanne's smile widens and David chuckles, shaking his head from side to side.

"Sure. Fourth grade. Miss Custer. Long dark hair, single, younger by at least 15 years than any teacher I'd had before. Also, the year I went to State with my science fair project."

"Impressive." Joanne feels her back begin to relax against the door frame.

"Yes. Body Language: The Natural Lie Detector."

"You made a lie detector? In fourth grade?"

"Not exactly. I tracked body language in people telling

lies and explained which parts of the brain are involved when lying. Or, rather, which parts were thought to be involved back then. I worked on a similar project, in college, that tracked activity with fMRI studies, and that study disproved my own award-winning earlier research. But fourth-grade me didn't know any of that yet and was pretty impressed with himself."

They smile together, Joanne picturing a young David brandishing a blue ribbon.

"So then, you've always been interested in how the brain works?"

"Huh," David considers. "You know, that science project may have been the start of it."

"So, fourth grade really was a big year for you."

Joanne's voice is soft and David feels warmed by it. Warmed by the idea of realizing something about himself and by the simple joy of sharing it with Joanne. When he doesn't know what else to say, Joanne jumps in, changing the subject.

"We're making pizza," she tells him. "And you're welcome to come have some with us. If you want to take a break?"

"Oh," David fumbles with his pencil, but he manages to hold her gaze. He's never eaten a meal with them or spent any real time with the girls.

"Not that you have to. If you're busy--"

"Oh, no," David rushes to interrupt. "I would actually love a break. I'm not getting anywhere at the moment anyway."

"About that," Joanne looks down at the book in her arms. She seems to be making a decision and David waits, giving her space. He feels a tinge of disappointment in knowing that she did come down here for another reason, for something more than inviting him to dinner.

After a long pause, Joanne steps forward, holding the book out toward David. "I found something that might help."

It's a large coffee table book. A collection of art by Salvador Dali. There's a familiar picture of bright shapes and melting clocks on the cover. David looks up at Joanne quizzically.

"It's not the book," she tells him. "It's what's in the book."

With care, she opens the cover and pulls a folded set of notebook paper from between the front pages. David recognizes the handwriting, even from this distance. His heart begins to race, but he does not reach for the paper.

Joanne's hand trembles. David's mind turns over the possibilities. When did she find the papers? How long has she been holding them back? What made her bring them to him today?

"Jo--" he trips on her name, almost shortening it, but quickly tacking on the second syllable. "--anne. Uh, let's just-- Why don't you sit down?"

Joanne perches on the edge of the empty chair, the book and papers resting uncertainly in her lap.

"Before we add anything new," he glances at the papers. "How are you doing now? With moving forward?"

Joanne sighs, her eyes stay downcast.

"The girls don't," she stops, reforming the words in her mind. "The girls aren't going to remember Jeff. Not for long. Not when they're this young."

A weight settles in David's chest. It's the same feeling he's gotten when working with Alzheimer's patients. With their spouses or adult children. It's the heaviness of a truth that he can't change or wipe away with a few kind words.

"Maybe not fully," he answers slowly, debating whether to add that they will keep some memories. That they will have stories and pictures. That they will have Joanne to help keep Jeff alive in their memories. But he knows that isn't what she's after.

"I can help them," Joanne looks up, leans forward, nearly reaches out for his hands. "We can help them remember."

David leans back with a long exhale and runs a hand over his nose and mouth. He's already begun shaking his head. Rejecting the idea.

"Jo," he forgets the formality, thinking only of her proposition. "They're just too young to go through this experience. I don't know how that might--"

"No," Joanne stops him, fingertips resting lightly on his knee. "Not them. I meant-- I mean that we could record my memories. Of Jeff. To keep for when they're older."

David looks into Joanne's eyes. He's drawn in by her sorrow, but also unsure, knowing how reluctant Joanne and Eleanor have been about recording their own memories.

"If you record your memories of Jeff," he begins slowly, testing the words as they come to him. "It won't be the same as them remembering him themselves. It might even distort, or replace, the memories that they do have of him."

"Maybe that's okay," Joanne's intensity causes her to

hunch forward, her fists pressed into her knees. "When Jeff remembered Isabella, the nurse, and I watched it... That memory is so real for me now, even though I know she wasn't even really there.

"And the birds. David," Joanne reaches out now, placing her hands over his. "You put birds in my head. Birds that didn't even exist. But now I can't remember that day without seeing them. They feel so, so real."

David presses his lips together, lets his thumbs and fingers lightly grip Joanne's trembling hands. "Jo," he doesn't like what he needs to say. "You and Eleanor were not happy about the birds. Or about Isabella. You hated the idea of someone changing your memories. Manipulating them."

Joanne pulls her hands away and sits up, looking sharply to the left. She knows he is right, but somehow it doesn't feel like the same situation.

"Well, I didn't. But--"

"But you're their mother?" Joanne looks back. "But you know better?"

Caught in their shared gaze, Joanne doesn't know how to respond. It *is* different, she wants to insist. It's a kindness. An act of love. It would be giving them memories that would make them happy. But the words won't leave her mouth.

A shrill buzzer sounds overhead.

They hear the basement door crack open and one of the girls calls down that the pizza is ready. Joanne calls back that she will be right up, and the buzzer stops ringing.

"I'm not saying no," David clarifies. "Just to think about it."

"I will," Joanne tries to smile, wiping her eyes even though they are dry. "It still needs to cool. The pizza. So, dinner in about 10 minutes?"

This time, David is the one to reach out. He tries to place a hand lightly over hers, but feels her press the folded papers into his palm. The moment his fingers curl around them, Joanne rises and hurries out the door.

The scribbled papers lay limp and unassuming in his grasp, but David already knows what they could mean. He's been noticing for some time that there seems to be a piece of the program missing. Something that Jeff may have held back or kept hidden whenever he was away from the system. These papers could be the answer. The key. The missing link.

Yet he hesitates. He needs to take a breath, steel his spine, before taking this next step. He needs to clear his mind of Joanne's worried eyes.

Unfolding the pages reveals a handwritten list of files found in a file system that has become quite familiar to David. Familiar, except for the addition of one directory David has never seen. A directory that may have been hidden. Or unmounted. Or deleted.

There are some short notes printed below the list that continue onto the second page. After scanning them rapidly, heart in his throat, David turns to the keyboard and starts typing.

Upstairs, Joanne mixes up the salad dressing while the girls set the table. She imagines David downstairs and wonders what Eleanor will say when she finds out that she has given him the pages. She watches the girls arrange silverware and tells herself that it doesn't really matter.

Whatever she owes Eleanor, she owes her daughters more.

Joanne is cutting the pizza when David opens the basement door. Her smile freezes when she sees the look on his face. His eyes are wide, his hair disheveled, his mouth twisted in an anxious frown. He scarcely looks toward the girls while stammering out an apology, saying that he won't be able to stay for dinner.

"Is everything all right?" Joanne can see the girls edging around the table toward the far side of the kitchen. She steps closer to David and lowers her voice. "Is this about--"

"No," David responds sharply, then makes an effort to soften his tone. "It's not about the, uh-- It's that I've been, um, called away. It's nothing serious, but something I need to take care of."

"At the lab?"

"No, a family thing. Just something I need to check into."

He looks around then, seeing the girls on the far side of the table, and gives them a smile that feels too bright, too big for the moment.

"Enjoy your pizza. Sorry I can't stay, but another time. Maybe. Okay?"

The girls nod in unison, wearing blank expressions, and David offers a hasty goodbye before seeing himself out the front door. The girls turn to Joanne and she forces a bright smile of her own, knowing that there is nothing else she can do.

CHAPTER TWENTY-FIVE

"She hasn't heard from him? At all?"

"Since you asked at the Monkey House?" Eleanor frowns at Andy. "No, she hasn't."

"It's been two days." Andy itches for a cigarette, but there's no smoking in this part of the zoo. Across the blacktop path, Joanne sits at a shady picnic table with the kids. Nolan is strapped in his stroller, waving a pinwheel in the wind, while Sarah and Ruthie unpack containers from the zippered cooler. Joanne faces Nolan, but her thoughts appear to be elsewhere.

"He said it was a family thing," Eleanor reminds. "Is he not allowed to have his own life?"

They are standing together in the long line at a frozen drink cart, sweating in the sun and being jostled by young kids who wriggle around their parents' legs. A woman in front of them grips the handles of a double stroller, pushing two toddlers, while quizzing her older son on the facts they've learned about different animals. She nods to his answers with a proud smile and speaks loud enough for those around them to easily overhear. Eleanor estimates that the boy is six or seven years old.

"I just want to get to it, you know?" They take two steps closer to the cart, as a family of four walks away with their brightly colored drinks.

"Mm, hmm." Eleanor lets her eyes drift over the other families. The normal families.

"He just stirred up all these memories and shit, about Mark. Going over the night he died." Eleanor turns toward Andy in surprise.

"What's to go over? You barely saw him that night, right?"

"Yeah. Well, Tyler thinks I need to remember some more. Try to get a clearer picture of it and shit."

"Excuse me," the woman ahead of them presses her lips into a tight smile. "Language?"

"Oh," Andy glances down at her son. "Sorry."

The line inches them closer to the cart as Eleanor looks across the pavement and grass toward their picnic table. The food is laid out, and Nolan is now kneeling on the bench beside Joanne. Sarah edges away from the table, pointing to their place in the line and carrying on an animated conversation with her mother.

"I don't see why you should fixate on that night." Eleanor crosses her arms over her chest and scowls at the lengthy order being given by the man at the front of the line. "There have been other important events in your life."

"Are you fucking jealous? Of Mark? Sorry," Andy shrugs when the woman turns around again. "Seriously?"

"I'm not jealous," Eleanor rolls her eyes toward the

sky, then turns to face Andy head on. "But there are other memories that I would *think* might be important to you. Things like, I don't know, maybe the birth of your own son."

"So now I'm a bad father? Again? Does every fucking thing have to-- Yeah, yeah, I'm sure he's heard worse, so just mind your own fucking business, okay?" The woman glares at him, then ushers her son up to the cart to place their order, leaving Andy to continue his rant. "I pay the damn bills, don't I? I put food on the table?"

"And that's all it takes to be a good father?"

Andy opens his arms, gesturing all around him. "I'm here aren't I?"

They stare at each other from behind their sunglasses. Andy's hands clench into fists at his side, while Eleanor's lips are pressed so tight that they have nearly disappeared.

"Aunt El," a thin voice calls out as Sarah and Ruthie appear at their side. "We're here to help carry."

The woman ahead of them pushes her stroller away then, shooting one last scowl in their direction. Andy takes her place at the cart.

"Hey, man. We'll take three cherry and two lemon, thanks." He whips out his wallet with a flourish, holding it in front of Eleanor as he pulls out the cash to pay for their drinks. Eleanor ignores him. When the drinks are ready, she hands one to each of the girls, then holds out a third. "Take this to your mom and tell her we'll be over in a minute, okay, love?"

She and Andy move away from the cart, each holding a slushy concoction, and watch the girls make their way across the grass toward the picnic table. Joanne looks back at them questioningly before gesturing for the kids to start eating.

"I make money, too," Eleanor responds gruffly, then bristles when Andy laughs.

"Yeah, your jewelry *business* really pays the bills."

"Damn it, Andy." Condensation from the plastic glass drips down the inside of Eleanor's hand. The sun is beating down, but she can't bring herself to cross over into the shade yet. Not with Andy by her side. "If you think so little of me, why don't you just fucking leave?"

"Why don't you?"

Andy sucks on his straw, drawing the red slush up to his lips. Eleanor sees the suggestion of a smirk and it makes her blood boil.

"Maybe I will," she threatens, though her voice is cool, calmer than the rage seething inside.

"Sure you will," Andy laughs. "But it would be a pretty stupid thing to do at the moment. Seeing as I'm about to be a pretty important person."

Eleanor stands in the heat of the sun, looking at Andy's full, scruffy face and growing beer belly. The sounds of kids are all around them. Some are laughing and playing, others are crying and being comforted by tired parents. Behind Andy, signs point back to different areas of the zoo. To the big cats, the monkeys, and the reptiles. Animals in cages. Eleanor looks up at Andy's grinning face and realizes that there's nothing left of the boy she once knew and loved.

"Here," Eleanor thrusts her lemon slush at him. "Go eat. I'm going to the bathroom."

The cement block building is about 20 yards down the

paved walkway, back toward the main zoo and away from the picnic area. Eleanor walks quickly. Hoping Andy doesn't follow. Hoping Joanne doesn't follow. There's a covered entrance on each side of the building, one for men and one for women. Instead of entering the bathroom, Eleanor walks straight through the covered passageway and onto a trail that leads toward the big cat enclosures. Crowds mill around one of the nearest fenced areas. They're looking down, some pointing, into a dusty pit.

"This seat's free," a voice calls from behind, and Eleanor turns to see a young woman smiling from a bench beneath a shade tree. "If you're looking for a place to sit."

The woman is around Eleanor's age. Blonde, tan, and very pregnant. There are bags from the zoo gift shop piled on the ground beside her, and Eleanor can see the yellow eyes of a stuffed tiger peeking out of the largest bag. She glances back toward the picnic area, now hidden from view by the cinderblock bathrooms, and takes a seat on the bench.

"Do they bother you, too?" The woman asks in a friendly voice, as if already in the middle of a conversation. Eleanor looks her way questioningly. "The animals," the woman clarifies. "In cages."

"Oh," Eleanor gazes across the walkway toward the people pointing cameras and jostling for better views. "I don't know."

"I'm not totally against zoos," the woman continues. "I have some friends who are really down on them. Want to free all the animals and turn the zoos into nature parks. I don't know about that. But, thing is, I haven't been to one since I was a kid, and it's not the same anymore. I look at the animals now and just feel sad."

Eleanor nearly asks why she's here, then thinks better of it. Instead she asks, "Are you here with your family?"

"My sister's family," the woman sighs, rubbing her hands over her distended belly. "My husband's out of town, so... here I am. They're over there somewhere, by the mountain lions. I said I needed a break, from the walking, but really, I just couldn't take staring down at more caged animals. Trapped in those fake pens. You know?"

But Eleanor doesn't know. It's the first time she's ever thought about how the animals are treated. She's never considered how they might feel about living in a zoo, secluded with their own kind, instead of hunting, or being hunted, on an open plain. She's about to say that maybe it's nice for them. They have their meals provided, they have vets to look after them, and they don't have to spend every moment focused on survival. But something stops her. It's the idea of them waking up to the same thing, day after day. Of filling their time without purpose, while others watch everything they do. She wonders if that's a luxury or a punishment.

"I don't mind my sister bringing her kids here," the woman keeps talking, unaware of Eleanor's thoughts. "And I'm not going to protest at the gates or anything. But I think this might be my last visit. Once this little one's born, I don't think I'll be bringing her here."

"It's a valid choice," Eleanor agrees half-heartedly, still stuck in her own thoughts.

"Yes," the woman frowns knowingly. "I've been thinking about that a lot lately, too. About the choices I'll make as a mom. It's such a big responsibility, you know? Making the right decisions. Setting the right example. Do you have kids?"

Eleanor nods, still watching the crowd and wondering which family belongs to this woman. "Nolan," she answers. "He's two."

"Oh, that's such a sweet age!" The woman smiles and clasps her hands in a way that no experienced mother would when describing a two-year-old.

"Sure," Eleanor smirks, knowing that sometimes it is. And sometimes it isn't.

"Do you just love being a mom?" There's a gleam in the woman's eyes. An excitement that Eleanor knows will be dampened within the first week of sleepless nights. But there's also a hint of doubt under her eager smile. A plea for reassurance.

"Yes," Eleanor answers honestly. "Nolan is my whole world."

But then her smile falters. She thinks of the machine in Joanne's basement and wonders what kind of world she is creating for her son.

CHAPTER TWENTY-SIX

Focused on his laptop, David doesn't notice as the apartment steadily dims around him. His search has turned up pages of superficial information, but none of the details he really wants to know. He could ask Joanne—perhaps should ask Joanne—but his desire to keep that promise has been overshadowed by his need to understand just what he has gotten himself into. Besides, he tells himself, it isn't worth upsetting Joanne, or Eleanor, if he doesn't have to.

Instead, David sits in the near dark, rubbing his neck with both hands and blinking against the glare of his screen. He needs to take a break. He needs to admit that he won't find these answers online. He knows that already, on some level, but his body hasn't caught up to that realization. His fingers grip the trackball and mindlessly scroll page after page. He's scoured social media, piecing together a web of relationships that mean nothing significant to his search. He has read through Mark's obituary a half-dozen times.

David is looking up the hours for the Parkview library, when he hears a knock at the door.

He freezes. Then waits to see if whoever it is will simply go away.

It must be Andy, he reasons. Or Joanne. They've both left messages over the last few days and he hasn't responded to either of them. He can't imagine Joanne leaving the girls to come see him. Or bringing them with her. He thinks Andy's knock would be louder. More insistent. More entitled to a response. There's a second knock, a little louder, and David wonders if it might be Eleanor. It seems more like her to track him down. To not be content with calling or leaving a message.

David knows he can ignore the knocking, pretend he isn't home, but his curiosity gets the better of him. He's in the hallway, halfway there, when a woman's voice calls his name. The sound stops him in his tracks. He looks down at his faded tee shirt and frayed cargo shorts. He feels the scruff on his cheeks and chin. There's a moment where he hesitates, despite knowing, without a doubt, that he will answer the door.

"Madeleine," he greets her from the jamb with the door cracked just wide enough to frame his body. The hall is brightly lit behind her, and she leans her head to the right, peering into the shadowy apartment within.

"Were you sleeping?" Her voice is kind, but curious. Probing. It makes David close the door a fraction of an inch more, hugging it tightly around him to block her view.

Madeleine is dressed in a silk, short-sleeved blouse and trim black slacks. There's a large black handbag slung over her shoulder and a thin silver necklace hanging around her neck. David realizes that there is something more polished about her appearance today. Something more put together. He fleetingly wonders if she dressed for him today. For this visit.

"Are you contagious?" She asks, when he continues to block the doorway. There's a coldness to her expression that makes it hard to read her intentions.

"Uh, no." The guilt of calling in sick washes over David, and he hopes that he does at least look sick. Mildly.

"Can I come in then?" Madeleine gestures impatiently, but David holds his ground. He looks down at her, imagining all the reasons why she might turn up on his doorstep. She inches a bit closer and looks up at him with the same inscrutable expression.

"Why are you here?" His voice is huskier than he intended.

Madeleine raises one eyebrow without smiling.

"You missed our meeting this afternoon."

Her sharp words hit David like a slap in the face. His mouth goes slack and he closes his eyes. The meeting. The meeting he and Madeleine had been planning for three weeks. The meeting where he was supposed to give a presentation of the progress they've made over the last six months.

Madeleine presses lightly on the door, and David yields, stepping back to let her walk past him into the dark living room. Recovering, he runs a hand over his scruffy face and flicks a switch at the left of the door. A halogen floor lamp flickers on from the corner, along with a second lamp on an end table beside the couch.

The room is sparsely decorated with a living room set,

a small dinette table, and a wall of packed bookshelves. A large picture window lets in the fading light and offers a view of the small shops across the street. The apartment is small and old, plain and utilitarian, but it offers plenty of space for one scientist living alone.

Madeleine glances toward his tiny kitchen, then down the hall that leads to David's bedroom and small office. She walks across the living room and lingers by the leather easy chair, as if deciding whether she wants to sit or stand.

"I'm sorry about the meeting," David apologizes. "Really."

"I handled it," Madeleine answers coolly, not entirely letting him off the hook.

"Well, how did--" David hasn't finished the question when Madeleine snaps an answer.

"It was fine." She looks at David then, sizing him up. "What's going on with you?"

"I, uh, I wasn't feeling well when I woke up and I completely forgot that today--"

"No." Madeleine crosses her arms, staring him down. "This isn't about today. There's been something going on with you for a while now. You've been distracted, and forgetful, and leaving work early. And, then, to top it off, some maintenance man comes around looking for you this afternoon."

"Maintenance?" David can feel the color draining from his face.

"Mm, hmm. Andy?" Madeleine cocks her head to the side and raises an eyebrow. "Jeff's friend, right?"

David curses silently, suspecting that Andy's appearance had been more of a warning than a genuine search.

"He's not a very good liar," Madeleine continues, when it becomes clear that David is not going to respond. "I've seen you talking with him before. Quietly. As if you don't want to be seen."

David runs his hands through his hair and turns to look out the window. The streetlights are on and most of the shops in the small plaza are closed, though light filters out from both the convenience store and the small bar on the corner. He turns back to Madeleine with a heavy sigh.

"What are you asking me?"

"Honestly, I'm not sure," Madeleine adjusts the strap of her handbag and glances back at the couch. David waits, neither inviting her to sit nor asking her to leave. Yet.

"When I first came in on this project," Madeleine speaks slowly, holding her ground. "I really admired you, David. Your dedication. Your ideas. And I thought it was, I don't know, nice when I saw you eating lunch with Jeff. Really down to earth, or something. And then I met him myself one night when I was working late. He came in to check the heater and we started chatting. He knew an awful lot about our research and had some very *interesting* ideas of his own.

"And that got me thinking about you. I started to wonder whether he'd been learning from you, or maybe…" she trails off meaningfully.

David wants to be offended. He wants to defend himself. But he's too tired and too distracted to care. A week ago, this would have been a crisis. Today, he just wants Madeleine, and the lab, and everything about his career to stop long enough for him to figure out what the hell he's doing.

As the moment stretches without a response, Madeleine begins shifting her weight from foot to foot, showing the first sign that she might not be as confident as she appears. David has the opposite reaction, beginning to feel emboldened by his own detachment.

"Is that it?" He asks coldly. "Did you say what you came here to say?"

"I--" Madeleine visibly pulls back, again reaching to adjust her handbag. Regrouping.

A part of David watches them both, berating himself for being cruel when he knows that she is actually right about him. Yet the larger part aches at the knowledge that she doesn't see him as someone who could challenge the established paradigm with his own creative brilliance. Despite his schooling, his years of diligent work, she would have an easier time believing his innovative ideas came from a college dropout maintenance man. And she's right.

David looks away with a pent-up exhale, losing the last of his patience. With her and with himself.

"Look, I'm sorry I missed today's meeting. I'm sorry you had to deal with the committee on your own. But I don't have to answer these questions. These *insinuations*." He walks back across the room, opening the door. "I think you should go."

For a moment, no one moves. Madeleine glances at her feet, then back at David's stony expression. She doesn't leave her place beside the chair.

"I haven't finished," she tells him simply.

"Really?" David sounds sarcastic now. "You have more to say than to accuse me of passing someone else's ideas off as my own?"

"David, I--" Madeleine's cool demeanor crumbles as she drops her hands to her sides. "I've said this all wrong. Can I start again?"

David stands by the open door. Waiting. He tries not to notice the way her silk blouse clings to her body or the way her breathing has become shorter and fuller.

"Look, we all get our inspiration from different places." Madeleine takes a step forward, a supplicating tone coming into her voice. "We have our muses, just like artists, and that doesn't mean the ideas that are sparked by them aren't actually our own. And maybe, working with Jeff, brought you outside of the box, outside of our project, where you were able to come up with something bigger."

"Madeleine," David wavers, letting his grip on the door relax, but still holding it open. Madeleine crosses the room, stopping within a few feet of him. Her eyes are bright and her face is more animated than he's ever seen.

"I think I know what's been going on."

"Do you?" The question catches in his tight throat.

"You're working on something on your own. In the off hours. Something that you came up with when talking to Jeff. But you haven't quite worked it out yet. And somehow Andy's found out, and he's using it against you now. Maybe he sees it as a chance to blackmail you? Threatening to tell Keller that you are using his resources on your own side project?"

David can only stare at her, struggling to calculate the angles of this new development.

"David," Madeleine lowers her voice, quieting it so much that David feels himself leaning in to hear her. She reaches a hand to rest on his arm. "Let me help you. Let me in on it, and we'll figure it out together."

David gazes down at her small, soft hand. He feels the burning in his eyes and a tremble in his stomach that reminds him he hasn't eaten since breakfast. But there's another sensation rising up from his chest as well. It's a feeling that swells and throbs, then erupts in a burst of laughter so strong that it steals his breath and stings his eyes.

Madeleine stares at him, pulling her hand away and tightening her grip on her precious handbag. But David merely struggles to stop laughing, to get control of himself.

"Oh, man," David shakes his head after several seconds, pressing one hand to his heart. "Your timing sucks."

The anger on Madeleine's face competes with her utter confusion. "What does that mean?"

David reaches for her shoulder, guiding her out into the empty hallway. The hollow laughter has gone away and left him with an aching head and heavy heart. More than anything else, he just wants her to leave.

"It means," he pauses, looking for an answer but finding nothing that makes reasonable sense. "It means that you should have talked to me three days ago. Or maybe you should talk to me three days from now. Or in a week. I don't know. But right now, it just means you need to go."

And he closes the door.

Back in his own cluttered office, alone, David snaps on a small desk light. He steps over to the wall where news articles and handwritten notes are taped up in a pattern that only he can explain. At the center is a square piece of paper with notes in his own handwriting. It reads, *"New memory, hidden directory: Jeff on the bridge at Landon's Hollow, Jeff pushes Mark off the bridge."*

CHAPTER TWENTY-SEVEN

Another night, another session in front of a glowing screen. This time at the local library where David sifts through microfilm images of past newspapers. He's had to wait three days for the library to fill his request. Three more days of not going to work, of not returning Andy and Joanne's calls.

Articles from the library's films span several days, but they don't answer David's most pressing questions. They report the facts. They say that a passing policeman stopped to investigate Mark's parked car. That he was looking for the car's owner when he came across empty beer bottles on the bridge and spotted Mark's body on the rocks and ice below. They talk about Mark's sister and his single mother, and they make a passing reference to a father who had "moved out of state" many years earlier. Later stories add that the case has been ruled an accidental death and that residents should note that the bridge at Landon's Hollow was not designed for pedestrians.

Mark's obituary is brief. It's the same write-up that David had found through the paper's online archive. It states the time and date of the funeral, lists the surviving family, and asks that donations be made to St. Peter Catholic Church in lieu of flowers.

However, a follow-up article about Mark's funeral goes on to report a large turnout. Quotes from classmates repeat the expected clichés about dying young. One comment, from an unnamed student, hints at Mark's reputation, "*I'm not like shocked, exactly, but I do feel bad for his family.*" There is also a quote from "best friend" Andy Wagner, both praising and defending his friend by saying, "*People didn't know Mark like I did, what a great guy he was, and now they won't. That chance was taken away.*"

David reads that line over and over, coming back to the words *taken away*. Did Andy think someone actually took Mark from him or was it a clumsy reference to fate? The police didn't seem to think anyone else had been involved, but there's little information about the investigation itself. There's nothing detailing the crime scene. There's no information about who the police talked to as part of their investigation. There's no mention of where any of Mark's friends were when he fell from the bridge.

Sitting back in his chair, David closes his eyes and pictures the fragmented memory he had found in the computer's hidden directory. A dark winter night. A tall, truss bridge up ahead. Its weathered, metal beams reflect the glare of headlights. The image doesn't last long, but there's enough time to see that the bridge appears empty. No parked car in sight. No sign of a dark figure between the shadows. And then an abrupt cut to the face of a tall teenage boy—a boy David now recognizes from the newspaper as being Mark Ferguson. There's an argument. Angry words that can't be heard and a surge of nauseous adrenaline that jabs into Jeff's gut. Yet the sensations are different than in the other memories. Less formed. They are more like fractured glimpses and disconnected emotions. Fear. Anger. Disgust. And then a shove, a feeling that stops at Jeff's trembling palms, followed by a moment of utter blackness. A blackness that gives way to one snapshot image of a body, stretched and broken, in a shallow gulch of icy rocks.

"Sir?" David jumps at the voice and his eyes snap open to see the librarian hesitating in the doorway of the small media room.

"Sorry," she smiles. "I just wanted to let you know that we're closing in about fifteen minutes."

"Oh," David glances back to the screen where Mark Ferguson's young face smiles back at them. "Thank you."

The woman nods, but she doesn't leave. Her eyes turn to the image of Mark and a sad frown comes over her face. "Did you know him?" She asks softly.

"No," David shakes his head. "I'm a, uh, sociologist studying the effects of tragedy on a community and someone mentioned this case to me. I was just looking into it to see if it might be relevant to my work."

It's the excuse David had prepared, but it sounds ridiculous when he hears the words coming out of his mouth. The librarian only nods, pursing her lips and cocking her head thoughtfully to one side.

"Did *you* know him?" He returns the question, in sudden revelation.

"Yeah," she hesitates. "I mean, small town, so everyone knew him. Or of him... after. But I knew him before, too." David is about to say something apologetic, but she keeps talking, her eyes glued to the face on the screen. "I was friends with his sister, Dee. Still am. It was hard on Dee, and their mom, especially with all the talk."

"Talk?"

She looks back at David, as if just remembering where she is.

"You're from the lab then? Out in Bristol?"

"Yes," David answers carefully, not wanting to mention the time he's been spending in Parkview. With Joanne. "David," he introduces automatically. "David Tyler."

"Linda," she shakes his outstretched hand awkwardly, then crosses her arms over her chest. "I guess you've never been out to the township then? Out to Landon's Hollow? Where the bridge is?"

"No," David lies. He'd driven out to the bridge two days ago, finding it after nearly an hour of wrong turns. He'd pulled into the makeshift clearing at the side of the road and walked the length of the bridge, feeling a déjà vu that he knew was based solely on Jeff's memory. He'd even stood between two trusses, holding on and looking gingerly over the edge at the gurgling ravine below.

"It's a local legend thing," Linda tells him with a shake of her head. "One of those spooky places kids go at night to drink and tell ghost stories. It made this harder, you know? All the kids spinning their own stories and the parents getting worked up over it. And then there were people who said--"

Linda abruptly stops talking and David leans in. "Said?"

"Oh, I don't know. People always talk after things like this."

David wants to know more, but Linda has waved the subject away and he senses that pushing won't get him anywhere. He says that he's finished with the films and she offers to pack them up for him, which gives him no reason to stay. At the door, he turns back and holds out a business card.

"If you ever want to talk," he offers awkwardly. "On the record. Or off. Either way, it might be useful. For my research."

Linda takes the card and tries to smile, but her furrowed brow ruins the effect. She reads the card while David lets his eyes trail back toward Mark's face on the screen. So young, he thinks while looking at the angular features and shaggy hair.

"Thanks," he tells Linda again, with a smile that tries to be sincere. "And I meant what I said. Call my cell phone, any time. It helps to talk, and it might help me out, too."

"With your *sociology* project?" Linda looks up from the card with an expression that raises the hackles on David's neck. He agrees mildly, thanks her again and leaves the small room. As he walks through the library, David wonders what she isn't telling him.

There's only one way he can think to find out.

CHAPTER TWENTY-EIGHT

"Was starting to think you were skipping out on us, doc." Andy lies back in the leather chair, electrodes stuck to his temples, and looks down appreciatively at the joint pinched between his fingers. "Didn't know you'd actually come to your fucking senses."

"Yes, well," David holds out a ceramic plate, glad that Joanne and the girls are out of the house.

Andy takes one more quick puff before surrendering it, then settles back with a contented smile. Smoke wafts through the small basement room. The drug goes against David's better judgment, but he sets his discomfort aside as he sets the thick yellow plate out of sight. It may be the easiest way to get Andy into a relaxed state, he tells himself. Besides, he needs answers and he'd rather Andy not be entirely alert when he gets them.

"Eyes closed," David prompts briskly while checking the settings on the computer one last time. He's followed the directions on Jeff's hidden notes and loaded the missing portion of the recording program, without revealing the memory file that was hidden along with it. He takes a seat in the rolling desk chair beside Andy and pulls out the notes he's compiled about the night of Mark's death.

"Begin to deepen your breath," he intones smoothly. "Long, slow inhale. Long, slow exhale. Good.

"Keep that breath as you think of the number 30. Begin counting back with each breath. Inhale, 29, exhale 29. Inhale, 28, exhale, 28."

In just a few minutes, Andy is breathing deeply and evenly, but the lines on the smaller monitor show that he is still awake. His mind is settled. Suggestible. David looks at his notes again and begins guiding Andy toward the memory.

"It is December 7, 2001. It's a Friday night and you are at a party with Jeff Simon. The party is crowded with high school friends. Music is playing. It's around 10 o'clock." David pauses his slow speech, giving Andy time to conjure the memory himself. "You're with Jeff now?"

"Mmm hmm," Andy murmurs assent, his eyes closed.

"Who else do you see?"

"Bunch a people. Mike, Greg, Jessica, Nicky. Megan Davies, and, damn, is she looking fine tonight." David makes notes in the margin of his legal pad. "That blonde hair, those lickable tits--"

"And is Mark there?" David pulls Andy back on course, pen poised and eyes narrowed.

"Nah," Andy's eyes shift rapidly from side to side, under his closed lids. His forehead creases. His face turns toward the left and then relaxes into a smile. "There he is. Coming through the crowd."

"How does he seem?"

Andy's brow wrinkles again.

"He looks pissed. Yeah," he draws the word out, with a slight shake of his head. "I know that look. Fucking Joanne. It's always fucking Joanne."

"Okay," David worries that Andy is pulling out of the memory, explaining too much instead of just observing. "But Mark is standing with you now. With you and Jeff. He's talking to you. Telling you something. Listen to him."

There's silence as David watches Andy's flickering expressions. His body tenses, yearning to know what Andy is seeing and hearing, but he needs Andy to focus more on experiencing it for himself than narrating it aloud. David watches the lines zig-zagging their way across the smaller monitor, then turns to see that the computer screen is now filling with a steady stream of hash marks. Jeff's method for showing that the program is actually recording data.

"You're still with Jeff and Mark?" David tries for a soothing tone, but a look of annoyance crosses over Andy's face.

"Damn it, Mark," he mutters under his breath and David sees the lines begin to spike across the small screen. Andy's breathing is speeding up and David eyes the jagged line anxiously. He leans closer, coaxing Andy through the emotional moment.

"It's already happened," David murmurs with one eye on the monitor. "Nothing you say or do can hurt him now. You're just watching. Just watching."

Andy's face tenses. His fists clench. David realizes that Andy may pull out of the memory to avoid this critical moment, the moment he thinks he let Mark down. And, if he does, that would stop the memory before he has a chance to see if Jeff left the party that night. In desperation, David leans in even closer, his lips almost grazing Andy's ear, and whispers, "It's okay. He's better off without her. You're his friend, tell him. Tell him and it will be okay. You're doing him a favor." David swallows hard, feeling a nauseous tremble as he adds, "He's better off without the bitch."

A long, low sigh escapes from Andy's lips and the lines on the monitor begin to smooth out.

"That's it," David croons, his neck muscles straining to stay stable as he slowly inches away. "You're a good friend. A good friend."

Andy's breathing steadies, his face relaxes. They sit together for another minute, in the damp chill of the basement, until David is sure that Andy is okay. That he will stay in the memory.

"Is Mark still there?" David asks cautiously, just above a whisper.

"Nah, he had to jet. But Megan," her name brings a leering smile, "Mmm, Megan is all alone and giving me the come-and-get-it."

"Mark went... where?" David bites his lip, glances back at the monitor.

"I dunno, man. I'm heading over. Eye contact all the way."

"Right, but..." David taps the pen point on his pad, weighing his options. "Is Jeff still with you?"

"Hey, there," Andy's voice is smooth and suggestive, deep in the thought of Megan Davies. David thinks through what he knows of the story. If Andy is talking to

Megan, where is Jeff? Is this when he slipped out of the party? He wonders if Andy actually saw Jeff leave, but never realized the connection. He wonders if looking around now would bring back a subconscious memory.

"Andy," David's whisper is barely audible. He feels sweat trickle down the side of his ribcage. "Megan isn't going anywhere. Who else do you see? Who else is in the room?" Andy frowns, lifting one hand slightly as if waving off a fly. David glances as the monitor, seeing that Andy is close to coming out of his relaxed state, but still in the recording zone.

"Just a quick look," David raises his voice, insisting. "Check the room. Who's there? Do you see Jeff?"

Andy shakes his head in small short jerks, but David can't tell if he's answering the question or trying to shut him out. Andy's eyes and mouth pinch tighter, as if struggling against something. Or maybe struggling to keep his focus. David is about to tell him to breathe. He's about to coach him back into a deeper state of relaxation, when Andy's eyes suddenly pop open. He blinks against the basement light, looks around the room and settles his gaze on David's pale face.

"Damn, doc," he says, before lifting his arms to stretch overhead. "That was intense."

"Uh," David fights to recover, jerking back and spinning to stop the recording. His heart hammers as he reviews the program's log file.

"Did it work?" Andy's voice is hopeful and David tamps down his own anxiety.

"I don't know yet," he answers honestly, but viewing the structure of the memory with the new tools he's discovered shows that something was recorded. He studies the screen for a few minutes, while Andy settles back into the chair behind him.

"Hey, doc?" Andy sounds hesitant now. "That was really fucking weird."

"How so?" David keeps scrolling through the data, though he's no longer reading it.

"Well, I remember what I was thinking... or remembering, or whatever... but I also remember just laying here, with you talking at me. A lot like watching Jeff's memories with you asking questions. You know? Really clear, like a video. That mean it worked?"

"It might," David's chest spasms and his mouth goes dry. He looks back at another sheet of notebook paper and types in a short series of commands.

"So? When do we watch it?"

"We can't," David answers matter-of-factly as he finishes typing. "Not yet."

Calmly spinning his chair to face Andy, David nods and brushes away his confusion.

"We captured a lot of raw data," he explains. "But now the program has to process all that information into a format that will work as a playable memory."

"How long does that take?"

"I don't know," David shrugs, fighting the quavering in his gut while making every effort to appear calm and in control. "But this is the first time we actually captured data that looks like it *can* be processed. Which makes this is a really big step forward."

"Hmm," Andy nods, but doesn't look happy.

"I thought you'd be excited to hear that."

"Yeah, I am, but…" Andy trails off. "There's something bugging me. Something I can't quite put my finger on, and--"

He stops, looks up sharply at David.

"I was in the memory, with Megan, and you kept pulling me away." David opens his mouth to respond, but Andy barrels ahead. "You were asking me to look around the room. You wanted me to look for Jeff. What was that about?"

"Oh, well," David turns to the monitor, but only a cursor blinks back at him. "You were getting pretty, uh, focused, and I thought it might help to ask about the background. To draw a more complete picture from your memory."

It isn't a lie, but everything about David's movement screams evasion. Andy watches him for a beat then lets it go.

"Yeah," he says with a slight frown. "Good thinking."

David hears Andy get to his feet and senses him walking over to the yellow plate. Andy lifts the remaining joint, sniffs it, then tucks it into his front pocket.

"How long do you think it will take?"

David is already shaking his head. "I really don't know. But I think we're looking at several hours. Maybe overnight. If it finishes at all."

"Why wouldn't it?"

David takes his hands off the keyboard and presses gently away from the table. The chair's casters roll and skid on the uneven cement floor.

"Any number of things could go wrong." David stands up, patting his pocket for his keys. "There's no point in sitting around here while it runs."

"But you'll come back tonight?" Andy narrows his eyes.

"Well," David hedges. The base of his neck has begun to throb and he can feel the acid churning in his stomach. "Maybe tomorrow would be better."

"Yeah, okay," Andy agrees after a long, weighty pause. The moment stretches between them until Andy sighs and heads toward the door, ready to go back upstairs.

"But it seemed clear?" David can't resist asking when Andy's back is turned. "You saw the party? And Jeff, and everything?"

Andy hesitates before looking back.

"Yeah," he answers with a wary expression. "It was just like I said. Mark left, angry. Me and Jeff stayed at the party."

David lets out a slow breath and nods, "Good." A smile starts to spread across his face. "That's a good sign. That it worked, I mean."

"Yeah," Andy agrees, but his smile is unsure.

CHAPTER TWENTY-NINE

The playground is quiet for a Saturday afternoon. A few kids hang from the jungle gym, two more sit on the covered platform above the highest slide. The air feels heavy. Sarah and Ruthie push Nolan in one of the baby swings. They stand close together, talking and taking turns as they half-heartedly reach out to keep him in motion. The way adults would. Joanne observes them from her place on the bench, but doesn't comment on it. She simply frowns, half-listening to Eleanor.

"How do you think it's going back there?"

Joanne doesn't want to speculate. There are birds overhead, cardinals perched in the tree branches. There is a light breeze and small clouds drift lazily across the sun. As she watches the birds take flight, Joanne notices that the leaves on the maple trees have turned upside down, waiting for rain.

"He seemed more confident today," Eleanor persists. Joanne tries not to listen, but she cannot ignore Eleanor's nervous energy. It's like sitting next to a kitchen timer that's about to go off. Eleanor shifts in her seat, one hand reaching up to pull nervously at her lower lip. "Do you think it will work this time?"

"Does it matter?" There's no emotion in Joanne's voice. There's no emotion in her body.

Eleanor opens her mouth, shuts it, opens it again, and then sighs.

"Doesn't it?" She asks at last.

Joanne shrugs.

"How can you be so calm?" Eleanor drops her hand, beginning to bite at her lower lip instead.

"It's not like it's you or me in the chair," Joanne turns to look at Eleanor for just a moment before swiveling her gaze back toward the kids. "It's not like Andy's hiding anything."

"I guess," Eleanor shakes her head. "Unless he remembers something. Something that makes him suspicious."

Joanne shrugs again, scanning the rest of the playground.

"He hasn't yet," she answers, but she isn't paying much attention to Eleanor. She's picturing a rainy night with Jeff. Lying in bed with him propped on one elbow, looking down at her. Flashing lightning and rumbling thunder punctuating his words. She remembers the look on Jeff's face as he offered up his version of what happened out on the bridge. A story that he had never told anyone else and one that Joanne had never repeated. Except to Eleanor.

"If he even suspected--" Eleanor stops talking. There's

no need to finish the thought. They both know that Andy would never keep something like that to himself. If he knew, they would know about it.

"So, there's nothing to worry about," Joanne crosses her arms over her chest and Eleanor agrees uneasily. They watch the girls lift Nolan out of the swing and follow him over to the smallest slide.

"If it does work," Joanne begins slowly, but the rest of the thought sticks in her throat.

"Jo--" There's concern in Eleanor's voice. Concern that Joanne hears as a warning.

"I don't remember my parents very well," Joanne lowers her voice, as if afraid someone will overhear. "It's just impressions now and even those are fading."

"That's--" Eleanor stops and sighs. "Jo, it will be different with Jeff. You're older and--"

"And the girls are younger," Joanne interrupts, her arms clenching tighter across her chest.

They sit with the idea for several minutes. Sarah and Ruthie are talking to another girl and boy who are about their age, while Nolan squats beside them to dig in the wood chips under their feet. They look so young in their jean shorts and tee shirts. Thin shoulders, small backs, but sturdy legs that let them stand their ground.

"Maybe that's okay," Eleanor says thoughtfully, keeping her eyes glued on the kids as well. "Maybe the memories have to fade as part of the healing. If the past didn't fade, how would we ever face today? Or tomorrow? How would we ever move on?"

"So, they forget their father?" Joanne's voice shakes. "And that's okay?"

"Well, no," Eleanor amends. "That part sucks. But we can't change that. We can't bring him back. So maybe letting the memories fade is part of accepting that and someday moving on."

"I don't want to move on," Joanne insists, but her voice has the same flat, detached tone. "Not from Jeff."

"Not yet," Eleanor agrees. "But someday. Someday you'll have to let him go just a little. Because he isn't here anymore, and you still are."

Joanne bites into her upper lip to keep from saying anything more. To keep from shouting. Or crying. Eleanor doesn't understand, she tells herself. Eleanor doesn't know what it's like to lose someone who made you a better person. Someone who made you more yourself than you'd ever been on your own.

As Joanne sits, lost in thought, darker clouds begin edging their way toward the playground. The wind picks up and parents call to their children that it's time to go home. The girls bring Nolan over without being called and Joanne reaches for them automatically. Her left hand cups Ruthie's upper arm, while her right brushes Sarah's hair away from her face. She smiles at them and they look back with passive eyes.

Is it the loss? Joanne wonders as she gets to her feet. Or is it the effort to hang on to the sadness that makes the girls seem so distant and out of step? Do they need to move on? Is she holding them back with her own grief? Maybe they need to make more pizzas and focus on building new memories. But the idea of new memories, without Jeff, makes Joanne feel sick to her stomach.

She watches Eleanor strap Nolan into his stroller and

wonders if she should admit to giving Jeff's hidden papers to David. She has a right to know, Joanne argues in her own mind, but she'll also know soon enough. Especially if the papers had made a difference.

"Mom," Ruthie calls from the far side of the stroller. "Did you know that jackrabbits can run 45 miles per hour? That girl told me. And she knows because she has two pet rabbits."

"But they aren't pet jackrabbits," Sarah clarifies. "Just the regular kind. But she says we can go see them sometime. Can we?"

A crack of thunder cuts through the sky as the rain begins to fall in large, heavy drops. Some kids shriek and run as their parents usher them down winding paths towards their waiting homes.

"Maybe," Joanne answers automatically, while urging them toward the wetly darkening sidewalk. "But first, let's get out of this storm."

CHAPTER THIRTY

Although the dark clouds swept in quickly, the rain is just beginning to fall when David pulls into his assigned parking place. The radio has gone to commercials, but he still pauses before switching off the ignition. His mind is back in the basement, still picturing Andy in the chair and still wondering what the memory will show. If it recorded anything at all.

David shakes the drops of water from his hair as he steps into his building's small lobby. There's a crack of thunder and the storm hits in full force. He lingers by the glass doors. Watching.

The rain drives across the pavement in rippling sheets as David pulls out his phone and glances down to scroll through his contacts. Her name jumps out at him, but his finger hovers over the call button. Unsure. He looks back at the rain, then retreats into the building, walking past the elevator bays to climb the three flights of stairs with his phone still gripped in the palm of his hand. The call unsent.

It's early afternoon, but his apartment is shadowed, despite its large windows. David turns on a small lamp and heads into the kitchen to pour a glass of scotch. He looks down at the phone again and calls before he has a chance to overthink what he will say. Madeleine answers on the third ring, just as David is taking his second sip of scotch. He swallows quickly, nearly choking, and coughs harshly before saying hello.

"Are you all right?" Madeleine asks with the sound of a smile, but David doesn't know how to answer that question.

"Can I ask you something?" He responds instead, ignoring the animosity of their last meeting entirely. "If you were working with a subject, on a memory project, and you came across some, uh, disturbing memories, what would you do?"

"Disturbing?" David hears music playing in Madeleine's background, a smooth rhythm over a walking bass. He hears the rain as well, but can't tell if it's through the phone or his own windows. "Something ethically questionable?" She clarifies. "Or do you mean legally?"

There's a pause while David hears a series of hollow clinks through the phone, maybe ice dropping into a glass. He tries to picture Madeleine's apartment, knowing that it's not far from here, in a building similar to his own. Maybe with the very same layout.

He tries to picture her in her own apartment. Maybe leaning against her own kitchen counter, drink in hand.

"Is anyone in danger?" Madeleine presses. "Is it an actual crime?"

"No," David responds to the first question. His mind

trips over the second as he wonders if it would still count as a crime after all these years. Would it matter after the person who committed the crime was dead?

"Well," Madeleine says the word briskly, assuming David had covered both questions. "I'd say it was time to find a new subject. Or at least a new memory."

"You would just ignore it?"

"Hmm." David has the impression that she's hesitating over her words, but not her decision. "We're not psychologists, David. We're not historians or lawyers. Our job is to discover how the brain works, not to get drawn into messy personal stories or emotional drama."

David finds himself nodding along. He takes another sip of his drink and forces his hand to loosen its grip on the phone. She's right, he tells himself, but there's another voice nagging in the background as well, and it comes with the image of Joanne's pale face and dark flowing hair.

He begins to walk around the apartment, wandering past the rain soaked windows, then heading down the dim hallway toward his empty office.

"But do we have an, uh, obligation? As scientists? To uncover the truth, even if it wasn't what we expected or intended to find?"

Madeleine sighs. "Has someone told you that they plan to hurt someone? Or hurt themselves? Is someone planning to commit a crime?"

"No, but--"

"Can you be sure the memory is even real?"

"Well, not exact--"

"I mean," Madeleine rushes on. "If we are discussing an *actual* memory. An *actual* project of some kind. If this isn't just a hypothetical discussion?"

The pause is heavy as they both wait to see what David will say. Time stretches as David's mind stumbles through half-formed explanations and imagines her possible reactions. He's on the verge of answering when Madeleine speaks again.

"Does this hypothetical mean that you're ready to tell me what you're working on?" Her voice glides through the phone, soft like the music playing behind her and smooth as the scotch in his glass, but David's throat clenches against the question. Resisting.

"You know what I'm working on," he answers lightly. "I believe we're already working on it together."

"Hmm," the sound is drawn out this time and David smiles at her disappointment. He's glad to have taken back the upper hand. The next pause gives him a moment to breathe. To regroup.

"It's good to hear from you, David."

"Is it?"

"I wasn't sure I would. Outside of work," Madeleine adds. "After the other day."

David looks down at his glass and swirls the remaining scotch with his free hand. He tries to picture Madeleine's face. Her clear eyes, her red hair. But Joanne stays stubbornly in his mind's eye.

"I wasn't myself that day," he admits cautiously, then laughs at his own words. "I haven't been myself for a while."

"Are you yourself now?" David closes his eyes, trying to erase the image of a green bridge and a jumbled argument. Trying to forget the feel of a shove.

"I'm trying to be," he downs the last of the scotch and sets the glass on the edge of his desk with a firm clink.

"What's stopping you?"

A crack of thunder sounds overhead and David looks up to see that he's standing in front of his wall of notes and pictures. His eyes wander over the constellation of clippings that are taped around Mark's obituary and come to rest on a print out of a profile he found on social media. Mark's sister. Dee Ferguson. Unmarried, but in a relationship. Waitress at Al's Parkview Diner.

"I don't know," David answers, when he notices the silence. "Maybe nothing," he adds carelessly, skimming back over the collection of articles.

"Maybe there's more to you than you knew?" Madeleine ventures, treading lightly.

"Maybe," David agrees, turning toward the office's small window. "Or maybe I just need to get some dinner."

CHAPTER THIRTY-ONE

Dust filters through the sunlight as it passes through the kitchen window. Joanne watches it, arms crossed over her chest, and is glad for the sun after yesterday's storm. The girls are playing in the backyard and Eleanor has taken Nolan home for his afternoon nap. The house is quiet enough to hear the air conditioning kick on, and Joanne hugs herself tighter against the coming chill. She should get a sweater, she thinks, then realizes that she could simply change the thermostat. It was Jeff who had liked to keep the house so cool. But she leaves the temperature set, rubbing her hands against her upper arms instead.

David hadn't stayed long today, saying that he had somewhere else to be, and Joanne hadn't asked about his plans. She puzzles over it now. He'd clearly been different since the day she gave him Jeff's missing pages. There was his unexplained absence over several days, his sudden success in recording a memory, and his surprisingly calm reaction to watching that memory play out. There was also something different in the energy between them. He had come back with something bothering him, but also with a distance that discouraged any questions.

The crunch of tires on gravel draws Joanne's attention back to the window, and she watches Andy's truck back down the driveway. As he drives away, she feels a gradually lightening sense of freedom. She is alone in the house. The girls are playing comfortably outside. Eleanor is occupied with Nolan at home. Andy has left the neighborhood. No one is watching.

Joanne turns to face the basement door, taking in its solid form just beyond the stream of sunshine. She moves down the stairs slowly, lightly gripping the railing, reminding herself to breathe with each step. The tingling has started. The pricks of sensation under her collarbones, at her temples, and in the small of her back. She stops in the doorway to Jeff's private room and looks at the empty chair. Her eyes move to the quiet machinery just behind it, then blink against the rapid beating of her heart.

She hasn't watched it yet—Andy's memory—but Joanne already knows what's in it. She had hung back while the others watched. Andy and David, even Eleanor. She could only shake her head when they offered, and no one pushed her to take the seat. She listened to their conversation about the memory, though it hadn't lasted long and hadn't included many details. That would come later. This was just an overview. Just a chance to see that it had worked. A chance to collect first impressions and marvel over what might come next.

But now, alone, Joanne needs to see it for herself. She needs to see him. Whether she is ready to or not.

The leather padding feels cold and stiff against Joanne's forearms. She tries not to grip the armrests as she forces her eyes to close. She recognizes the house the moment she sees it. She recognizes the shabby furniture and the groups of teenagers who mill around with bottles and plastic cups. And she recognizes Jeff.

He's so young, Joanne sighs as she feels the tears begin to gather. His thin shoulders, *so thin*, hunch up as he looks around, squinting at the crowd. Her heart aches. He doesn't want to be there, Joanne knows, but his head bobs slightly with the music and he nods, more firmly and half-smiling, at someone he recognizes in the crowd.

"*Who else do you see?*" The thought whispers through her mind before her gaze—Andy's gaze—swings away from Jeff, scanning the crowd. Joanne struggles behind his eyes, willing Andy to look back at Jeff, but he continues to pan the room, stopping on a blonde in a low-cut tank top. *Megan something*, Joanne thinks to herself, a moment before the name *Megan Davies* floats into her thoughts. She isn't sure who remembered the name, whether it came from her memory or Andy's, but that doesn't matter because suddenly he is coming through the crowd.

Mark is tall and wiry, all angles and hard lines. Joanne's stomach drops at the sight of him. Her entire body breaks out in a cold sweat. The smell of him fills her senses: smoke, musk, and cinnamon gum. He parts the crowd, getting closer. Closing in. Joanne wants to shut her eyes, or look away, but he's already there, behind her eyes, in her mind.

Her eyelids part for a moment, her breath shallow and rapid. She darts her gaze around the drab basement, reminding herself where she really is, but he's there, too, a persistent overlay. His nasal voice pulls her back into the darkness behind her eyes. Back into the memory.

"*Hey, man,*" Mark nods a greeting to Andy, lips pressed in a tight line, and barely glances Jeff's way. He shouts to someone passing by, snatches his cup, and downs the contents in a single gulp.

"*What the fuck, dude?*" The other guy scowls, but lets his friend pull him away. Mark ignores them both. His gaze hovers somewhere over the crowd. Scanning.

"*She here?*" He asks, and a tremble runs through Joanne's body.

"*Naw, man,*" Joanne feels Andy speak the words, as if they're coming from her own throat. Her fingers curl around the arm rests, nails digging in. "*She ain't been around.*"

"*Something happen tonight?*" The words, the soothing voice, seep into Joanne's mind, sinking through her, grounding her. She silently begs Andy to turn toward Jeff, but he glances in the opposite direction, eyes on Megan again. When he finally turns back, Mark's eyes are narrowed in Jeff's direction. Mark stares with intensity for a moment, jaw set like stone, features unreadable. And then he relaxes, with one corner of his mouth lifting in a smug smile.

"*Nope,*" he keeps his eyes trained on Jeff, sending a silent warning. "*We're good. Just need to sort out a few things.*"

Joanne's eyes jerk open.

She sits up, yanks off the electrodes and stumbles into the adjoining bathroom to sink to her knees in front of the toilet. Gagging. Clutching her stomach. Waiting for the nausea to pass. When it does, she sits back against the wall, drawing her thighs into her chest. Breathing. Gasping. Shuddering with an effort to get air into her lungs.

His face swims behind her eyes. His voice lingers in her ears.

We're good.

We're not good, she thinks. We were never good.

She closes her eyes and pushes Andy's memory aside. She lets her mind travel back to earlier that night. At Mark's house. In his living room. Him standing on one side of the room, her on the other. Keeping her distance.

"This isn't working," she'd told him. "It isn't what I want."

And he'd laughed.

"Because you want to fuck Jeff." She can still hear his words, hear his laugh when she denied it. "You think I don't know you? That I don't know him?"

He was fast then. Darting forward faster than she could jump back. His hands grasping hers, then crossing her thin wrists together in the grip of one hand, the bones pressing painfully together as he pulled her close. His free hand wandering up the back of her shirt, a single finger sliding under her bra strap.

"Do you think I care who you fuck? Do you think I don't know that you're a fucking slut?" And then leaning down, breath hot in her ear. "You can do whatever you want, get it out of your system, but you'll end up back with me. Because we, you and me, we're forever."

The tears run down her face now, in the memory and in the present. Her stomach clenches again, roiling against the emotions. Her eyes are closed, her breath held, and her head shakes from side to side, denying it. Shutting him out. But the memory is too strong and his lips are wet as his voice echoes through her head.

"There's nothing you can do that would make me leave you. Ever. But you think it through. You fuck Jeff and they won't find his fucking body. Do you understand me?"

The knuckles of both fists dig into Joanne's forehead as she focuses on the feel of the cold tile under her hips and feet. "It's 2012," she mumbles under her breath. "It's 2012. I'm an adult. I'm in my house. I'm a wife. I'm a mother."

And then her litany stops.

I'm alone, she thinks in horror. *I'm a single mother.* She can't bring herself to say the words out loud, but the idea grounds her. It brings her back to the basement bathroom and lets her ease her fists open, seeing the deep crescent shapes from her fingernails pressed into her palms.

With a ragged breath, she forces herself to think through what happened next. Telling herself it's just a story. Not real. Not now. Just a story. They were interrupted, she remembers, by the sound of a key turning in a lock. The front door had opened. Mark's mother and sister had come in, giving Joanne a chance to break away. His mother had been surprised to find Joanne in tears, but Dee merely stepped aside, leaving the door open for Joanne to hurry out.

It wasn't until she'd hit the front porch that Joanne froze. She'd drawn her shoulders back, turned to Mark's mother and said, "*I'm sorry, I-- I won't be--*"

And then she'd looked at Mark, her eyes hardening like stone. "I came to tell Mark that I won't be seeing him anymore. It's over."

And then she'd walked out the door.

CHAPTER THIRTY-TWO

David watches Madeleine smile at the representatives from the oversight committee as they exchange small talk in the hallway. He feels a mix of gratitude and shame, knowing that she had carried their part of the presentation, but he's relatively proud of his own performance as well. It was worth spending most of Sunday and Monday prepping for this meeting, he decides. It was good for his career, he tells himself, and good to spend time with Madeleine.

He tries not to think about how it had also given him some needed time away from his secret life in Parkview.

Their small group begins to break up, with Dr. Keller excusing himself to get back to his office and Fletcher quick on his heels. Madeleine offers to see the committee out and David stays by her side, beginning to like the feeling of being a pair.

Now that he's actually recorded a memory, David feels a step closer to legitimizing the project. A step closer toward recreating Jeff's machine in the lab, maybe with

Madeleine's help. Maybe even a step closer toward eventually untangling himself from Andy, if he could just let go of a few nagging doubts.

David brushes the thought aside, turning his attention back to his guests. He's shaking their hands, thanking them for their time, when David catches sight of Andy watching them from the far end of the hall. Keeping his expression neutral, David assesses Andy's wide-legged stance, noticing how his hands bury deep into his pockets. He stands his ground. Staring. Waiting to be acknowledged.

Deciding that Andy isn't going away, David politely excuses himself from the group, carefully ignoring Madeleine's quizzical side eye. He holds his friendly smile until Madeleine has ushered their visitors in the opposite direction, leaving David and Andy alone in the long hallway. A brief moment passes before David grimly closes the distance.

"What is it?" David lowers his voice as a door opens and an intern hurries by. "Has something happened?"

Andy continues to stand firm, cocking his head to take in David's expression before saying, "You tell me."

"Okay, look," David glances back down the hall nervously. "I don't know what this is about, but this is not the best time. Or place."

"You enjoy your dinner Saturday? Did you like the pie?"

"What?" David knows exactly what, but he tries to paste a look of confusion over his face.

"See, you barely come by on Sunday, after our big breakthrough," Andy explains, step by step. "And you say it's because of work. So, I let it go. But then I stop by

Dee's diner last night and hear the damnedest thing. You know Dee, right?"

David presses his lips together, refusing to answer.

"Mark's sister. She works at a diner," Andy continues tightly. "And she said there was this clean-cut guy there on Saturday who kept watching her the whole time he was there. Like he knew her, or like he wanted to say something, but he never did.

"Looked like the type who would work at the lab, she said. Wearing a blue t-shirt with the name of a softball team on it.

"Which is funny," Andy goes on, leaning in closer. "Because I seem to remember you wearing a shirt like that on Saturday. What was that team name again? Was that a college thing? Or do you play with some of these lab guys? A little beer and ball on a summer night?"

"Andy, please," David strives for a soothing tone as two more people pass by. It's an early sign of the end-of-the-day rush, making David feel exposed and vulnerable in the lab's main passageway.

Looking over Andy's shoulder, he watches as a door opens at the far end of the hall and a small group of people emerge, laptops and travel mugs in hand. They pause, waiting for someone who is still inside the room.

"Don't hold out on me," Andy encourages, in a slightly louder voice. "I just want to know where you played softball. Is that too much to ask? Is softball a state secret?"

"All right, stop," David interjects more firmly, looking to see if anyone overheard.

"No problem," Andy pulls his hands from his pockets,

cracking his knuckles. "But I do have some other questions."

"Fine." David eyes the group down the hall, making a quick decision. "But not here."

He leads Andy down a side hallway and into the nearest men's room, rapidly scanning the partially opened stalls to be sure that they are alone. Andy hangs back, watching David's search before following him to the far end of the sinks.

"You hiding from someone, doc?"

David waves off the question, catching sight of himself in one of the mirrors and quickly looking away, though he doesn't know where to send his eyes. The overhead lights cast a fluorescent glare on the pale gray tile and porcelain sinks. Andy seethes in front of him.

"This about my memory? Of the party?" Andy scrutinizes David's face before shaking his head. "But it started before that," he adds, without waiting for David to speak. "You were working as usual, and then you weren't. And then you knew how to record the memory. So, what changed?"

"I don't know," David shakes his head, avoiding Andy's eyes. "I just took some time and figured it out."

"Bullshit," Andy shakes his head in short, tight jerks. "You didn't just figure it out. So, what? You found something? Something of Jeff's? Yeah," his words come faster, putting it together. "Yeah, you found something you'd been missing. Notes or something in the computer. But what's Dee have to do with it? Something in the notes about her, too? About Mark?"

"No," David grits his teeth, thinking furiously.

"No? No about Dee? Or no about Mark?" Andy badgers, the questions coming faster and louder. "But not no about the notes? There were notes, right? Or something? You found something?"

"All right, fine," David tosses his head back, looking up with a determined glare. "Yes, I found some new information and it cleared up some questions about how the process might work. But the rest is... I just stopped at a diner for dinner. If Mark's sister works there, it's news to me."

"Nah," Andy shook his head. "Doc, it's too late for that shit. I saw your face when I asked about Dee. You keep forgetting that I'm not as stupid as you think."

"I don't think you're stupid," David responds, buying time.

"Right," Andy frowns. "So, prove it. Tell me what the fuck you're up to."

David clasps his hands together, twisting his fingers as he sorts what he should and shouldn't share. He'd been concerned, and maybe there were still doubts, but seeing Andy's memory on Sunday had changed that. Jeff had been there, in the background, after Mark had left. It was entirely possible that Jeff had been at the party the whole night, and not out on the bridge with Mark at all. The choppy, erratic quality of Jeff's hidden memory alone suggested that it was somehow different. Maybe it was a dream manifested from Jeff's guilt over being in love with his friend's girlfriend. Or maybe it came from the guilt he'd felt in being glad that Mark's accident had cleared the way for him and Joanne.

"David?" The sound of his first name, coming from Andy, snaps David back to attention.

"It doesn't matter," David runs his hands across his jaw and down the back of his neck, looking toward the ceiling before dropping his arms with a long exhale.

"What doesn't?" Andy's face is like stone, but his eyes are bright. Intense.

"I was just tense about getting the memory," David gazes down at his feet before forcing himself to look up. "About figuring it out," he clarifies. "The setbacks were making me crazy and making me think crazy things. But we got it now. We can move on."

"Move on?"

"Yeah," David nods encouragingly. "You wanted to remember that night and you did. So now we can move on to other memories. Happier memories. Maybe about your childhood? Or about Nolan?"

David forces a smile onto his face, pushing aside his suspicions and trying to get the project back on track.

"So that's it?" Andy rocks on his heels. "You're not going to say why you were at the diner? Or what you were up to?"

David hangs his head, calculating.

"I'm embarrassed," he says with his head still down. Andy waits, arms slack by his sides, eyes zeroing in. After a moment, David lifts his head and shrugs his shoulders.

"I got pulled in," he admits, glancing around as if unable to meet Andy's eyes. "I got curious about what it was like, for you, for Jeff, for Joanne. It was morbid curiosity, and a distraction," he looks at Andy then, his eyes widening, "and I'm sorry."

Andy crosses his arms, slowly, not saying anything for a full thirty seconds. When he speaks, his voice is musing, almost sarcastic.

"So, you were just curious? Personally curious?" Andy nods, but his frown puts David on edge. "See I have a different theory.

"My theory is that you were back on that memory integrity thing. You wanted to check the facts and be ready to see if my memories held up. So, you've been doing some digging."

David shakes his head, but Andy ignores him.

"You looked into Mark, and the accident, and found out he had a sister, and started poking around to see what else you might find out. Even though you said you wouldn't. And you found something, didn't you? Something that made you really want to know what Jeff was doing at that party."

"Andy, I--"

"No." Andy's fists clench at his sides. "See you were making a pretty big deal about me looking around to see Jeff. So, why? What did you think was happening?"

"Well, okay, I may have had some concerns," David's throat goes dry and he begins to wish they were back out in the hallway. "But that doesn't matter now. Your memory shows that Jeff was at the party with you, so--"

"But you thought maybe he wasn't? Maybe he slipped out? Followed Mark to the bridge? Is that it?"

"Well, I--"

"Why?" Andy persists. "Did Jo say something? Did El?"

David swallows, staying very still. Andy steps closer.

"Did you *find* something, David? Something in Jeff's notes or--" He stops abruptly as their eyes lock under the yellow lights. David shakes his head, refusing to admit anything else.

"Jeff was at the party with you," he reminds Andy. But Andy laughs, then backs up. He moves to one of the sinks, braces his hands on either side, and looks into the mirror above.

"You know that suggestion thing, doc? The birds?" Andy talks into the sink, then slowly turns to watch David's face. "See you kept asking me if I saw Jeff at the party. And I saw Jeff at the party. But ever since then, something has been different."

Andy lets go of the sink, standing upright.

"When I picture that memory, there's something just kinda tugging at me. Kinda bothering me now. So, last night I had this dream, and it was like that memory, but no sign of Jeff after Mark left."

David's heart begins to pound, but he keeps his mouth shut, letting Andy go on.

"And all day it's in the back of my head, until I remember something else from that night. When it was time to go, I couldn't find Jeff. I went all over the house, asking around. No Jeff. Then I found him out front, talking to some people who were taking off. But what if he hadn't just walked outside with them? What if he'd just come back from somewhere?"

The moment stretches until David realizes that he's shaking his head in tight, nervous jerks, as if warding off Andy's confession. His phone vibrates, audibly in the quiet of the men's room, but he doesn't answer it.

"Jeff left the party that night, didn't he?"

"We don't know that," David holds up his hands, attempting to diffuse the situation. Fragments of Jeff's hidden memories leap into his mind, but they mingle with images of Joanne. Images of the Jeff he had known at the lab. The Jeff who couldn't have done that.

"We don't?" Andy's nostrils flare, but he's holding back now. Looking to David for answers.

"The police investigated," David reminds him. "They ruled it an accident, so they must not have found any evidence of anyone else being out on that bridge."

"Fuck the police," Andy mutters, even as he's nodding. Considering. He lifts his eyes and David is surprised by the pain, and the pleading, that he sees in them. Andy's voice is calm, controlled when he asks, "What did you find, David?"

Without hesitation, David looks Andy straight in the eye and says, "Nothing." He pictures Joanne's dark hair and sad eyes. He feels the softness of her hands resting in his. "It was just an idea. Something I imagined, between the lines."

Andy squints, peering into David's eyes, then pulls back, clasping his hands on top of his head. He turns in a slow circle, looking at the empty stalls, the door, the mirrors. He stops to see something in his own reflection. Something that makes him press his hands onto the edges of the sink again.

"Maybe we just have to let this go," David tells him gently. "We can move on to something else. Another memory. We have a whole future ahead of us."

David's phone begins to vibrate again. He pulls it out of his pocket, but doesn't recognize the number.

"I need to go," Andy mumbles. "I've got to get out of here."

"Andy, wait," David tries to stop him, but it's not enough. The door silently closes itself as David hesitates.

The phone continues to vibrate and David answers it without thought.

"Who is this?" He asks, then pales at the answer.

CHAPTER THIRTY-THREE

Eleanor looks out the kitchen window as she sips a cup of raspberry tea. Thick clouds have drifted across the sky all afternoon, but for the moment the sun is shining brightly. She watches the girls playing in Joanne's backyard and remembers summer days like this when she was growing up. Days when the clouds were so thick that there was a noticeable chill each time they blocked the sun. Moments when she'd close her eyes and bask in the returning warmth, appreciating the sun all the more for its brief absence.

As she watches, the girls crouch at the edge of the driveway and begin sifting through the gravel. They are back by the wider part of the shared driveway, where the gravel spreads out to give access to the adjacent garages at the back of their property. After a few minutes, they stand up and trot around the far side of their garage with large chunks of rock in each hand. Eleanor can no longer see the girls, but she imagines that they are painting the rocks or using them as pieces in some made-up game. She knows that Jeff's truck is parked in that garage now. Out of sight.

Eleanor is still looking out the window when Andy's truck rumbles into view and stops by the kitchen door. She frowns to see him home early and suspects that his parking in the driveway means he plans to go back out soon. To the bar. With a sigh, she takes her tea mug to the sink and jumps when the kitchen door bangs open behind her.

"Jeez, Andy! You're going to rip it off the hinges."

By the time she turns, Andy has shut the door and is leaning against it with his gaze unfocused toward the center of the room. His arms hang heavy at his sides, an open beer in his right hand.

"Were you drinking that on the way home?" Eleanor's tone is sharp, but Andy barely acknowledges her.

"Just a little," he mumbles while pushing off from the door and setting the beer on the table. The faraway look stays with him, making Eleanor's anger turn to an uneasy concern.

"What is it?"

Andy releases a heavy sigh, takes a seat at the kitchen table and pushes the half-empty bottle aside. Outside, the sun disappears behind another cloud and the room dims around them.

"When did they get together?" Andy asks without moving a fraction of an inch, using a low, steady tone that matches his rigid posture.

"Who?" Eleanor knows who he is talking about.

"You always said it was a couple of months later. At that Valentine's thing," Andy goes on in a heavy monotone. "That fucking stupid dance we just had to go to, as friends. You remember. To get our minds off Mark. But maybe I was the only one even thinking of him by then. Maybe Jeff and Jo weren't thinking of him a lot sooner than that."

Eleanor can feel her heartbeat speeding, but she forces herself to breathe and relax her shoulders.

"What are you talking about?"

"Jeff left the party that night," Andy looks up at his wife as the words leave his mouth. He's watching for a reaction, any reaction, but none comes.

"The night Mark--" She stops herself. "What does that mean?"

"It means he followed Mark out to the bridge."

"Just because he--" Eleanor is shaking her head, but Andy interrupts.

"He told the cops he was at the party, but he wasn't."

The sentence fills the kitchen. Eleanor shakes her head weakly, but Andy doesn't notice.

"Where else would he fucking be?"

They pause there. Andy sits at the table, Eleanor leans against the kitchen sink. They both silently process the situation. Eleanor's eyes slowly go out of focus, just as Andy's gaze sharpens. He studies Eleanor's crossed arms and the way she is chewing the inside of her lip. There's a soft grunt from the monitor, but neither react.

"See, at first I wasn't sure," Andy keeps talking in a light, almost conversational tone that only makes Eleanor's heart pound harder. "I mean, it's fucking crazy, right?

"But then," Andy reaches for the beer bottle and mindlessly rubs his thumb over the label. "I had this whole drive home and all the pieces just started coming together, you know?"

"Andy, you can't really think that Jeff would--"

There's a sudden crash as Andy pitches the bottle straight into the kitchen cabinets. Beer and shattered glass spray over Eleanor as she turns away, covering her head with both arms. A wailing cry pierces through the monitor and Eleanor quickly snaps it off, afraid of what Andy will do next.

"It wouldn't take much," Andy responds in the same even voice, as if nothing had happened. "Two angry people, shoving. An icy bridge."

Eleanor looks down at her body, her arms and legs, and gently feels the side of her face. She is damp with beer, but doesn't seem to be bleeding. Nolan's crying has stopped. For the moment. With a glance toward the window, Eleanor sees the girls wander out into the middle of their backyard. She looks away quickly, plotting how she can get to Nolan and still escape through either the front or back door.

"This is all in your head," Eleanor lets her irritation show, hoping it seems natural, and starts wiping up the glass and beer with a kitchen towel.

"Maybe," Andy answers lightly. "Unless he recorded it…"

The towel stops moving. Eleanor goes still as a statue. Andy watches her settle her shoulders and sit back on her heels before facing him with a calm expression.

"Have you seen a recorded memory?"

The left corner of Andy's mouth curls into a sneer and Eleanor forces herself to wait for his answer. Careful not to give anything away.

"Something made David suspicious," Andy shrugs off the question. "And I know Jeff left the fucking party."

Upstairs, Nolan begins to call out from behind the baby gate on his bedroom door and Eleanor stiffens. The plastic gate rattles against the door frame. Eleanor shakes her head, trying to look unconcerned, and says, "Andy, I don't know anything about this."

When he doesn't respond, she steps over the broken glass and takes steady, deliberate steps out of the kitchen, hoping to get Nolan and take him out the front door before Andy notices. But she only makes it to the front hall before he grabs her by the upper arm.

"I think you do," he tells her. "You've been against this from the beginning. Protecting your fucking privacy. So, what the fuck've you been trying to hide?"

"You're crazy," Eleanor tries to pull her arm away. "Mark was alone. He fell. Or he jumped. Either way, Jeff was not out on that bridge."

"And how do you know that?"

Eleanor turns her head away as her lips press together. Andy squeezes her arm.

"El?"

"Because he was looking for Jo," she finally snaps in exasperation.

Nolan cries louder, shaking the plastic gate, but Andy refuses to let Eleanor go.

"Look," her eyes flash resentment. "Jo broke up with Mark that night, but he didn't want to accept it. That's why Mark was looking for her. That's why Jeff was looking for her. And that's why she was hiding out where I was babysitting. That's it. End of story."

Eleanor tries to pull away, but Andy only grips harder.

"Wait!" He narrows in on one idea. "How do you know Jeff was looking for her that night? Did he tell you that? Did you know he'd left the party? Back then?"

"Moooommmmmyyyy!" Nolan's wail is punctuated by kicks against the plastic baby gate. Eleanor calls up that she'll be right there, but Andy isn't finished with her.

"So, we were covering for him? With the police? You and Jo *knew* we were covering for him, but *no one told me*!"

"Andy, we didn't tell you because--"

"Because I wouldn't have fucking gone along! That's why you didn't tell me. The cops would have looked at Jeff more closely. Fuck. El, that asshole may have killed Mark and I was his fucking cover!"

The realization loosens Andy's grip enough for Eleanor to pull away, but she stands her ground, too angry now to keep from shouting what she's known for years.

"Mark was a bully, asshole, rapist and he deserved whatever happened to him!"

The punch comes faster than the thrown bottle, leaving Eleanor no time to react. Andy's fist sends her stumbling backward, where her head hits the corner of the stair post before she drops to the ground with a sickening thud.

"Oh, fuck." Shock at what he's done instantly chases Andy's anger away. The curses continue under his breath, as if in prayer, as he kneels down to assess the damage.

"Come on, babe, talk to me, please," he begs helplessly while reaching to cradle her head. There's blood on his hands.

Having finally pushed down the baby gate, Nolan sits high on the staircase and stares down at the scene below. Tears flow freely over his small cheeks, but he is too afraid to move.

CHAPTER THIRTY-FOUR

The diner is busy for a Tuesday. Families fill booths for an early supper, while solo diners line the long counter. David hesitates, just inside the glass door, scanning the room for a certain waitress. His right hand grips his phone, as if it will guide him, and his shoulders tense at the sound of a crying toddler just two booths from the door.

Dee spots him first. With a few soft words, she hands off her tray to another waitress and rapidly crosses the room. She doesn't smile. She doesn't frown. Her features remain neutral as she confirms David's identity, then leads him to an empty booth in a relatively quiet part of the diner. As he slides onto the vinyl seat, David takes in the clean, but smeary table and the crusted ketchup bottle centered between a pair of glass salt and pepper shakers.

They sit across from each other, silently, and David resolves to let Dee lead the conversation. She called him, she chose the location. Yet she keeps her mouth shut and lets her eyes rove over David, taking in his features, his clothes, and his fidgeting fingers.

"Nice place," David offers, without meaning to speak.

"Mmm," Dee shrugs. "We do all right."

"Well," David wonders if she expects him to order something. Coffee, maybe. His mind runs over the possibilities, thinking of every tense diner confrontation he's seen in movies or on TV, until Dee interrupts.

"You're not very good at this." David looks up sharply. "At snooping into people's lives," she clarifies.

"Snooping? Oh, uh," Dee's raised eyebrow stops his stuttering.

"You're a sociologist? But you give out a card that says you're a…" She looks down at something she's pulled from her apron pocket. "A cognitive neuroscientist?"

She lays his business card on the table and slides it toward him, adding, "My friend, Linda. At the library."

"Uh, yeah, I remember her--" The room feels warm as David wonders exactly what Andy and Dee have discussed.

"And you were here over the weekend," Dee reminds, pausing for a confirmation that she doesn't need.

"Good pie," David quips without a smile.

Dee leans forward, frowning, hands clasped on the table.

"What do you want with my dead brother?"

David flinches.

A woman passes by their booth carrying a toddler toward the double bathroom doors. The little girl waves shyly over her mother's shoulder, her face and fingers covered in what looks like strawberry jam. David stares until the door closes behind them and is still left searching for an answer.

"Don't bother," Dee rests back in the booth, satisfied by something in David's expression. "I'm better at it than you are, and I know more people in this town.

"You been spending a lot of time in Parkview. A lot of time at Joanne Simon's house." She waves away his attempted explanation, "I'm not judging. Who Jo screws is none of my business."

"I'm not--"

"But my brother is my business," Dee talks over his interruption. "So, what? You worried about her track record? Dead husband. Dead boyfriend. Gonna up your life insurance?"

"Now wait a minute--" David feels his face flush, but Dee jumps in again with a humorless chuckle.

"Calm down. I already said that's none of my business. But do you really think Jo wants you snooping into her past? Not the best way to start a relationship."

"That's not--" David cuts himself off, unsure how else to explain his interest in Joanne's past and wondering again what Andy may have said to cover up their real plans.

As she waits, Dee sits across from him, her soft body held rigid and her tired eyes trained on his every movement. In that moment, David senses the pain that hovers under her skin. A pain that she lives with, breaths with, sleeps with, every day of her life. It's a repressed pain that he's seen before. In Andy. In Joanne.

"She feels guilty," he says the words softly, feeling his way and hoping that he isn't making anything worse. "About the, uh, accident."

"Yeah?" Dee narrows her eyes. "That's not news."

The mother walks out of the bathroom, passing by

with her cleaned-up daughter, and smiles a quick hello at Dee. David waits until she's gone to slowly shake his head no.

"Not to you," he ventures carefully, but something about his answer makes Dee's eyes harden.

"What did she say?"

"Nothing," he tells her. "Not really."

"Okay," Dee leans in. "What did she *imply* then?"

"Well," David manages only the one word before Dee's face flushes with anger.

"She say it wasn't an accident?" She spits the words across the table in a harsh whisper.

"No," David raises both hands as if warding her away, but then caves. "Not exactly."

"Not exactly?" Dee sits back.

She taps her finger on the table, considering.

"She's not going to tell you the truth," Dee admits matter-of-factly. "I know Jo and she'll never tell you the truth."

"Okay," David can only nod, waiting.

"But she'll tell you something she shouldn't," Dee continues, letting her eyes drift out of focus. "She's too eaten up to let it be. Already has you thinking there may be more to the story. More than an accident."

For the moment, Dee seems to have forgotten that David is there. Listening. He sits as still as he can, hoping she'll say more. Instead her eyes come back to him with a sudden intensity.

"Why are you dragging this up? Why do you care? Really?"

"I don't know."

The honest answer relaxes David's chest, letting him breathe deeply and look Dee in the eye. He asks himself the same questions. Again. And as he does, David's mind pictures the little girl with the jam on her face, held in the arms of her smiling mother. That's where he should be, he tells himself. Home with a young, normal, healthy family of his own. He shouldn't be here playing amateur detective, and he shouldn't be letting a decade-old tragedy distract him from the biggest breakthrough of his career.

"Look," Dee draws David's wandering attention with a heavy sigh. "You have nothing to worry about and there's no point in bringing it all up now. Okay? He was alone out there and it was an accident. Case closed. I don't need you stirring this shit up again, so let's just pretend you were never here."

"Right," David agrees, almost ready to leave, until he realizes what Dee just said.

"Why did you say he was alone out there?"

"What?" Dee straightens up, but her eyes flare. "Because he was."

"Dee," David hunches forward, glancing around to make sure no one is within earshot. "Was Jeff on the bridge that night?"

"Jeff?" There's a dismissive scowl on Dee's face and David sees her instinctively reach toward her apron pocket, rummaging for something before returning her empty hand to the table. "What does Jeff have to do with anything?"

"Well, I--"

"Oh," Dee's brows relax with understanding and her mouth drops slightly open. She turns toward the empty aisle and curses under her breath, making David realize that he's somehow gotten everything wrong.

"Jeff was here."

Dee is still looking across the aisle, out the plate glass window over another empty booth. Outside, a family crosses the parking lot, heading toward their car. An older couple passes them, hand in hand.

"He'd been out looking for Jo that night," she confesses, "but not at the bridge. He was worried about her. And more worried when I told him she'd broke up with Mark that afternoon. There was a pay phone then, in that corner by the door, and he kept getting up to call Jo's house. Or El's. And I kept pouring him coffee and saying everything would be all right."

"Then Jeff wasn't..." David lets the thought trail off and Dee closes her eyes for a moment.

"Jeff wasn't," she confirms with no emotion.

"But you don't think he was alone out there?" David's thoughts swim around the idea. Not Jeff. Not Andy. Who else? The answer creeps into his stomach first, clenching and churning, before making its way to his disbelieving brain.

Dee's hands come back together, clasped on the tabletop. David watches her fingers curl in against her knuckles as the sounds of the diner fade into the background.

"You know about Jo's parents?"

"Her parents? They died in a car accident."

"Yeah," Dee bites her lower lip and shakes her head. "Another accident."

"What does that have to do with any of this?"

"It doesn't," Dee agrees. "But before that, her mom

was a cop and her dad a lawyer. Jo's lawyer was her dad's partner, the cops were all their friends, and Mark, well," she sighs, the pain glimmering in her eyes. "Mark had gotten into a lot of trouble over the years."

"You think Jo was out there?" The question slips out the moment it forms in David's brain. "You think Jo was out there, with Mark?"

David's breath catches, holds as he waits. He wants to shake Dee, to make her talk. But she only stares at him cryptically before fishing a pack of cigarettes out of her apron pocket and glancing toward a side door near the bathrooms.

"Doesn't matter what I think," Dee shrugs. "But it's hard to believe he slipped on his own. And he wouldn't have jumped."

Her last words come with a warning and David knows better than to cross that line with her. He thinks through what he knows of that night.

"But Jo was with Eleanor. Babysitting."

"Yeah," Dee scoffs. "And you don't think El would lie for her?"

"But she just broke up with him," David persists. "Why would she go looking for him out on the bridge if they just broke up?"

"Yeah, she broke up with him," Dee agrees, but with a pained expression that David has seen before. On Andy's face. "But that wasn't going to be the end."

She shakes her head silently before looking David straight in the eye.

"He was obsessed with her," Dee admits, "absolutely. But she was just as caught up in it. Like a sickness.

Whatever it was that kept them twisted up together. She couldn't stay away either. Much as she wanted to."

The thought sinks in as David considers everything he's learned. His mind coming back to the question of why Jeff might try to create a fake memory of that night. It didn't make sense. Unless Jo had been there. Unless Jeff had wanted to convince someone else that it had been him, if it ever came out. Unless he thought the fake memory could replace Jo's real memory, somehow taking away her guilt and pain.

"We done here?" Dee cuts into David's speculation as she taps the cigarette pack against the table. She shifts toward the end of the booth, clearly itching to get outside.

"Wait," David reaches out to her. "One more thing and I won't bother you again. Does Andy know about this? About Jeff being out looking for Jo? Or about your... suspicions?"

Dee shakes her head, pausing at the edge of the seat.

"If Andy even *thought* something was going on with Jeff and Jo before Mark died, it would have killed him. Or he would have killed them. Either way, I wasn't going to give him that pain."

"Shit," David snaps to attention, his gut sinking with dread. He remembers the look on Andy's face when he left the bathroom at work. The anger. The despair. "I've gotta go."

CHAPTER THIRTY-FIVE

There's a stuffed duffel bag slung over Joanne's shoulder and a large suitcase clutched by her side as she crosses the driveway. David hurries up from the street, scanning the area as his breath comes in short, fast huffs. His eyes barely rest on Joanne before they dart toward Andy's house, then peer around her toward the garage. Joanne pauses for just a moment, taking in his disheveled hair and nervous hand-clenching, before resuming her steady pace.

"He's not here," she tosses out the answer before David has a chance to ask.

"Was he?"

One withering look is enough of an answer. He had been here. And it wasn't good.

David catches up at the back steps, ready to follow Joanne up and into the house, but she stops just before the bottom step, setting the heavy suitcase down on the gravel path and flexing her fingers. David stays a pace behind, noting the way her right shoulder droops under the weight of the duffel bag.

"What happened?"

There's worry in his tone, but the question feels inadequate. David's mind spins with possibilities as he notes the absence of police or emergency vehicles. Unless they've already come and gone. But they couldn't have, he tells himself. Andy couldn't have gotten here more than an hour or so ago. *What could happen in an hour?* And then he sees the slight shake of Joanne's head.

The subtle movement causes his stomach to pitch well before she pivots to face him with hard, cold eyes.

"What do you think happened?" Her voice is tired, resigned.

David's lips part, but he doesn't know what to say.

"Well, Andy was a bit upset," Joanne's fists rest on her hips and her words have a sarcastic edge that David has never heard from her before. "As I'm sure you can imagine."

Her hair is pulled back in a messy bun and David is unnerved by the way her contained hair makes her face appear more angular, more stern. She hardly seems like the Joanne he has come to know. Her lips disappear in a white line and her eyes blaze anger.

"What did--" David stutters to a stop.

"What did you tell him?" Joanne counters. "Huh? What could you have possibly said?"

"It wasn't-- I didn't--"

"You know what? No," Joanne cuts off his sputtered explanation with a flash of her eyes. "I don't want to know what you said or what you think."

She turns back toward the house, reaching for the suitcase, while David stays rooted to the spot.

"Jo, please," he doesn't entirely know what he expects from her, but his heart skips when she straightens up, leaving the suitcase in place. He watches her shoulder blades settle down her back before she shrugs the duffle bag strap higher on her shoulder. She's waiting, giving him one chance.

"Is Eleanor okay?"

He watches Joanne's thin neck as her head bows, then shakes slowly from side to side. A cold fear spreads through his body. David is about to step forward when Joanne's next strained words hold him in place.

"She will be."

They stand together in silence. David looks past Joanne toward the waiting house, wondering if Eleanor is inside. With Nolan. With the girls. The sunlight is fading, but it's bright enough to turn the windows into mirrors, concealing whoever may be watching from within.

"Look, Jo, I know that you don't want to hear…" David casts around for the words that will keep her talking. "Well, anything from me. But I do care. About what's happened. About Eleanor, and about you. And there's something that you need to know. That Andy needs to know."

Joanne turns again, this time reaching for his arm and swiftly walking them both back toward the driveway. Away from the house. David feels the stuffed bag swing between them and graze the back of his upper thigh. Once they're across the driveway, Joanne looks up at him intently.

"You found something." It's not a question, but

there's uncertainty in the statement.

David instinctively shakes his head no, but then stops. When he looks into her eyes, he can see past her anger to the tough vulnerability that never fails to draw him in.

"I did," he admits cautiously. "But I have to tell you something else first. I just came here from talking to Dee Ferguson."

"Dee?" Confusion washes over Joanne's face. "How? When?"

"Now." David resolves to tell her everything, no matter how it affects the way she sees him. "Just now. She called and asked me to come to the diner."

"Why would Dee call you?" Joanne's eyes narrow and her arms fold over her chest. And then realization lights her eyes.

"You tracked her down," Joanne's gaze drifts beyond David. "You were checking into Andy's memory."

"Not exactly." David tries to untangle the pertinent facts before deciding that the details won't change anything. "But essentially, yes. And Dee heard I was looking into what happened.

"She said that she knew I've been spending time here," he continues. "That she has friends who see things."

Joanne's arms tighten across her chest. She scans the houses across the street, as if expecting to see her neighbors lined up with binoculars and cameras. She sinks back, as if the slight movement toward Eleanor's house would be enough to shield her from prying eyes.

"She thinks that you and I-- Well, that we--" But he can't finish the sentence without his cheeks tingling and his throat choking on the words. Joanne ignores the insinuation.

"What did she tell you?" She asks flatly.

David straightens up, responding to her businesslike tone.

"That Jeff was at the diner that night," he admits freely. "That Jeff couldn't have been out on the bridge with Mark."

There's a pause as Joanne considers this information, her eyes trained on David's face. She doesn't seem to notice that the duffel bag is still weighing down one shoulder, but David wishes she would set it down or let him carry it for her.

"Why would you think Jeff was out on the bridge that night?"

Joanne's question is slow, deliberate. David has no intention of keeping the truth from her now, but her steady wariness puts him on edge. He wonders whether he should tell her about Dee's suspicions as well, or whether she already knows.

"Jeff left a hidden memory."

The direct approach seems best, but the short statement drips with deeper meaning. A flicker of a question passes over Joanne's face, but is quickly resolved with a subtle exhale.

"It was hidden on the computer, but I found it with those last, hidden notes. From the art book," David clarifies. It was a memory of being on the bridge. That night."

"But Jeff wasn't--" And Joanne stops. Something clicks into place as her fingers lift to cover her mouth.

"It wasn't a memory," David rushes in. "It couldn't have been. Dee remembers Jeff being at the diner. With her. And she says Mark was out there alone."

He stumbles over the last words, a flush coming to his face. Joanne sees it and her eyes harden.

"Does she?" The cold has come back into Joanne's voice. "And what do you think?"

"I--" David hesitates, thinking rapidly before looking back with confidence. "I think there are a lot of ways Jeff could have recorded something like that without it being an actual memory. It has a different quality, choppy and fragmented, which leads me to suspect it was a dream. Or a nightmare.

"Maybe he recorded himself while sleeping. Maybe he purposefully let his mind wander over the memory of a dream. Or maybe it was a daydream borne from guilt, or regret, or grief. But that doesn't mean it happened."

"And now you know Jeff wasn't out there?" Joanne confirms, opening a door for him to say more. She raises one eyebrow and lifts her chin, as if daring him to repeat Dee's suspicions.

"I think Mark was alone on the bridge," David responds, with more conviction than he feels.

Their eyes cling, ignoring the sound of a car passing by and the chirp of a bird from the small plum tree beside Eleanor's back porch.

"And that's what you told Andy?"

David drops his eyes, feeling the weight of responsibility come rushing back. He tries to remember what he did tell Andy, exactly, but the conversation is cloudy now, shadowed by Dee's revelations and by whatever Andy had apparently done when he had gotten home.

"No," David manages softly, before getting the courage to look up again. "I mean, I didn't tell him about Jeff's memory. The hidden one. But he had questions, and he thought maybe Jeff had left the party, and I couldn't confirm that for him. Either way. Because I hadn't talked to Dee yet, so I didn't know."

Joanne's eyes have lost focus again as she looks out across the driveway. David wants to give her space to think, but the lengthening silence begins to wear at his barely maintained calm. It feels as if Joanne has drifted away from him and David begins to feel a desperate need to pull her back. He wants her here with him, even if she's angry, even if she never forgives him.

He reaches for Joanne's arm, first lightly grazing his fingertips over her skin and then nudging gently to get her attention.

"Jo, what do we--" David clears his throat, deciding that this is his responsibility. "No, I did this. Andy has the wrong idea, but I'll find him and set him straight. I'll confirm that Jeff was at the diner that night. Without a doubt."

Joanne's eyes clear, but David isn't sure if she really heard him. She reaches for the strap of the duffle bag and rotates her shoulder under its weight. When she speaks, it is with a new urgency.

"Yes," Joanne takes hold of David's arm and begins guiding him back down the driveway, clumsily shrugging the bag on her aching shoulder every few steps.

"That's how you can help," she tells him. "Find Andy and keep him away for the night. Away from El. Okay? Keep him at the bar until closing, at least, or, even better, take him home with you for the night. Don't tell him about Jeff though. Just say that El needs some space tonight. That she's staying with me."

"Okay, so you don't want me to tell him that Jeff--"

"No," Joanne interrupts, but her eyes shift rapidly from side to side, still working out her thoughts. "Not yet. It would only raise more questions. And you can't mention Dee. Just calm him down. Okay? Buy some time until we decide the best thing to tell him.

"Can you do that?"

David hesitates for only a moment. He looks down into Joanne's pleading eyes and feels himself nodding agreement. It's okay, he tells himself. It's Joanne's story and she knows what's best.

CHAPTER THIRTY-SIX

Nolan is asleep in Ruthie's bed by the time Joanne goes upstairs to tuck the girls in. His cheeks are flushed, his mouth hangs open and one foot sticks out from under the covers. It's early for the girls to be in bed, but they were eager to retreat and Nolan wouldn't go to sleep alone. They nestle on Sarah's side of the room with their heads resting on pillows at either end of the narrow bed. Sitting on a chair beside them, Joanne smiles softly in the dim glow of the night lamp.

"Are you ready for bed?" She asks, even though they are already in their pajamas and under the covers. "You brushed your teeth?"

They nod and Ruthie adds, "We read to Nolan until he fell asleep."

Joanne reaches to stroke her hair, "Thank you, pet." Then, as if remembering, turns to pat Sarah's leg as well. "And thank you, too, love."

Sarah frowns at the praise, her mind elsewhere.

"Will Aunt El get a divorce now?"

The question sounds like a challenge and Joanne knows that Sarah has been wanting to ask it ever since Andy had helped Eleanor stumble into their kitchen, a dish towel pressed against the back of her head. Joanne hesitates, glancing toward the other end of the bed. Ruthie's eyes are fixed on the closed curtains, but Joanne knows that she is listening. Joanne meets Sarah's eyes.

"Yes," she says firmly. "Aunt El will get a divorce now."

"Will she and Nolan live with us?" Joanne sighs then, looking down at her hands. "It's okay, if they do," Sarah adds quickly. "As long as Uncle Andy doesn't."

"Will Andy go to jail?" Ruthie asks so softly that Joanne barely hears the question.

"Of course he will," Sarah answers angrily, then wavers, looking toward their mother. "Right?"

Joanne bites her lip. They haven't called the police. She and Eleanor haven't talked about what they will do next. There was too much else to do. Piecing the story together, calming Nolan, sending Andy away. Stopping the bleeding. Joanne pictures Eleanor sitting at the kitchen table with a bag of ice against the lump on her skull. Then she pictures the stolen equipment filling her basement.

"It's a little more complicated than you think," she begins slowly, as Sarah crosses her arms and Ruthie turns her gaze up to the shadowed ceiling. She wants to tell them that everything will be all right, but there are too many variables. Too many things to consider.

As she looks at their shadowy forms, Joanne realizes that her daughters don't always need to know the details behind her grown-up decisions. They don't have to see her wallow through the cosmic whys or the practical options. They only need her to take charge.

"Don't worry about that tonight," she tells them. "Aunt El and I will figure it out. We always do. But, first, the three of us need to take care of Aunt El and Nolan. And that means getting a good night's sleep. Okay?"

Joanne leans over to kiss Sarah, then Ruthie. She's halfway across the room when she hears Ruthie whisper, "I hope he goes to jail."

Downstairs, Eleanor sips at a cup of tea. She's sitting at the kitchen table with her knees hugged to her chest and both feet perched on the edge of her chair. Her face is swollen and beginning to bruise. Her clothes smell faintly of spilled beer. Walking toward the opposite seat, Joanne notices that the curtains are closed and a second cup of tea is waiting beside the steaming kettle.

"We should go to the hospital," Joanne repeats. "You may need stitches."

"The bleeding's stopped," Eleanor cradles her teacup and closes her eyes as the steam warms her face.

"You probably have a concussion."

"I was only out for a minute. Less probably."

"Still."

It's a conversation they've repeated several times over the last hour. Each time, Eleanor has put her off, saying "later." After Nolan has calmed down. After the kids have eaten dinner. After the kids are safe in bed. Now that they're in the later, Joanne waits for the next excuse.

Instead, there is only silence as Eleanor carefully sips her tea.

Looking around the softly lit kitchen, Joanne feels trapped in a time loop. So many nights spent drinking tea with Eleanor at this same table. She doesn't remember exactly when it began, but she knows it was her grandmother who started the tradition. Whenever they would come home from whatever social event dominated their weekend, upset about some teenage tragedy, Joanne's grandmother would put on a pot of tea and sit them down to talk it out. She'd pour the tea with a gentle smile, saying, "*Any problem seems smaller with a cup of tea in your hand and a good friend by your side.*"

Tonight, Joanne looks around Eleanor to study the dark cabinets with their dated brass handles and worn, loose hinges. It's too dim to make out the wallpaper, but Joanne could see it with her eyes shut. Brown and tan stagecoaches racing across a yellowing, beige background. She knows where its seams and corners have been re-glued. She knows which brown flecks are stains, and not part of the design. The weight of the room feels heavy on her tired shoulders.

"He can't get away with this," Joanne's voice quakes with the effort to be firm. Eleanor's eyes swing her way with a dull, detached look.

"What did you have in mind?"

The question hangs between them and Joanne is the first to break their stare. Her eyes drop to the table and her fingers tremble as they brush over the raised design on her teacup. Her grandmother's teacup. Eleanor sighs, setting her own cup onto its saucer with a soft clink. Joanne knows that Eleanor loves this tea set as much as she does. Their shared tea set, their shared problems, contained and repeated in the shared kitchen of their childhood.

"You're right," Eleanor admits at last. "I know you're right, but it's not that simple anymore. I have Nolan to think about."

"I'm thinking about Nolan."

Joanne doesn't have to elaborate. Eleanor releases another sigh and nods, though Joanne doesn't look up to see it. There's no point in saying that Eleanor never should have married Andy. Marrying him had seemed inevitable, after so many years. His friends were her friends; his family was her family. And Jeff had been loyal to Andy. After Mark. Andy had fit in their lives, a tradition as much as this tea set.

It has to be a clean break, Joanne tells herself. But she wavers at the thought. She remembers the sight of Andy holding El in his arms, in this very kitchen, just moments after waving a cigarette in her face. She remembers his angry tirades when El would talk to other boys at basketball games. She remembers the time he slammed her into a locker for saying she had to study with Jeff instead of going to a movie with him. But that one wasn't El.

That memory was her own. Of Mark.

Joanne drops her forehead into her hands, breathing through the ringing clang of metal behind her ears and the spasming tension in her tired neck.

"You can't go back to him," Joanne says with more determination, speaking from behind her hands.

"I know," Eleanor agrees, but the hopelessness in her voice makes Joanne lift her head. She sits up straighter, glaring now.

"No. I mean it. You cannot go back to him."

They stare at each other across the table.

"Yeah, well," Eleanor sets the damp, bloody, ice-filled towel on the table. "Where's a good bridge when you need one?"

The air sucks out of the room. Joanne's body trembles. Her tears jump into Eleanor's eyes, though neither lets them fall.

"That's not funny."

Eleanor shrugs, blinking to clear her eyes.

"Well, if anyone has a right to joke--"

"Stop it!"

Joanne shoves her chair from the table, rattling the teacups as she spins to face the basement door. She hears David's words echoing in her mind, "*Jeff left a hidden memory.*" A memory of the bridge.

It only takes a moment for Joanne to gather enough courage to twist the knob and hurry down the stairs. The machine is waiting for her. Jeff is waiting for her.

Joanne flips on the power strip, grabs a pair of electrodes and fumbles to untangle their long, thin cords. She wants to see it for herself. She needs to see it for herself.

But as the computer whirs to life, Joanne settles into stillness. She sits on the edge of the leather chair. The electrodes dangle from her limp fingertips.

She could find Jeff's false memory, watch it, and let it confuse, or possibly even replace, her own. She could show it to Eleanor, let it do the same for her. Maybe it would change their past, shift some blame, and open the door to a new future. Yet, sitting here beside Jeff's masterpiece, she realizes that it wouldn't work that way. Because, maybe, it already works that way.

"*Memory is associative*," she reminds herself in David's voice. Memories are reformed over and over. New details coming in, old details fading away. She doesn't need to replay Jeff's memories to cast doubt over that night. Or over any other memory.

Memories are just stories, Joanne decides in a sudden flash of insight. Memories are stories that we tell ourselves in whatever way we want to remember the past.

There's a creak as the door opens wider and Eleanor steps gingerly into the room. Joanne turns to meet her gaze, unaware of the tears that roll freely over her cheeks. She feels the house breathe with her, as if sighing with her release.

"It's my turn," Joanne tells Eleanor. "You protected me. Now I'm going to protect you."

CHAPTER THIRTY-SEVEN

David drives through the quiet streets of Parkview in a state of heightened awareness. Every blue truck draws his attention. Every police car speeds his heart. He has driven by Joanne's house and through the surrounding neighborhood. He has worked his way to the edge of town, driven out to Landon's Hollow and cruised past Dee's diner. His phone rings, but David ignores it when he sees Madeleine's number. Again. He doesn't have an explanation for not being at work.

The past night is a blur of endlessly searching these same roads. Andy wasn't at the bar. He wasn't at the bridge or at the diner. His truck wasn't parked anywhere that David could see, and it wasn't back in the shared driveway on any of David's frantic passes.

Eventually, David had driven home, making a careful loop through the near-empty lab parking lot on the way. When he'd woken up from a fitful sleep this morning, there was a text message waiting on his phone. A single response to the many messages he'd sent Joanne during his fruitless search. It simply read, "*Say nothing until you talk to Doug Mitchell – atty.*" Followed by a phone number.

The message had jolted David out of bed and into a cold sweat. It had come in at 5am, an hour before he woke, and there had been nothing since. No follow-up messages and no knock on his door.

Studying the phone, David had wondered who was going to come looking for him with questions that he wasn't supposed to answer. The police? The lab? David had hesitated over the underlined phone number in the text, but he hadn't made the call. Instead, he'd hurried into clothes and stumbled out to resume his search. As if finding Andy would reset whatever had happened in the night. Whatever had prompted Joanne to send him to a lawyer.

Driving now, nearly two hours later, he was no closer to knowing what to do next. He'd stopped at one point, halfway between the lab and Parkview, to get a bagel sandwich and two large cups of coffee. He'd eaten in the car, watching the passing traffic for a glimpse of Andy's truck and cringing when two police cars passed by.

What had happened? He didn't text Joanne for answers, but he did scan the morning news for a breaking headline. *Had Andy gone back? Had Eleanor died in the night?*

Nearing Joanne's house, David glances in the rearview mirror again and again. No one is behind him. No one has found him. David slows carefully and his heart pounds at the sight of Andy's truck parked brazenly in the gravel driveway. At last. Pulling to the curb, David clutches the steering wheel. He looks at his phone, perched on its hands-free mount, and sees a new text message come in from Madeleine: *Call ASAP!*

He considers calling, for a moment. He imagines that her urgent message means something is happening at the lab. Perhaps the mysterious someones, the ones who will have questions, are looking for him there. Perhaps they are asking Madeleine those questions instead. But David only feels a faint twinge of regret for her discomfort. He knows that she can only speculate.

Slipping the phone into his pocket, David leaves the car and walks steadily up the driveway. He passes the front porch, glances into the empty truck, and shifts his eyes rapidly between the two houses. Nothing moves. No one speaks. Instinctively moving toward Joanne's kitchen door, David catches sight of sunlight glinting off some broken glass on the back steps. The door is ajar.

"Joanne?" David calls out as he tentatively eases past the door.

There is no one in the kitchen, but the basement door is standing wide open. The house is quiet around him. Unfamiliar without the sounds of the girls watching TV or Joanne rustling around the kitchen. Stepping to the wide doorway, David looks through the dining room and into the still living room.

"Joanne?" He calls out again, as if proving his good intentions to the empty rooms. "Eleanor? Are you all right?"

There's a soft thump in the distance, below his feet. David crosses back into the kitchen and descends the stairs. His hand grips the phone in his pocket. He hesitates on the bottom step, trying to think clearly, but the buzzing in his head chases away his common sense. *It's all right*, he tells himself, *I'm here to help.* As he rounds the corner, a large body blocks his path. Grabs him with thick, calloused hands.

"Where is it?" Andy shouts at him. "Where is it?"

David swivels his head as Andy grips his upper arms, shaking his body for answers.

"Are you in on this?" Andy demands. "Was this your idea?"

The narrow hall around them blurs as David struggles to keep his feet on the ground. Andy pivots then, pushing David's back against the nearest wall, giving him a moment to breathe against its solid support. Andy's face, flushed and trembling, fills David's vision, but there's uncertainty there, too. Andy's eyes search David's wild expression, weighing his role in whatever had happened during the night.

"It wasn't him," David chokes out the words that he's been waiting to say all night. "He wasn't on the bridge that night. It wasn't him."

Andy eases his grip, then backs up as he releases David completely. There's confusion on his face as he blinks rapidly. And then realization dawns.

"Jeff?" Andy asks with his head cocked to one side, still puzzling over something. David nods, leaning into the wall, and Andy runs both hands over his mouth and cheeks. He turns toward the doorway into the unfinished back room, bites his lower lip, then spins to face David. He's about to speak when feet thunder down the stairs beside them.

Time speeds, then slows, as two uniformed men burst

into view. David's vision hones in on the raised guns and his hands fly into the air, fingers spread wide. Andy responds to a different instinct. He barrels forward, trying to force an opening between the two men.

David flattens his body against the wall and looks sharply away, waiting for gunshots that never come. After a brief struggle, Andy lies prone, his wrists pinned behind his back. David watches, fascinated, as the handcuffs are snapped into place.

"Andrew Wagner," one of the men says in a gruff voice. "You're under arrest for the assault and battery of your wife, Eleanor Wagner. You're also being charged with grand theft."

As the charges dissolve into the familiar reading of Andy's rights, David gradually lowers his hands. Both men are focused on Andy, who is struggling against the cuffs and cursing between sputtered shouts of innocence.

David swallows hard, finally turning away from the dramatic scene to peer mindlessly into the back room. His eyes widen as his brain comprehends Andy's first frantic question. *Where is it?*

David takes a careful step forward, sweeping his eyes over the small room. Jeff's old computer sits alone on the wooden workbench. The racks of additional equipment, the second monitor, the video camera, and the electrodes are all gone. The leather chair is pushed against one wall and a small stack of notebooks, about half of Jeff's collection, rests on the shelf below his secondhand text books. The room is neat and clean, shocking in its ordinariness.

By the time the officers turn their attention to David,

his head is swimming. One of them rests his hand heavily on David's shoulder, telling him that they'd like him to come answer some questions, and David can only nod. They are back in the kitchen before David feels the weight of the phone in his pocket and calmly tells them, "I'd like to call my lawyer."

CHAPTER THIRTY-EIGHT

They sit at a small table toward the back of the donut shop. Caffeine already buzzes through David's veins, but another cup of black coffee sits in front of him. Doug pours cream into his own paper cup, taking his time. He sighs. It's been a long night and he's losing patience for the conversation that still has to happen. He wants to go home.

Yet David has been surprisingly cooperative, quietly waiting while Doug arranged for his release and not asking questions on their short drive from the police station to the donut shop. His quiet compliance has earned a grudging respect, and Doug finds himself softening toward the scientist.

"You must have a lot of questions," he eases in, as David continues to stare into the depths of his untouched cup. Doug stirs his own coffee, contemplating. "Well, maybe it's better if you don't ask them," he continues. "Maybe it's better if I just review what's happened."

David nods, now staring just past Doug's head.

"Jeff was interested in neuroscience and saw you as a sort of mentor," Doug begins laying out his case. "He had some theories and you encouraged him, hoping he'd finish night school and pursue his dream. When he died, Joanne offered you Jeff's notebooks, and you struck up a friendship."

David sighs heavily, but Doug ignores him. He glances out the window as a car pulls into the parking lot, then resumes his story with a steady voice.

"You knew that Jeff had told Andy his theories, too. And you knew that Andy thought you could turn those theories into a money-making reality. But you didn't know that Andy had stolen equipment from the lab and hid it in his basement."

"In *his* basement?" David visibly startles, causing Doug to frown and narrow his eyes.

"Yes," Doug confirms deliberately. "Those *hypothetical* questions Andy had asked about how Jeff's research might work were his way of finding out which equipment to steal. It's shocking, of course, since you had no idea whatsoever that Andy planned to engage your help in making some sort of actual… *thought* detector.

"Drink your coffee," Doug adds, seeing David's consternation. He takes a sip from his own cup, settles back in his chair and waits for David to follow suit. He nods when David drinks, then continues more conversationally.

"Of course, Andy had been doing the same thing to Jeff. Asking questions and taking equipment. Naturally, Jeff was upset when Andy surprised him with the scheme, and tried to get Andy to return the equipment. But then Jeff had his accident."

David chokes on the coffee, coughing harshly as it dribbles down his chin. Doug passes him some napkins, leaning in to show concern, yet also glancing around apologetically at the customers standing in line.

Lowering his voice, David whispers, "You're not implying that Andy had something to do with--" But Doug waves the rest of the question away.

"I'm not implying anything," he says dryly. "People form their own conclusions."

David sits back in his chair, taking in Doug's casual collared shirt and fatherly features. He looks like a family man. Someone who plays golf on Sundays and is home for dinner every night. Yet there is something hard under his genial expression. A determination that David didn't appreciate until just this moment.

"It was a pipe dream, of course," Doug goes on, in a dismissive tone that David imagines working well on a jury. "Pure science fiction. Not that Jeff's research wasn't valuable," he corrects quickly. "But Andy was delusional to think that he could use those theories to create some kind of get-rich-quick scheme."

David finds himself nodding along, fascinated by the unfolding story. He can hear his own words from just two months ago, the words that accused Andy of the same thing. For a split second, he doubts his own memories of everything that has happened in the weeks since.

"Eleanor had become suspicious though," Doug confides sadly. "She was worried and confronted him after finding the stolen equipment, hidden under a tarp in the back room of their basement."

David's eyes widen in dread, seeing the story come together.

"Andy became violent during their argument, then fled. Which is, of course, when Joanne told you what had happened. You were worried and didn't know what to do, especially when you didn't hear from her again.

"Concerned, you came by to check on them this morning, not knowing that I had taken Joanne and Eleanor to the hospital during the night. You found the broken door and Andy in the basement, but had no idea that my wife was hiding upstairs with the children, or that she had called the police as soon as Andy had broken in."

"Your wife?" David echoes, stumbling over this added piece of the story.

"She stayed with the children last night," Doug explains. "While I was at the hospital with Jo and poor Eleanor. Who is lucky to only have a mild concussion."

David nods dumbly, accepting that as fact and feeling vaguely glad that Eleanor had been to the hospital. But the rest of the story has left his body cold and his mind reeling.

"Does that about sum it up?"

David meets Doug's eyes and sees their hard determination. He remembers Dee telling him that Joanne's lawyer had been her father's law partner. He wonders how much Doug actually knows, about this and about everything that has happened in Joanne's life. He wonders how much Doug knows about that night on the bridge and if he knows whether Mark was really alone.

"This equipment that I didn't know about," David begins warily, hearing an edge of anger that he doesn't entirely feel. "The equipment that no one but Andy knew about. What are the police going to find on the hard drives?"

Doug stirs his coffee again, then removes the plastic stir stick, placing it on his napkin.

"There were no hard drives in the computers. No tape in the video camera."

"I see," David looks back at his own coffee, assuming that the hard drive in Jeff's old computer may be similarly found missing, if anyone cared to look for it. He pictures his own office at home. He imagines the news clippings in his trash can and the sticky tape marks on his wall. He thinks of his home computer and the USB stick that has been quietly transporting files over the past two months. His thoughts turn to the chance of a search order, but he decides not to mention it. Directly.

"The police will have more questions for me?"

David had been polite at the police station, compliant, as he sat quietly nursing a cup of bad coffee and waiting for Doug to appear. He had been allowed to use the bathroom and, as the time ticked by, asked if he would like to use the vending machines. When Doug finally entered the room, there had been a swift apology from an older detective followed by brief questions confirming David's employer and the fact that he had been at the house out of concern for Joanne and Eleanor. The detective had shaken his hand then, thanking David for his cooperation, and saying that they would be in touch if needed. And that, had been that.

"There may be," Doug doesn't seem concerned. "Depending on whether Andy accepts the terms of his deal."

"Deals wrap things up neatly in this town," David observes, although Doug only shrugs.

"Deals are made in every town."

"I guess that's easier when you have friends in the right places," David's exhaustion comes out through his bitter tone, but Doug doesn't seem to mind.

"It always helps to have friends," Doug answers amiably. "And to understand when it isn't worth making the news."

David thinks about that, assuming the conversation has shifted from the assault charges to the grand theft. The lab could make an example of Andy. They could investigate and find out whether David, or anyone else, had helped Andy take the equipment. Maybe they could even implicate Jeff to get out of their settlement with Joanne. But the explosion had brought negative publicity at a national level. Another controversy, particularly one that could raise more questions about the explosion, might be well worth avoiding.

The thoughts make David curious about the kind of deal Doug has in mind for Andy. He assumes that it will involve jail time, and a faint thread of guilt wraps its way around his twitching stomach. He doesn't want to know the terms.

"Eleanor will be all right?" He asks instead, effectively putting an end to the subject.

"Yes," Doug relaxes and offers a soft smile. "She was released from the hospital early this morning."

"And Joanne?"

"Joanne is a survivor," he answers firmly, but David hears sadness behind his words.

They drink their coffee slowly. Quietly. Two police officers enter the shop, but they take no particular notice of David and Doug. They ask for coffee and donuts to go, then joke with the cashier while she prepares their order. David watches them warily. There's a knot in his stomach and he suspects that it is a feeling he should learn to live with.

Once the uniformed men have left, David asks if they can go to Joanne's house now. Doug presses his lips in a firm line, looks at the table, then slowly meets David's questioning gaze.

"I'll take you to get your car," Doug tells him. "But Jo won't be there. Neither will Eleanor."

David nods, sensing that there is more to the answer.

"They're moving on," Doug continues after a thoughtful pause. "They're taking the kids and heading somewhere else. Getting a fresh start."

There's a challenge in Doug's tone, an unspoken warning to stay away, but David scarcely notices it. He is too distracted by an overwhelming sense of relief.

CHAPTER THIRTY-NINE

The rhythmic thrum of tires on pavement lulls Joanne into a meditative state as she sits upright behind the wheel. Eleanor rests in the passenger seat, silently watching the blur of trees on the side of the highway. In the backseat, the girls smile at a favorite movie, their ears covered by large headphones, while Nolan sleeps soundly in his padded car seat. They're headed south, steadily extending their distance from Parkview with each passing mile.

The idea of settling into a new town, a new home, frightens and excites Joanne. She thinks of the cities and towns they've circled on the map. The places they plan to try out over the next few weeks. She imagines the apartments and small houses that they will rent, the places they will visit and the people they will meet. She doesn't let herself think about the home that she is leaving behind.

The house was just a place, she tells herself each time her mind flashes back to her familiar kitchen, her sunny living room, or the bed that she shared with Jeff. She tells herself that the memories she made there, the stories she tells herself, are portable. They are stories that she can pack up and bring with her if, and only if, she decides to keep them.

It feels right to begin an inventory of those memories as the miles pass and the sun begins to set. Joanne thinks about a picnic with Jeff. She thinks about the birth of her daughters. She thinks about drinking endless cups of tea with Eleanor by her side. She lets memory after memory, image after image, flit through her mind, picturing them being filed away in a long row of drawers. And then there are the other memories. The ones that are better left in Parkview.

Of the many memories she no longer wants, one in particular has no place in her future life. As Joanne drives, gripping the wheel, she decides to leave that memory here. She decides to replay that night now, just one more time, before letting it drift out of the car to be lost in their tailwind.

The night comes back to Joanne as it always does: in fractured snapshots. She's sitting on a pink couch in a stranger's house. The couch is faintly patterned and springy beneath her, as if its firm cushions don't want to accept her weight. Eleanor is with her, holding her hands and shaking with anger. Anchoring Joanne to the spot. There are dried tears on her cheeks and, as Joanne remembers the feel of them, her stomach sinks with the realization that Eleanor will never understand. That no one will ever understand. It's the feeling that pervades the memory, giving it shape and form.

She had left Mark. She had chosen Jeff. It should have been over. But it wasn't.

Sitting on that couch, trying to explain through her misery, Joanne had known with absolute certainty that what she wanted didn't matter. His voice was too loud in her head. She can sense the feeling now, an echo brought back by the memory. The unequivocal knowledge that she could never be free of Mark. The whisper that she was inextricably tied to him. The promise that he would always come back and always get what he wanted. The resignation that he was inevitable.

And El hadn't understood.

Through dry-eyed shame, Joanne had sat on that couch and said that she'd made a mistake. That she was being selfish and putting Jeff in danger. That the best thing would be for her to give up, give in, and let Jeff go. But Eleanor had refused to listen.

"*Mark doesn't love you.*" She said it over and over, burning the words into Joanne's memory, but never breaking through her certainty. "*He hurts you. That isn't love.*"

It hurts Joanne to remember those words. It hurts to know that she believed them, even then, but that they weren't enough. She knows that they sat on that couch for a long time, but the memory has faded, cutting to a later moment. The moment of panic when Joanne had come out of the bathroom to find that Eleanor wasn't in the living room. She wasn't in the kitchen and she wasn't checking on the sleeping kids upstairs. She wasn't outside, and Joanne's car was gone.

Glancing over at Eleanor now, Joanne sees that she has fallen asleep. She hears the girls whispering as they load a new movie into the player and Nolan snoring gently. The sky grows darker and a sign by the side of the road says that they are less than an hour from their hotel.

Keeping a steady grip on the steering wheel, Joanne takes a slow, deep breath and lets the rest of the memory come back in careful pieces. Pacing the strangers' living room. Seeing the flash of headlights in the driveway, not knowing whether it was Eleanor or the kids' parents coming home. And then, at last, Eleanor stumbling up the icy front walk and pausing to throw up in the bushes.

Joanne brings her focus back to the road. Deep breaths. There are less cars around her now.

Keeping her eyes forward, Joanne lets herself remember the terror in Eleanor's eyes as they dropped onto the pink couch together. She lets her mind replay fragments of Eleanor's story.

"He said you were his. His! Like he owned you… He laughed… He said… And I hated him… And I shoved back…"

It's all she has to remember. All she needs to picture everything that came after. The fear, the plan, the stories. Everything that had made that night become a different reality for everyone else. Everything that had made that night a secret in her mind, and in Eleanor's, alone.

Eleanor's words echo in Joanne's memory now. Words she's never repeated out loud. *I shoved back*. But Joanne doesn't cry to remember them now. She doesn't regret. She breathes in. She breathes out.

She lets them go.

She decides to believe a new story.

ACKNOWLEDGMENTS

While starting to write a book is easy, completing that book is a serious undertaking. This book, my first, would not exist without the support and encouragement of several close friends, nor would it be finished without the inspiration I find in so many around me. Each day I see friends who are not afraid to pursue their dreams. They create amazing art, run their own businesses, develop technology that shapes our future, and selflessly share their expertise with others.

There are many who have inspired me, simply by living their own lives to the fullest, and many who have encouraged me, simply by believing that I could—and would—finish this book. Thank you to you all.

Special thanks to my friends and family who were kind enough to read early drafts of *The Insistence of Memory*. In particular, Jennifer Brown, who read my earliest chapters and told me to keep writing; Wendy McMullan, my own best friend forever, who dropped everything to read the full book in two days and call me with gushing excitement; Jim Beaver, my father, who offered his insight on multiple drafts; and Angel Fischer, who not only gave extensive and continuing feedback, but also designed this beautiful book cover.

Thanks as well to Ursula Cox, whose guidance of my yoga journey, both as a student and teacher, has nurtured the confidence I needed to embrace my authentic voice; and to Jen Pool, who is always there when I need honest advice, professional headshots, or time to low-key hang out.

To my husband, Peter, there are not words to describe all you do to support and encourage me. Beyond this book, you are part of me. We have grown together, like entwined vines, and I am stronger for having you by my side.

In the larger picture, beyond writing this book, thank you to everyone who has touched my life in a positive way. Family, friend, acquaintance, or stranger passing by, we're all in this world together. We can all find inspiration in each other, if we simply take time to look.

ABOUT THE AUTHOR

Susan Quilty is an avid reader and a freelance writer who has written articles, advertorials, and essays for a wide range of both print and online publications. *The Insistence of Memory* is her first novel. In addition to writing, Susan is a certified yoga teacher, who has practiced yoga for over 10 years. You can learn more about Susan by visiting her website at: www.SusanQuilty.com.

Made in the USA
Columbia, SC
22 October 2017